THE
IMMORTAL
GAMES

ANNALIESE AVERY

Published in the UK by Scholastic, 2023
1 London Bridge, London, SE1 9BG
Scholastic Ireland, 89E Lagan Road, Dublin Industrial Estate, Glasnevin,
Dublin, D11 HP5F

SCHOLASTIC and associated logos are trademarks and/or registered
trademarks of Scholastic Inc.

Text © Annaliese Avery, 2023
Cover illustration © Tom Roberts, 2023
Map illustration © Julia Bickham, 2023

The right of Annaliese Avery and Tom Roberts to be identified as the author
and illustrator of this work has been asserted by them under the Copyright,
Designs and Patents Act 1988.

ISBN 978 0702 30609 9

A CIP catalogue record for this book is available from the British Library.

Printed and bound in Great Britain by Clays Ltd, Elcograf S.p.A
Paper made from wood grown in sustainable forests and other controlled
sources.

3 5 7 9 10 8 6 4

www.scholastic.co.uk

For Linda Rosemary Spendlove
Who once taught me the secret to immortality.

*"The measure of a man is
what he does with power."*

—PLATO

ANCIENT GREECE

EPIDAMNUS
LYCHNIDUS
LAKE LYCHNITES
ILLYRIA
APOLLONIA
ORICUM
CHAONIA
CORCYRA
CORCYRA
MOLOSSIS
EPIRUS
THESPROTIA
DODONA
ELAEA
AMBRACIA
AMBRACIAN GULF
ANACTORIUM
LEUCAS
IONIAN SEA
PALE
SAME
OENIADAE
CEPHALLENIA
ZACYNTHUS
ZACYNTHUS

MACEDONIA
LYNCESTIS
AEGAE
PELLA
MYGDONIA
BEROEA
THERMA
ORESTIS
CHALCIDIC
ELIMEIA
PYDNA
METHONE
OLYNTHUS
DIUM
POTIDAEA
MOUNT OLYMPUS
CAMBUNIAN MOUNTAINS
MENDE
PERRHAEBI
MAGNESIA
TRICCA
LARISSA
THESSALY
PAGAS GULF
PAGASAE
SCIATH
ACHAEA
PHTHIOTIS
PINDUS MOUNTAINS
OREUS
LOCRIS
AETOLIA
MALIS
DORIS
PHOCIS
EL
DELPHI
LOCRIS
MOUNT PARNASSUS
NAU PACTUS
CHALCIS
PATRAS
BOEOTIA
THEBES
AIGOSTHENA
ACHAEA
HERAION
MEGARA
ATT
ELIS
SICYON
ELIS
ORCHOM ENUS
PHLIOUS
CORINTH
OLYMPIA
ARCADIA
ARGOLIS
AEGIN
DIPAEA
OENOE
SAR GU
LEPREUM
TEGEA
ARGOS
TROE
THYREA
HERMI
MESSENIA
LACONIA
HALIESIS
STENYCLARUS
GULF OF ARGOLIS
PELOPONNESE
PYLOS
THURIA
SPARTA
METHONE
GYTHION
HELOS
PARNON MOUNTAI
GULF OF MESSENIA
MYR S
GULF OF LACONIA
CAPE MALEA
CYTHERA

1

THE BLOOD MOON MORN

The villa is still and cold in the dawn, but not as cold and still as the bed next to me. I look at it, the pillow untouched, the bed sheet still tucked in.

It's been five years since my sister last lay in the bedroom beside me, but I still catch my breath every morning; I still ready myself as I turn to face the emptiness. And this morning, this day, I feel her absence more deeply than usual.

I sit up and swing my legs out of bed; the terracotta floor tiles are cool under my feet. I quickly discard my nightdress and let it fall, then cross to the chair by my dresser and pull on the tunic that's waiting for me. Our housekeeper Ida must have left it out while I slept. I secure my leather belt in place and quickly plait my hair, tying it with a length of leather thong. The small clay offering jug I left on my dresser is still there and I snatch it up in my hand. It fits perfectly, the red wax of the seal holding in the rich wine that I decanted into it before bed last night.

I slip it into the fold of my tunic. My sandals have been placed under the chair and I scoop them up as I tiptoe to the door and slip out.

I cross the mosaic tiles of the hall swiftly, making my way to the front door. I'm just about to turn the handle when I hear my father call out. "Ara!"

I hesitate for a second, then walk into the reception room at the front of the villa. The doors on to the veranda are open and the weak dawn light is all grey shadows. My father blends into them as he sits behind his desk, an oil lamp casting a soft amber light on the papers he's studying. If there is any warmth in the light it runs out before it reaches his face.

"Are you ready?" He doesn't even look up. I don't need to ask him what he is talking about, what I need to be ready for.

A shiver runs through me as I stand in front of his desk with the toes of my bare feet pressed into the hard floor, my sandals swinging in my hand, and suddenly I feel like a small child of six rather than a young woman of sixteen.

"I'm ready. I was just going for a run, to leave an offering at the temple."

My father's eyes still haven't left his paperwork; I wonder if he truly sees it, just as I wonder if he ever truly sees me.

"Good, an offering is always welcomed by the Gods, and a run will keep you in shape. I don't know why the instructors insist on declaring the day of the Blood Moon one of rest. Surely today of all days preparation is called for."

"Yes, father." What else can I say? "I'm going to meet Theron at the training grounds. We're going to spar before they start to prepare for the festival." I wince as I hear the hope in my voice, the hope that he will praise me, that he will notice me.

I see his face in the flicker from the lamp. The five years since Estella was taken from us have made me a woman and our father an old man. His beard covers a chin too fond of wine and his once brown hair is grey with the worries of a man twice his age.

"Theron is a good fighter, and the Gods shine favourably on the boy; you can learn a thing or two from him, Ara." My father says, and I quickly agree. He finally looks up and when he does, I get the feeling that he is not looking at but through me. "It's Theron's last chance is it not? It will be a shame if the Gods do not choose him; a young man like that would make Oropusa proud." I feel the sting in his words. "He'll make a good husband one day, and if the rumours of his birthright are true then maybe there is some worth in this friendship that the two of you have." He looks at me then, just for a moment, and I feel my cheeks run hot. I try not to think of Theron in that way and know too well that my father only sees one element of worth in me.

He looks back to his papers and I stand in the silence of the room, waiting. The nothingness engulfs me as I stand in the centre of it. I remind myself to relax, to surrender to it. I have been in the shadows since the day Estella died. I should be comfortable in them by now and most of the time I am, but today … today I thought it might be different and that small spark of hope burns me as I feel it gutter and die.

My father says nothing, so neither do I. I turn from him, from the small glow of light in the room and back out into the hallway. I close the door of the villa behind me, silently, and stand in the morning air taking in a big breath. I fill my lungs with the morning and hold it in till it burns, and small stars appear in the daybreak. Then I let it out and breathe normally as I secure my sandals and start running.

I set off at a sprint; for the first few moments my body is fine because it hasn't realized what's happening yet. But it soon does. I push on, urging my limbs to keep going, to keep up the punishing pace. I feel energy surging through my body and I feel alive as the fields rush past me; the ground, and the crops – a dull grey in the dawn of the day. But green slowly fades in as I run towards the treeline that edges the field and creates a natural barrier around the farmland and the stream that makes my father's land so rich and fertile.

Apollo's fingers are stretching in the sky, pink tendrils reaching up into the gathering blue of the heavens, and I watch as a large eagle circles high and slow, one of the signs of Zeus. I wonder if he is watching me. I hope so.

My pace naturally slows as I reach the stream and run along the undulating bank, my footfalls irregular as I navigate the rocks and vegetation. The tall trees are blocking out the sunrise and the coolness of their branches is welcome as the sweat runs down my body making my tunic damp.

The stream flows into a pool and I stop here, kneeling to cup my hands in the icy fresh water, sending ripples across the surface as I wash my face. Drops fall from my chin into the pool. I stay there and stare at it like Narcissus. I see myself reflected, but unlike him I am not enamoured by what I see. On display are all the parts of me that I shared with Estella and all the parts that I didn't. Our cheekbones and jawline were the same, but my nose is my own, fuller and round at the end. Hers was perfectly straight and small, and her eyes were delicate and shapely, the soft brown of an old oak tree. My eyes have always been too big for my face, but the colour I've always liked, a rich chestnut brown that reminds me of autumn.

Estella never had a scar on her cheek like I do, either. I run my fingers across the thin line of silver white that is never kissed by the sun. It looks stark and bright against my skin in the reflection and is a little raised beneath my fingertips. I'd received it in my first week of training, just a few days after Estella was murdered by the Gods.

My father is a stoic man; he knows the training will not keep me safe, but it might give me a fighting chance, something he had not thought to give to Estella. My mother was already defeated and beyond my tears of protest at that time.

There was no easing into it. The instructors were not paid to be kind to us. They were hard on us so that we would become hard. Over the past five years I have become as unyielding as the marble of the temple that houses my dead sister's body.

I remember that first day. We were navigating a field full of obstacles, myself and the other children whose parents took the Blood Moon and its threats seriously. Back then I couldn't run without getting out of breath or falling over my feet. I tripped and stumbled my way through the training field and when I came to the obstacles, I could hardly lift my body over them. I fell at the first one, a simple balance beam comprising of a felled log. I can somersault across that log now, and all the others. But back then my balance and core strength were non-existent. Blood ran down my cheek, dripping off my jaw, mixing with the tears, but I didn't stop. I was headstrong even then. My muscles burned, and my body ached, and I cried my way around the course, but I still didn't stop. I thought of Estella. I thought of how she had not been ready when the Gods chose her to play their Game. I knew that I would be: I would be prepared, and I would be strong, and I would be ready for them, ready for Zeus.

The unthinkable had happened to my family and I. Estella had been chosen to play the Immortal Games, and she never came back to us, not whole, not alive. And just like my father, I wasn't about to let the Fates have their say without me having mine too.

There is always speculation as to why the Games happen. Some say it is to honour the strongest among us, and the fact that the winners and survivors are treated like demi-gods afterwards suggests that might be true. But others say it is the Gods' way of controlling us, of letting us know that they can take anyone that they choose at any time.

Before Estella had been chosen on the evening of the Blood Moon, there were only a handful of children in our village whose families sent them for training. It had been so long since the Gods had chosen a token from Oropusa that we had forgotten to fear the lunar eclipse and the possibility that the Gods were not only watching us but walking among us, ready to take one of us as the moon turned red. This was a mistake that was soon rectified but also soon forgotten.

As the years passed and the Blood Moons came and went without any of the other children being chosen by the Gods, the anxiety dwindled, not for all – not for me or my family – but enough that fewer and fewer children are now sent to train.

Usually, the instructors drill us from early morning to sunset, sometimes beyond. Some of the trainees have chores, expectations on their time and they train around them. I am thought of as one of the lucky ones – my whole life is dedicated to training. Every day I get up, I train, I eat, I sleep, I repeat, and all so that I have the best odds of surviving, so that if chosen, I have a fighting chance.

I push myself up from the side of the stream, knocking the dry dirt from my hands as I start walking through the gathering morning in the direction of the training grounds. I doubt that any of the others will be there, except Theron. Theron has always been there; he was there before Estella was chosen by the Gods, training every day, hoping to stand out and be selected.

Theron's mother is a beautiful woman, the most beautiful in Oropusa. It is said that Aphrodite herself blessed her at birth, and that she had been wooed and seduced by a king. The king then refused to marry her and cast her out of his kingdom carrying Theron.

Theron has definitely inherited his mother's blessing, and the way he is always so certain of himself makes me believe the rumours around his royal birthright. He and I are alike in one way – we both want to catch the attention of the Gods. For him being selected for the games is his way of proving his worth to his absent father, and for me being selected is an opportunity to avenge my sister.

But unlike Theron, tonight is not my last Blood Moon. I have two more chances left to be honoured by the Gods.

I let out a snort as the thought passes through my head and I catch the smell of something sweet and light. Following the scent, I soon find a tangle of wild peonies pushing their stems through the solid greenery of the bushes that line the river.

I stop and breathe them in then curl my fingers around the stem of one of the beautiful blooms, snapping it off.

I gently place it in the folds of my tunic on the opposite side of my body from the offering to Zeus.

THE OFFERINGS TO THE GODS

I can see Theron in the training grounds. With his back to me and a blunt sword in his hand, he spars with wooden foes, the metal resonating on the poles, his grunts of exertion drifting across to me on the light breeze. Slipping into the shadows of the temple before he notices me, I watch from the pillar as he moves his body effortlessly, his shoulders square and feet steady, his arms flexing with each strike. He's strong, stronger than me, but I'm quick and nimble.

I smile as I think about the few occasions when I've managed to best him while sparring. It always surprises me, but I try not to let it show. He always tells me that he let me have that one, but the ones he lets me have are getting more and more frequent lately. He pauses and runs a hand through his light brown hair and, as if he can sense me watching, he turns to look at the temple. I swiftly push my back up against the column and imagine him squinting in my direction, raising a hand to shield his eyes as the quizzical look that I know so well crosses his face.

The Temple of the Zodiakos has twelve sides, as is the tradition, each representing one of the houses of the zodiac, I scoot around the temple, away from Theron, and stop when I reach the twisted pillar decorated with scuttling scorpions. Two pillars hold up this portion of the fanned roof. On the triangular apex of the roof the word SCORPIO is inscribed and above it the constellation of my sign is carved into the stone. Making my way up the steps, I pass into the wedge-shaped chamber. My eyes are drawn, as always, to the mosaic floor. A scorpion, scattered with white tiles to mark the stars of the constellation, sits in a backdrop of deep blue. Small niches are carved into the curved walls, most already full of offerings to the Gods. By this evening, the offerings will be trailing out of the chamber and down the stairs.

My sandals slide over the smooth stones as I approach the arch that leads into the centre of the temple. I pause on my way through and put my hand in my right pocket. The clay offering bottle, sealed with red wax, is warm in my hand. I've scratched my name on the bottle and next to it the name of the God I hope will choose me. I clutch it, my fingers pushing hard on the fired clay.

As I place the offering in one of the niches in the wall, I speak out loud. "Hear me, Zeus, God of all Gods. I stand before you, a humble servant and a worthy token ready to be chosen, ready to play the game and to win."

I have long since held the belief that Gods cannot know the inner thoughts of mortals — if they did I would have been struck down the night my sister had been returned – and as I stand in the temple and call to the most powerful of all the Gods, I am glad of that small protection. Glad that my intentions remain unknown to all but me.

I wonder if my offering is enough to catch his attention, I wonder if *I'm* enough, and a shiver runs through me: *what if I am?*

I continue under the arch and into the circular inner hall. At midday the light will shine straight down through the oculus in the roof, spreading through the space and into the crypt below. But the sun is not yet high enough, so I take a candle from the side of the room and light it from one of the offerings already burning, then make my way down the curving stone steps in the centre of the room.

There's a chill in the crypt. I shiver as my sandals crunch the grit and dirt beneath my feet. There are five sarcophagi down here, the resting place of those from Oropusa who had been selected by the Gods over the years to be their tokens in the Immortal Games. Five teenagers, four were not victors, but one was: she got to live to a ripe old age, dying when I was six. I can remember the festivities that were held as her body was interred in the temple with the other tokens.

There was nothing like that when Estella was placed here, her burial a sombre affair, conducted in the darkness with the stars of the zodiac watching over her. Mother had collapsed on the stairs that lead into the Gemini entrance of the temple and Ida had stayed with her, encouraging me to follow my father down to the crypt. I remember walking across the mosaic floor, the twins looking back up at me. I knew the loss of Castor and why his brother had sacrificed divinity for him. I didn't know it then, but now, standing before Estella's sarcophagus, I realize that I have gladly made the same sacrifice; my life from that moment till now has been spent pursuing the chance to honour my sister.

Her sarcophagus is cut from stone and on the top lies the cold hard image of my sister in marble said to have been provided by the Gods and fashioned by Hephaestus himself. The rendering always floors me. She looks just as she had on the morning of her selection, a true likeness preserved in stone for all time. She was so very beautiful, the fairest girl in all Oropusa, everyone said so. The Gods obviously thought the same; some said that when she was taken it was in honour of her beauty and I can't help but think the same as I take in her fair face. I run a finger down a rigid white marble curl of hair, once so soft and dark with a scent of roses. I remember the small, warm smile dancing on her lips, a smile that was gone when she was returned to us.

From the left pocket of my tunic, I take out the soft flower from the river path. Placing it at Estella's feet, I read again the inscription beneath, "Estella token of Zeus."

I will make him pay for what he did to you, I tell her in my heart, but not out loud. If the Gods are watching and listening, my plans will remain out of their reach even if I am not.

3

THE GOD OF THE UNKNOWN

Hades stands on the steps that lead out of the underworld and up to Mount Olympus.

"You can't come with me," he says to Cerberus, stroking one of the hound's heads. Cerberus looks up at him, one face expectant, one sad, and the other looking away pretending not to be interested in his young master leaving.

"You're much better off staying here," Hades says, and he means it. Cerberus starts to lick him, while another face nudges his other hand for affection.

Hades crouches down, the folds of his long dark robes gathering around his feet, and strokes Cerberus, kissing each of his three heads.

"I'll be back soon." Hades smiles. "Go on, go home." He stands, but the hound sits at the foot of the stairs, resting one head on the lowest step with a sigh, as another looks up at Hades with big flame-filled eyes.

Hades begins walking. The climb is long, and he is already late.

Cerberus wags his tail, beating it on the ground, the sound filling the entire underworld. The God of the dead glances over his shoulder briefly, then turns and continues upwards.

Olympus, the home of his brother Zeus, is far above him. He has the long climb to ready himself for the pomp, for the politics, for the pathetic whims of his godly family. He will do as he always does during the Games: he will choose his token, aid them in the ways that his conscience allows, and then he will care for all the tokens who fail the quest and end up in his realm. It is the same every time the Gods play the Immortal Games. Even to Hades the irregular summoning of the Blood Moon feels like the whim of the Gods, although he knows there is a cosmic rhythm behind it, a pattern in the firmament forged by Gods older than him, Gods long forgotten.

Hades sweeps a hand through his night-black hair and as he climbs higher begins to squint in the shining light of Olympus. The very building appears to emit a radiance so different from that of the mortal earth. Different, also, to the golden glow of the skies in Elysium – the blessed isle deep in the underworld where all the spirits deemed worthy are sent to live out their afterlives, slowly forgetting that they were ever truly alive.

The light of Olympus is too bright, too white and artificial for Hades to feel comfortable. It has no single point of radiating brilliance; instead, it comes from everywhere, irradiating all it touches, even him.

His pale skin looks almost translucent in this light, and his black hair is almost as dark as some of the motives the Gods hold. He readies himself as he continues to venture upwards, the surety and calm that the darkness of the underworld gives him is slowly being replaced by trepidation and worry. It is like this each and every time he is summoned to play.

They are my family. He tries to remind himself, but he has very little in common with them now and over the eons there is less and less that he respects or likes about them. He checks himself – he is being unkind – some of them are not all bad.

Hades slips unnoticed into the great house of the Gods. He has a knack of being inconspicuous, and he likes it. He keeps his distance from the knot of Gods gathered in the middle of the vast room, the room where they will play out the game. Beyond the pillars holding up the roof there is nothing but open sky, and far below that the realm of the mortals. Around the room sit twelve marble slabs resting on plinths, surrounding a large central table on which the world of the mortals is depicted. The molten marble of the table shifts at the Gods' command; mountains and cities rise up in an instant, reflecting the lands that are of interest, only to be replaced at the wave of a hand. This is where the Gods will play – the pieces moved, the die rolled. All action taken on the table will influence the world of mortals below.

Hades stands as still and silent as the pillar he is resting nonchalantly against and watches as beautiful Hera moves close to the game board. She smiles at Poseidon, who waves a hand over the board. It ripples with the waves of the ocean, a chain of islands reaching up from the cresting peak. Poseidon leans in close to one of the smaller islands and it swells and expands to cover the board, the shoreline is magnified and on it a group of men and women pull in a catch from the sea, their boats bobbing in the moving marble just as they do in the sapphire blue waves on the Earth.

Hera leans in close to Poseidon, she speaks and he gestures to the board, then her hand touches his arm lightly as she laughs at something he says. She looks around her, no doubt checking where her husband is, but Zeus has not yet arrived. She lets her hand drop but carries on the private conversation.

Hades sighs, his breath carrying the weight of a dying wish before the grave. The tension between his brothers, Poseidon and Zeus, has always been obvious to Hades and no doubt to Hera too. She uses it to her advantage when she can; the power of a God is not without its limits and sometimes a little creativity is necessary.

Hades has long since stopped aligning himself with his brothers' ambitions. It is often as if he alone remembers the last war they raged against the Titans, against their father. And even now, Hades is still dealing with the repercussions of their actions.

He moves closer to the party, lifting a cup of ambrosia

and sipping its sweet nectar, although it does nothing to remove the bitter taste in his mouth.

He had readily joined Zeus when his brother called them all to action; he had gladly donned his armour, reached for his helm of darkness, and readied his fiery bident. Hades was as much to blame for the way of things as any of the other Gods were, maybe even more so.

He sighs again as he thinks of the destruction, of the continued pattern of ruin that seems so familiar and easy to his kin.

Tonight, the moon will bleed ... and then, shortly after, the tokens will too.

THE TRAINING GROUNDS

I squint as I step out of the temple, lifting my hand to shade my eyes as they adjust to the light; Apollo is a little further along in his course. Theron is no longer at the wooden fighting poles. He's sitting on the steps two pillars down, making an offering of his own to the stars of Capricorn.

I walk down the steps and head in the direction of the training grounds. Theron doesn't say anything as he joins me, matching my footfalls as we approach the sparring ring.

"Swords or sticks?" he asks as we get close to the circle of fine dirt.

"Swords," I say. "It is a special occasion after all."

He laughs and gives me a large smile, but his laugh is hollow and his smile stops long before his eyes. I know him well enough to see behind his bravado; I know what is at stake for him this evening.

I grab a sword, feel the weight of it, and then I reach for a shield.

"Oh, we're not playing today!" he says, snatching up a shield too.

"Only the Gods play today," I answer.

We take up our positions in the training circle. I plant my feet the way that the instructors have taught me and relax my muscles, letting my limbs extend and lengthen under the weight of the sword and the shield before I raise them both.

I wait for Theron to attack me. He always makes the first move, unable to stay still for too long, unwilling to exist in that space of concentrated anticipation. I know by the drop of his right shoulder which way he is going to bring down his sword and I move mine to block him as he pulls back and shifts his foot. I know his next move before he makes it and block again, this time with my shield as I bring my sword around and strike his forearm.

The swords are blunt, but he'll get a bruise.

"Easy, Ara, I don't want to be carrying an injury this evening," he says as he takes a step back and shakes out his arm.

"You know there's no holding back with swords," I tell him with a knowing look, as I repeat the words of the instructors: "Unleash the might of the blade."

"I should have insisted on sticks!" Theron says, the good humour back on his face as he gives his arm a final shake.

I wait patiently for him to move again, striking to the right. We develop a rhythm now – swords, shields, lean, reach, tilt. I get close enough to hook my leg around his and I pull it out from under him. As he falls, he clips my shield with his and pulls me on top of him. The air rushes out of him in a mighty puff as he's sandwiched between the dirt and our shields which are tightly pressed under me. I roll from him and get straight back to my feet as he lays there for a moment. I offer my hand and he grabs it but only to pull me down again.

"Not fair." I punch him on the shoulder, not hard but he fakes injury.

He looks at me, the same way he did a few days ago when it was raining and the instructors had sent us on a run. We'd found ourselves alone. Just like then I feel myself leaning towards him. But then I stop; just like with the swordplay, I can wait. I expect him to fill the gap between us, to attack first, but instead he bites his lip and shakes his head before resting it back on the dirt.

I push off him and sit up, our shields and swords cast around us.

"What do you think the quest will be?" he suddenly asks.

It's a question he asks every Blood Moon and it usually leads to a long discussion as we speculate over which God might be in charge of setting the quest for those particular Immortal Games and what trials the twelve chosen tokens will face along the way. But this year I just shrug. "Does it matter? They're all the same really, all designed to entertain the Gods and test us to destruction. I guess it's best to plan for the worst, and what's the worst?" I shrug again. "For us it is probably that we won't be chosen."

Theron is shaking his head from side to side, and he has a wide, smug smile on his lips. "Maybe you won't, but this is it; I can feel it. Tonight, I will be chosen as a token." His voice is flat and serious.

I stand up, hands on hips and look down at him. "Really? How do you know?"

He drops his hand as my shadow casts over him, blocking out the glare of the sun and the bright cloudless sky. He shrugs. "I just know. I've felt it for a few days now and this morning I just woke up knowing."

"Knowing or hoping?" I ask as I try to assess how I feel. Nervous obviously, determined and eager, but that look of surety on Theron's face – I definitely don't feel that.

"I know," he says, pushing himself up on his elbows and looking straight at me with that intensity again. "Tonight is the last Blood Moon before I turn nineteen. They took their time, but I'm going to get my chance to prove myself to everyone, to my father." He looks away. I sit down again, close to him, his long body still stretched out on the dirt as he gazes at me.

All the other Blood Moons we've faced together and he's never spoken like this – with hope yes, but not surety. I try to think back to the morning of Estella's choosing and wonder if she felt different, if she knew that she was going to be chosen. If so, she didn't say anything.

"But *how* do you know?" I ask, my voice high. I need to know what it feels like; I need to know why I don't feel the same way that he does.

He smiles at me. "I just know, Ara. I feel calm and ready and … I can't explain it, I just know it deep in my being, deep in my spirit. Like I've been called."

"Are you sure this has nothing to do with you hitting your head just now when I put you on your arse?" I ask.

He smiles and sits up, lacing his fingers in mine, and I feel a little thrill of excitement run through my fingertips and up my arm.

"It will be all right. I will be all right," he murmurs like a mantra.

"Well, yeah, I know that." His face falls and I realize that he thought my questions were out of concern rather than curiosity. "You've been training with the best," I add with a little raise of my eyebrows, and he's smiling again in that easy way he has.

Then he's looking at me and it makes me feel nervous and excited all at once. Like I'm stuck in that long moment of anticipation – and for the first time I understand what Theron must feel when we're sparring, when he is so overcome with tension that he has to move.

I shoot to my feet. "I'll see you tonight," I call to him over my shoulder as I run out of the training grounds. I don't need to look back to know that he's running after me, but I'm faster than him.

I hear him skid to a halt and I look back to see him

shake his head with a smile and call out, "Tonight!"

I keep running and don't stop till I get to the stream.

"It was supposed to be me! You were supposed to choose me!" I shout up to the sky.

I start crying then, great heaving sobs, as I realize that my chances are fading. If Theron is right then I'm likely to lose him as I did Estella. Then I may soon have two lives to avenge, and another God to kill.

5

THE PREPARATION

The water is cool by the time I step into it. I shiver before I rally myself, bending my knees and letting my back slide along the cold metal of the small bath, dunking my head under.

Opening my eyes, I look through the distorted surface, the lavender oil lingering on it in a film of colours. I count as I hold my breath. Even though I can feel the small bumps on my flesh I stay under the water. When my vision begins to blur and small stars race towards me, when I struggle to remember which number comes next and my lungs start to burn, I resist the urge to sit up.

Two more, I tell myself and I count a slow *one, two* and then shoot up through the water, gasping for air as my head breaks the surface. The oil has coated my skin and small droplets of water run from me as if I am impervious to them.

It takes three deep inhalations before my breathing returns to normal; I've learnt the hard way that recovery is almost as important as being able to push yourself. Making sure that you can pick yourself up and run if you need to could be the difference between victory and failure, or life and death in the Immortal Games.

I think about lowering myself into the freezing water again but realize that I should already be dressed and on my way to the temple.

I grab the cloth and the rose-scented soap and begin to scrub the dirt from my skin that the oil has covered. Then I lather the soap in my hands and spread the foam through my hair.

I remember how Estella would massage my hair as she washed it, then brush it and curl it for me – plaiting and pinning it in place. She was a year younger than I am now when she played the Games. I looked up to her so much, and she guided me so well. When she was gone I stopped following the way she had shown me, not because I had wanted to, but because I didn't know the way. The Blood Moon is the only time when I take pride in my appearance, the only time I feel Estella telling me to sit up straight, to smile sweetly or to brush my hair.

I'm always so focused on how strong or weak I am, how many injuries I'm carrying from training, how much improvement I've made in my physical abilities; I rarely stop to think about how I look, and each time I do it is only to note the parts of me that look like Estella.

I step out of the bath and pick up the strigil, using sure swift swipes to scrape the beads of water from my body, then stand in the room as my damp skin dries enough for me to rub the lavender and rose oil over it. I add some to my hair and rake it through with my fingers before brushing it. My hair has a natural wave to it, and I twist the strands as Estella would have done to enhance the curls around my face, then I set about plaiting and placing the hair up on the top of my head in what I hope is a delicate cascade. I peer at my reflection in the mirror – I guess it might pass for something beautiful if the lighting is dim.

I look over at the soft green chiton that hangs on the back of the chair, and I sigh. I face competitors in the training fields all the time: boys twice my size, girls who would bite my ears off if I gave them the chance, and yet none of them fill me with as much fear as this piece of flowing fabric.

I muster my courage and dress. As I pull the fabric over me, I can't help but be delighted at the way it slips over my sun-bronzed body, the oils intensifying the colour of my skin with a shine that makes it glow next to the pale green of the dress.

I cross to the dresser and look at the necklace and bangles that have been left out for me. I wonder if my mother helped to pick them out, but I know that it was most probably Ida. I don't reach for any of them; instead I open the box that I keep on the dresser and from inside pull out the golden chain with the small disc on it. As I twist it in my fingers the sign of the Gemini catches the light as does the inscription, ESTELLA TOKEN OF ZEUS.

I place it over my head and feel the cold metal sit on my chest. I have worn it to every Blood Moon since Estella was returned to us with it hanging limply around her neck.

I am caught off guard by a knock on the door.

Ida doesn't wait for my reply and bustles in. "The festival starts soon. Your mother is saying that she will not go, and your father is saying that she cannot stay." The sudden motion and noise makes me dizzy. She looks up at me and her voice fades. Something flits across her face, and I wonder if she is thinking about Estella.

Ida smiles at me gently then leads me to the chair. I look at her blankly as she encourages me to sit with a smile that is kind if a little pitying. She pulls at the golden pins in my hair and unplaits my messy braids. Her fingers work quickly as she deftly picks her way through the weapons available to her, weapons that I realize I have little mastery over.

Ida combs out my locks and runs more oil through the patches that have frizzed as they dried. She starts to hum a lullaby, one she sang to my mother when she was a baby, then to Estella and me when she became our nanny. Now I sometimes hear her sing it to my mother on those nights when the memory of Estella makes her slip from us.

I match her tones, and before I realize it, we are singing together, tears gently rolling down my cheeks. As she finishes my hair and begins to pick through the jewellery on the dresser, I know for certain that it was her, that she had picked out my clothes, had chosen the necklaces and bangles. My voice breaks as she takes my face in her hands

28

and wipes my tears, then she kisses my cheek and reaches for a pot of powder.

"Close your eyes," she says, and I obey. Her fingers dance over my eyelids and it feels so good to surrender to her, to know that she is there for me; it's been so long since I've felt properly cared for.

Mother was consumed by her grief and father removed by his.

In this brief moment, I realize I have been blinded by my own grief, driven solely to avenge Estella. No one pointed me in the direction I now find myself lost in; no one told me to try and kill Zeus. But in the moment when I woke up and found Estella next to me – with the token that now hangs at my neck around hers – all I could think about was how Zeus had taken her from me. And as more things were removed from me – my mother, my father's affection, the life I had led with my sister – I knew that I had to make him pay.

I feel myself getting upset again, and try not to cry, not wanting to spoil all that Ida is doing to prepare my face.

"You can open your eyes now," Ida says, as she turns away and picks up a pot full of the brightest red I had ever seen, dabbing it along my cheeks and then over my lips.

She steps back and tips her head to one side before smiling. "There," she says with a nod to the mirror.

I stand up, a little hesitant to look, but she nods encouragingly.

I'm not sure who the young woman is before me,

although I know she's me. Maybe she's some other version of me. The Ara I have forgotten to be.

I twist from side to side, and I realize that I like the me in the mirror. She smiles easily, her eyes are bright and bold, and she looks happy; she looks as if she has a life full of joy, and for a moment I allow myself to pretend that I am her and I almost start crying again.

"You look so beautiful, Ara." Ida is crying.

I turn and throw my arms around her. "Thank you." My voice is thick. "Not just for this, but for everything. For all the care you show mother, and me." I realize that if I am selected this evening then this might be my only chance to say thank you.

I suddenly think of my parents and ask where they are.

"Your father has already left for the temple and your mother is in her rooms."

I place a hand on Ida's arm. "I'll speak with her, but let's not make her go if she doesn't want to. I'll explain to father."

I know the way the Blood Moon makes me feel; I can't even begin to imagine how incredibly hard it is for my mother, or my father.

Ida nods and leaves the room as I reach for my old sandals, forgoing the ones that she had left out for me.

When I get to my mother's door, I place my ear up against it and listen. All is quiet inside. Sometimes I fear silence more than the times when she howls and rages, when she cries wildly to the Gods and curses them, when she breaks everything that she can get her hands on, dashing it to the floor and stepping on the pieces, covering the wreckage with her blood. She will never be whole again, I know that; we all do, especially her, and I think that makes it all the harder for her to bear.

I push the door open a crack and slip into the cool abyss of my mother's room. All of the shutters are closed to the approaching night.

The room is still and orderly, the clothes that Ida has laid out for her remain untouched, her bath cold and clear. I make out her bleak shape in the bed, the blankets covering her like a shroud, and creep closer. Her eyes are closed, and her hair is whipped out around her. I brush it from her face, and she sighs deeply. I hope that her dreams are full of happier days than today and kiss her cheek, feeling the salty tears that she's shed before her slumber. I wonder for a second if they are for me, if they are for what might happen to me this evening. But I know who they are for.

I close the door then make my way out into the evening.

The sun has only just set and the air is still warm. Artemis, however, has been swift this evening. The moon is already above the horizon, full and ready, her pale face caught in a scream at the horror that is about to unfold in the Immortal Games.

I walk quickly, my old sandals gripping the ground below my feet.

I hear movement behind as Ida hurries to catch me. "Lift your skirts or they'll get all dusty," she says. For a second I hesitate. I don't want her to see my old sandals, but I know she'll grab my skirts and hold them up herself if I don't. She gives a small smile and shakes her head as she notices my choice of footwear.

"I didn't want to wear the new sandals in case I'm chosen," I say, and I hear her inhale sharply. "I know I can run in these; I can walk for days in them if I have to, and they won't cut or blister." My voice is even but inside I'm trembling as I keep my eyes on the moon.

I start to walk, and Ida falls into step beside me, holding in each of her hands a basket. Taking one from her, I smell honey rolls and my belly growls.

"That's very sensible," Ida says, her voice a little thick and distant as she reaches into the basket and hands me a roll. She doesn't tell me that I'm being silly, that the Gods won't choose me. We both already know that anything is possible otherwise Estella would be with us now, and mother too.

We continue on, through the quiet streets of Oropusa. I can see the fires burning, lighting up the twelve sides of the temple, each one full of offerings. Not many of those offerings are like mine; almost all of them say, "Please don't cast your eye my way; please do not take me for your token."

6

THE WAGER

It is not that Hades dislikes the shining glory of Mount Olympus; he merely prefers the dark. It has been his companion for longer than he can remember. Even before he became master of the underworld, back in the days of the Titans, he would walk unseen through the world of mortals and monsters and Gods, wearing his helm of night-time and darkness, visiting the places others cowered from but in which he found quiet solace.

The darkness is the only place where light can be seen for what it is, for without the dark, the light would have no meaning, and from the shadows Hades currently stands in, he sees that the light holds many things that he is fearful of.

"How now, brother?" he calls to Zeus as he steps forward, squinting only a little as he forces himself not to baulk from the light.

"Ah, so you have finally come. It is like you to be late," Zeus booms, his voice as large as his smile, which is as empty as his words.

"Not late, brother, on time. The moon is only just risen and the bleeding of the eclipse is only just about to begin."

Hera brings Hades another cup of ambrosia and smiles sweetly. "Yes, you might be just in time for the start of the Games, but you have missed much of the merriment."

Hades nods his head to her and takes the glass. "I am sorry to have missed your company." He means it. "Forgive me, sister, I have been much detained by the dead." He lowers his eyes and his lips to the cup, noticing, but not acknowledging, the shiver that Hera gives at the mention of the inhabitants of the underworld.

"Indeed, I imagine that they occupy much of your time and energy, brother." She links her arm in his and walks him across to the great table where the Games will be played, around which sit thirteen chairs. "Now, have you any insight into this Blood Moon's Games?"

"Come, Hera, you know that it is against the rules to gain knowledge of the Games before they are played."

Hera waves her hand. "Gossip and speculation are never facts. If you had arrived at a proper time, you would have heard Hephaestus recount how a while back Hermes employed him to manufacture twelve keys all the same but each one unique. What do you think of that, brother?"

"I think that as the God of travellers and doorways, Hermes has no need for a key to anywhere. But I also know that he is a clever and bright fellow, far more intelligent than I, and that if he made so marked a point of asking for twelve then it was so that Hephaestus would report it here, leading us away from any true element that Hermes had been devising for the quest."

"You see!" Athena calls out. "Hades and I are one in our thinking: the keys are nothing more than a ruse." The Goddess of wisdom lifts a cup to Hades then pats the chair next to her, bidding him to sit.

He gives a small smile, hardly a twitch of his lips, but she notices it not and as he sits next to her she leans into him.

"He also visited Demeter and asked her to grow him twelve saplings of the largest, strongest oak trees the world has ever seen."

Demeter calls out from the other side of the room, "Yes, and when the saplings were as tall as you, Hades, he came and collected them, spiriting them away on his winged shoes." She raises her eyebrows at him. "And I watched him, he headed west."

Hades lets his twitch of a smile slip again. "West, you say?" He sips the ambrosia from his cup.

"West!" Demeter says with a forceful nod. "What could he mean to do with them? Hades, do you know of any fertile lands to the west where these trees might grow?"

Hades nods. "Many fertile plots, but I don't think their location will help you in finding out anything about the quest."

"See, Hades and I are of one mind on this subject too," Athena adds. "There is no point in speculating." She gestures across the hall and beyond the pillars and the steps leading down the mount to the realm of the mortals. "The blooming draws near and so, thank Zeus, does Hermes. He can put us all out of this misery of not knowing."

The other Gods begin to cheer and welcome Hermes as he flies towards Olympus. Hades stays in his seat, watching them from afar as he often does. He sighs as he feels another mortal pass into the underworld; the thought of the twelve young contestants who are about to be plucked from their lives to face the Immortal Games weighs heavy on him. Soon he would be welcoming the majority of them into his realm. He drains his cup as Poseidon occupies the seat Athena has just vacated.

Poseidon is tall and graceful, his muscles long and taut beneath the folds of blue fabric, his eyes the deep blue-green of the ocean. His long beard reminds Hades of fields of soft brown kelp, his bald head of the smooth interior of a shell.

For a moment Hades remembers how he, Poseidon and Zeus smashed the skull of their father Kronos, claiming his world and splitting it between the three of them.

"Brother, how goes it with you?" Hades asks.

"Well, I am excited for these Games," Poseidon says, staring at Zeus, who is at the centre of the knot of Gods eagerly awaiting the arrival of Hermes.

Hades feels something stirring in the depths of those fathomless sea-green eyes and leans in closer. "Which games exactly are you speaking of, Poseidon?"

"These Immortal Games for sure, but also the great

game; you know, the rivalry the three of us are always playing, this constant sibling one-upmanship we three find ourselves locked in."

Hades sighs and leans back in his chair. He'd feared as much. "Two of you are locked in such a conflict, brother. I removed myself from the fight for Olympus many eons ago. I am content within my dark realm and do not desire the throne of our father."

Poseidon snaps his head towards Hades, his gaze full of the force of a storm-driven tide. "The throne our brother Zeus has sullied. He does not rule, he plays – this rivalry with us, that game with the mortals, any form of amusement that catches his fancy – and we are all players under his control."

"And what would you do with the throne, brother?"

"I would remind the mortals of the greatness of the Gods. You must have felt the waning of tribute, the lack of respect and prayers being offered to us. They grow too bold. And Zeus is oblivious, thinking only of his sport with the humans; they are his playthings, when they should be treated…"

"Like his children."

"Cattle … I was going to say cattle."

"Of course, brother!" Hades says, with a dark edge to his voice.

Poseidon stands abruptly and then turns, lowering his face in line with Hades, the smell of warm sand and salty swells filling Hades' nostrils.

"Will you play your part? When the time comes? When our brotherly rivalry begins?" Poseidon's voice is tense. "It is a game for three and would not be played with any more or any less, a game we have played from the crib and will be playing till the last star burns in the heavens."

Hades' eyes darken. "It is a game I must play, although it brings me no joy."

Poseidon clamps a hand down on Hades' shoulder and smiles, teeth as white as pearls. "The time is soon. Come, brother, let us choose our tokens."

Poseidon leads the way across to the throng of Gods gathered around Hermes, who flies into the room on his winged sandals, his caduceus high in the air – the two twisting serpents writhing around the bottom of the winged staff.

"Do you have your favourites selected?" Poseidon asks over his shoulder.

"You know full well that I don't have favourites," Hades replies as he comes to a stop close to Zeus. "I leave my tokens to the Fates."

Zeus lets out a laugh that peals its way around the halls of Olympus. "Hades, you might need to speak to the Fates as I fear they do not hold you in their favour. You have never won a Game."

"Indeed, brother, whereas you have won…"

"Oh, too many to count but many more by far than all of the other Gods put together. But who's keeping score?"

Hera humphs. "Who indeed, husband?"

A trill of laughter runs around the hall, and sparks light in Zeus' eyes.

"I dare say I would have won more yet, if I had sometimes not let my heart choose my token over my head."

Another ripple of laughter echoes but Hera throws a dangerous look at her husband.

"I wager that you won't add this one to your tally." Poseidon's voice is nonchalant but Hades notes that his brother's chin juts out just enough to betray his true feelings.

"Ah, so you are planning on ending your losing streak, are you, brother?" Zeus shoots Poseidon a smile. "It has been what, seven, no eight, Blood Moons since a token of your choosing won? Do you like your chances in these Games? You fancy you can win against me!"

"I did not know the competition boiled down to you alone, brothers," Hades adds as he stands next to Poseidon.

"Quite right. We all have the same chances to win," Athena says.

Hades pities her for her honesty and good intentions, but it would seem that the Goddess of wisdom is not always wise to the motivations that are moving around her.

"What would be your wager?" Zeus asks as he turns to Poseidon, a glint in his eye.

"What are we playing for – you to lose or one of us to win?" Poseidon gestures towards Hades, drawing him firmly into the rivalry.

Hades feels his shoulders droop at the thought of it,

the constant tug between them, with no one ever truly winning and everyone, everywhere, suffering for it.

Zeus is thoughtful for a moment. "Very well, if one of the three of us wins then we win this wager; if none of us win, then the wager is off."

"That hardly sounds fair to poor Hades." Hera's comment sends another light chuckle around the assembled Gods.

"Ah, Hera, sweet wife, Hades knows how *this* game works; he knows his part." Zeus winks in Hades' direction.

Hades raises an eyebrow, a small shift on his otherwise impassive face. "Who knows, brother, this might just be my Games?"

Zeus' laughter is full, the others joining in the joke. "Ah, come, brothers, what will we wager on the outcome of these Immortal Games?"

"My throne."

At Poseidon's announcement, the Gods fall quiet.

Hades feels the change in the halls of Olympus ripple through him. "Your throne, brother," he says quietly. "That is a mighty prize indeed."

"Yes, yes, it is," Zeus says with a smile, and turns to Poseidon. "And that you would willingly give it to me."

"I will hardly be giving it to you. You might be the most successful winner, but you are not the *only* winner of the Immortal Games."

Zeus raises an eyebrow. "Still, I prefer my odds to yours and definitely to Hades'."

"My odds are none of your concern, I am sure." Hades casts a dark look at both his brothers, the gravity of the stakes already weighing on him.

"Come, a brotherly wager," Zeus says dramatically. "To the victor of these Games, the thrones of the other two will pass. And who knows, you may have another chance to win it all back next Blood Moon, when I am sick of the dark and the dead."

"And what if someone other than you three were to win?" Hephaestus asks.

"No, this is between the three of us only. If you should win then the victory is yours, but our thrones remain our own," Zeus commands.

"Now that definitely sounds like a plan of your devising, husband," Hera says.

"Dear wife, you know full well that he who owns my throne will wear my crown as chief amongst us and I would not have *you* rule over me, nor any other of you but my brothers – if they prove they are worthy and equal to it."

Zeus takes a step forward and grabs Poseidon's forearm. "It is a pact!" He extends another arm to Hades. "But only if the three of us are united in it."

Hades looks between his brothers, hesitating. Zeus so sure of himself and Poseidon ... there is some plan lurking in the depths of his actions that Hades cannot fathom.

"I can command you," Zeus says.

Hades, knowing he could never let it come to that,

reaches out his arm and unites with Zeus and Poseidon in the wager.

A large clap of thunder sounds through Olympus.

For the first time ever, Hades realizes that he is going to have to actually play the Immortal Games, even if still on his own terms.

"Now this truly will be entertainment worthy of the Gods. Hermes, what do you have planned for us?" Zeus asks.

Hermes stares at the three Gods, shaking his head in disbelief, then he smiles mischievously. "These are my finest Games yet. I would not be so sure of your victory, my lords Zeus, Poseidon." Then he adds in a stage whisper, "I shall save my breath for the chances of the other brother."

The pantheon of Gods hoot in laughter. Hades narrows his eyes and the sky of Olympus instantly drops into darkness.

"Shall we get on with the selecting of the tokens?" Hermes says. "The moon is soon to turn!"

"Yes, let's!" Zeus adds, clapping both of his brothers on the back.

"You all know the rules for this part of the Games," Hermes says. "You will select your choice from the twelve tokens, each of which show a symbol that represents one sign of the zodiac. Six are iron, six are copper. You will then fulfil the requirements of your token. You may only pick a mortal who is between the ages of thirteen and nineteen. No demi-Gods, mortals only." He wags a playful finger at Zeus. "You may only choose a mortal born under the Zodiac sign you have selected. If your token is made of copper then you must choose a girl, if iron then a boy. Choose well, your chances in the Games depend upon it. And for some, your thrones too!"

Hermes releases his caduceus and the wings on the top begin to beat, holding it in mid-air; he then produces a golden cloth bag from nowhere and holds it open.

As is the custom for the start of the Games, the winner of the last chooses first.

Zeus places his hand into the bag and pulls out an iron disc. Cupping it in both his hands he peeks at the symbol on its face. His eyes light up. "Ah, I have just the mortal in mind!"

Hades knows that Zeus is not the only God to have a list of favoured mortals, watching them closely and assessing their chances as tokens.

The other Gods take it in turns to select a token so the bag empties, until it is Hades' turn. Hermes tips up the bag and the one remaining copper disc falls into his outstretched hands.

7

THE BLOOD MOON

"Are you ready, Ara?" Theron asks, his excited smile covering half his face.

I'm more ready than he will ever know. As we sit on the dry grass at the far end of the training grounds, away from the festivities and the temple, the people of Oropusa watch the sky and wait. I look up at the moon, the slim crescent of red on the silvery orb reminds me of a fingernail dipped in blood. I shake back my hair, smile, and then turn towards Theron.

"Am I ready to participate in the Immortal Games? To be the playing piece of a God? To face impossible trials and dangers unknown for the chance to win a place among the stars and the life of a hero? For the chance to win a favour from the Gods, to ask for anything I want, anything at all? Oh yeah, I'm ready." I look him up and down. "Are you?"

He laughs. "Me, I was born ready, but honestly, Ara, you have no chance against me. I mean they never choose tokens from the same place, the odds of us both being selected are…"

"Cruel," I say. He links his fingers with mine and I feel that little rush of excitement run up my arm. I look back up at the moon, the sliver of red a little thicker now. "So it's definitely possible." If there is one thing that I am certain of when it comes to the Gods it is that they love mortal misery: it is like a siren song to them.

I feel a bolt of terror run through me and I drop Theron's hand, standing up quickly. "We should get back."

Not looking at him as I start walking back to the temple, my sandals move quickly over the earth, the dust kicking up and clinging to the bottom of my dress.

His strides are longer than mine and he doesn't need to walk quickly to catch me. When he does, he grabs my wrist, his fingers circling it. I stop in my tracks, and he pulls me to him. I look up; his smile's gone, and his eyes are serious. I think about how this is his last Blood Moon; after this he is out of chances.

What will await him tomorrow? What will he do if he's not chosen?

I don't think that possibility has ever entered his mind, but I know that he won't stay here; he'll go in search of a way to prove his worth. He'll leave Oropusa one way or another and he'll leave me here waiting not just for the next Blood Moon but for him to return.

In a heartbeat I glimpse the way that life could be, so easy, so full of all the things that are around me but that

I know I'm not really part of. I see me and Theron and the life we could have together. And as I'm staring into his eyes, I think he sees that too. My head is stretching up as Theron arcs his neck towards me, his hand on my cheek, his lips dangerously close to mine, and I inhale as the anticipation runs through my body, and the distance between us diminishes to nothing.

His lips are soft and still, pressing upon mine with a lightness that feels like it is almost not there. I open my eyes and the first thing I see is the eclipsing moon, and I realize that if he's right, if he has been chosen, then he might not be here for very much longer.

I push my lips against his, fierce and desperate, as if my kisses can keep him here, can keep him with me.

As he snakes his arms around me, binding me closer to him, I hear shouting.

We both look across the training grounds beyond the festival at the small temple alight with flames, and start running towards it.

There is a hive of activity around the temple as people desperately try to account for everyone while attempting to smother the flames. I see Ida close to the steps of Taurus, walking around the burning portion of the temple and calling out. As I get closer, I realize that she is calling my father's name.

"Father!" I shout as I join Ida.

"Ara, Ara!" Ida clings to me when I get close enough. "He went in to pay his respects to your sister..."

I don't stop to think, running to the opposite side of the temple where smoke is billowing but no flames are licking.

As the air becomes thicker, I throw my hand up in front of my face. I twist one of the fabric folds of my dress over my mouth and hold it there while extending my other hand to feel my way in the smoky gloom.

"Father!" I call out as I make my way up the steps of my zodiac sign, past the niche with the offering of wine I made that morning and out into the circular inner chamber. The smoke is thicker here and I can see flames leaping out from the sections of the temple ahead.

Looking up, I see the smoke flowing out of the circular hole in the roof, and beyond the Blood Moon, the red eclipsing shadow covering almost three quarters of the orb. I find the stairs and call down as I feel for the edge of the steps through the soles of my sandals.

Time is drawn out; it takes me forever to descend the stairs, but with every step I take the smoke clears a little, although I pull some of it along behind me as I make my way towards Estella's sarcophagus.

Father is slumped over the marble, his head resting on my sister's stone chest. As I reach him I turn him over.

"Father!" I shake him and he rouses, his eyes unfocused, and begins to cough. I hold him up as his body shakes.

"Your mother, where is she?"

For a second, I just look at him.

"She's at home. Come on, we have to get out of here."

"No, your mother, she's here, I saw her, she did this,

she started the fire." He starts coughing again and I leave him while I call out to my mother.

I search the sanctuary of the fallen tokens looking for her behind each of the other sarcophagi, but there's no sign of her. By the time I return to my father the smoke is beginning to fill up the subterranean crypt.

"Come on, she's not here," I tell him, and I wonder if she ever was, or if it's just the shock and smoke talking. I grab his arm and help to lift him up.

"We need to get out," I say, and he understands, allowing me to guide him to the stairs and up. As we reach the top, I see a shadowy figure in the smoke and for a moment I think my father might have been right about my mother, and then I realize who it is.

"Theron!" I call out as I half pull my father up the last steps and into the burning temple. Bright flames are leaping over most of the building now; even the section that I entered by is glowing.

Theron hooks an arm around my father's other side and begins to pull him towards the arch heading to the sign of Sagittarius, where there is less smoke and no flames.

We move together, coughing as we enter the chamber. I can see the steps and beyond them the townsfolk moving as they try to temper the flames.

I don't know why I turn, or what makes me look behind and across the temple through the smoke towards the chamber of the Gemini, but there she is silhouetted in smoke, with the bursting flames behind her.

I don't know if she can see me, if she knows that I am watching her as she walks into those flames.

"Mother!" I call as I let go of my father, trusting him to Theron.

The smoke shifts and I lose sight of her. I hold on to where she was a second ago and I head for it, calling and coughing as I do.

The heat from the fire is stifling, and I can smell the burning of the flowers and the offerings that line the temple. I raise my arms to shield me as I see her, standing close to the top of the stairs that lead out of the temple and on to the training grounds, flames all around her. Beyond the roar of the fire I can hear her cries, wild and desperate.

"Mother!" I shield my face from the intense heat and move towards her, scooting around the burning offerings in my way.

She turns to look at me, her eyes large with wonder. "Estella!"

"No, it's Ara!" I call out as I near her and I see the disappointment on her face.

At an ear-splitting crack, I let out a scream. The column covered in crabs has fallen and is now leaning against the column of the Gemini. The roof and the columns are flexing and moving and I can see what is about to happen, how it will fall and crush my mother who still stands at the top of the stairs.

I run forwards as a tearing sound fills the air, like the world has been ripped in two. My hands outstretched,

I push her as hard as I can down the burning stairs and out on to the ground, watching her roll and people rush towards her. Just as I turn to face the column falling on to me, my last thought is of my sister and how by the grace of Hades I will get to see her again.

8

THE FATE OF HADES

Hades watches as each of the Gods rushes off to secure their tokens, but unlike them he does not stop his journeying when he reaches the realm of mortals; instead, he continues down into the underworld, into his own realm.

"Cerberus, down boy," he murmurs as his dog jumps up at him.

He strokes each head, running his fingers behind its ears, and scratching deeply into the thick fur.

"I was only gone a short time; did you really miss me that much? Come, want to go for a walk?" Cerberus lets out a great bark that rattles the mighty gates as they open for the lord of the underworld and his hound.

There are many gates that give passageway both to and within the underworld, each large and imposing, each forged from time and starlight and the blood of beings now extinct.

Hades commands each of these gates; they open and

close at his touch. Others have access to some gates, but Hades is the lord of them all. He walks through the underworld, the darkness bringing him comfort. But the inky black is not everywhere; some regions of his land shine brighter than the sun and light the underworld with a glow that is more wholesome and caring than a lover's embrace. Not all is dark in the darkness.

Hades slips his helm on his head and places a hand on Cerberus as they walk through the fields of Elysium, the golden summertime land where the world is in a perpetual state of warmth and rich harvest, and the spirits of mortals live their carefree afterlives in bliss.

Hades smiles as he and Cerberus pass unseen, hidden from the souls of his realm. He often walks among them, invisible, with the aid of his helm. And as he journeys he observes, watches and tends to his godly responsibilities.

He walks past an old man and woman, the couple sitting under the shelter of a small grove of olive trees, lazily huddled in each other's company. The woman is reading aloud from a book of poetry as the man lovingly sketches her likeness in his notebook. The sky is clear and warm, birds swoop and call to one another and Hades takes a moment to look about, unseen by all.

He can't help but feel a swell of pride for this corner of his land and he worries what shadows may pass over it if either of his brothers were to win the wager he just agreed to. He walks on, Cerberus at his heel, and feels foolish for being pulled into their folly.

It is not long till he comes to a large, secluded lake fed by a cascading waterfall. Cerberus jumps in and happily swims the waters as Hades makes his way to the waterfall and the cave behind it.

The dwelling of the Fates is cast in dancing rainbows as the light from Elysium splits its way through the waterfall and pushes deep into their cave. Hades moves with it into the cave with its smooth, warm rocks that sparkle and shimmer in the spectrum of light.

Before him is the loom of life, large and vibrant, running along the curved wall at the back of the cave. To one side of it sits Clotho, at her spinner, pulling the thread through the needle and casting each one in a different colour that she plucks from the rainbows as they waltz through the air. Her nimble fingers constantly move to pinch out numerous colours, weaving them together to form a unique hue of thread that she passes to her sister, Lachesis.

Lachesis then moves along the loom, weaving and teasing the threads from Clotho, entwining, separating, pulling and stitching them along the tapestry of the living. Their sister, Atropos, moves along beside her holding a pair of small golden scissors and snipping the threads, before pulling them from the tapestry, ready to pass them to Thanatos so that he might collect their mortal souls.

"Ah, young Hades, it is time for another poor soul is it not?" The voice is as soft as a summer breeze rippling over diaphanous fabric.

"I am afraid so, Atropos. The Gods of Olympus will have their games and we all have to play them."

"So, what will you have this time, Lord Hades?" Clotho says, as she leaves her threads and ventures forward.

Hades holds out his copper token.

"A Scorpio. It's been a long time since you selected one of those; the last time you did you almost won." Lachesis weaves a few loose threads into the tapestry, tugging to the front a grey-blue thread the colour of pre-dawn light.

"It is not always about the winning," Hades says. "Although this time…"

"It may not ever be about the winning for you, but I bet your mortal tokens would have something different to say about that," Clotho says, with a chortle that sounds like the clatter of the loom.

"We heard about your wager!" Atropos says, as she snips another thread. "Are the parameters of your choosing still the same?"

"Yes, I see no need to change my morals now. I will require a mortal that fits the conditions of the token: a girl aged between thirteen and nineteen born under the sign of the scorpion; and for my conditions she must be close to death, you must be about to cut her thread loose. Life is precious. I would not want to take a life for the sport of the Games that was not already at risk."

"Not even when so much is at risk for you, for your realm?" Clotho asks.

"Especially not then. If we change who we are, our

morals, our values, the fundaments of our nature for the sake of winning then we have already lost," Hades says.

"You are an odd God, Hades, not at all like your kin, not like us old ones, or the Titans, either," Lachesis says.

"I sometimes worry that I have spent too much time in the company of mortals. They all come to me and my realm eventually and when they do they become my charges for eternity or until they choose to walk through the fields of Asphodel and forget their lives ready for a new one. They live a mayfly life in the air, but here with me in the underworld they live a life that is marked by the slow turning of the cosmos. There are souls in my realm that I have been acquainted with for longer than some of the stars have shone. And even if they are reborn, their threads rewoven into the loom of life, they come back to me in an instant. New threads are always being woven, and my realm expands. I am only saddened that when they reach me the richness of their threads has often paled."

"Yep, he's definitely an odd one," Lachesis says, and her sisters laugh like the tinkling of pins falling to the stone floor. "Come." She beckons Hades close to the weaving and points to a knot in the fabric of the loom, running a finger over three thick strands that shine with a lustre that makes all other threads look weak. She gestures to each thread in turn, her fingers tracing the lines, one thread of gold, one silver, one bronze.

"These threads belong to you and your brothers, and this knot is the wager you three have made. Can you see how it sticks out from the weaving of the world, how it pulls on all the other threads, how it puckers the fabric that was once smooth and flowing?" There is an edge of annoyance in her voice.

"There is something about this wager between the three of you that is unsettling to us," Clotho says, as she passes a new thread towards the loom for Lachesis to weave.

"We, the Fates, can see all – we know the past, the present, the future of all things – but this knot in the weaving of the world was not created by us and the threads are pulled too tightly for us to unpick."

"Can you not cut the threads free and pull out the knot?" Hades asks.

Atropos smiles at him and he feels like a small child before her. "I cannot cut the knot, to do so would kill a God, or three, and my scissors are not sharp enough for such a task."

"This game you are playing, this foolish brotherly rivalry of the Gods, it is more important than any of the petty rivalries and wagers you and your brothers have ever had, Hades. We cannot see the outcome, but we know that if the knot remains then all the other threads will be pulled into it and many, maybe all, will snap."

"All threads, Hades – yours, ours, everyone's," Lachesis adds. She runs a finger over the knot and Hades watches it grow, the threads twisting more tightly, drawing together.

"You must find a way to unpick the knot that you and your brothers have made."

"Why me?"

"Because, Hades, you are the morning star and the evening light, you are movable and transient. You have a foot in life and another in death; you have knowledge that neither of your brothers do because they do not value death and they do not value life."

"I came for a token, and you give me this."

"You gave this to yourself, Hades. The knot is made of three Godly threads; without you it wouldn't have been. What is it you say to the dead when they rebel against their punishments in the underworld?"

Hades groans, not appreciating the use of his own words against him. "I tell them to own their deeds and face their choices, to make amends if they can and to forgive themselves if they cannot."

"We would offer you this same advice," Atropos says.

"And now for your token." Lachesis teases the dawn-coloured thread towards the knot.

Clotho leaves her spinner and leans close to the loom. "Ah, I remember spinning her thread," she says. "It is strong and yielding and her colour is deep and varied, but the edges of her thread are scattered. Beware, Hades, that she does not catch and fray!"

Atropos places her scissors in her pocket and instead pulls out a stitch picker. She tugs at the morning-grey thread and moves it across the surface of the weaving, then pulls at Hades' thread. He lets out a short sharp gasp as the Fate twists the two strands together.

"There, I have not cut her thread as I should have, but I have linked it to yours for a while. She has a second chance of life now, and if she makes it through the Games, her thread will stay in the loom, and she will be blessed with a long and smooth weaving."

"Thank you," Hades says, as he rubs his chest where he felt the tug. "You have given me my token and much to think about besides."

"Remember, Hades, knots can be tricky things, and this one will require you to actually play your brothers at their own game this time."

Hades looks thoughtfully at the three sisters of Fate; he understands the seriousness of their words. As he turns to leave, he hears the snip of the scissors, the spin of the wheel, the clack of the loom. If the knot were to break all the threads, then there would be no more weaving.

Hades walks through the waterfall and once on the other side looks down at the token in his hand, running a thumb over the name that has appeared there – Ara.

9

THE TOKEN OF HADES

The roar of the fire is replaced by a silence so deep and complete that it is deafening. I open my eyes to find that the light of the blaze has been extinguished, sucked out completely. I shiver with the loss of its heat.

It is then that I feel a searing pain rush over my arms, my face, my legs. I cry out and stumble as the adrenaline that was sustaining me floods from my body. Collapsing to the ground, I find that I'm on a short flight of broad stairs, the tread deep and the riser shallow. I wonder if these are the steps to the underworld, and I try to manage the pain and panic as my chest rises and falls sharply. Part of me is surprised that death is so painful; the other part of me is not surprised at all. I spent most of my life secretly cursing the Gods; this fiery pain might just be my punishment.

But still, it is excruciating. I cry out again, shaking my head, unable to imagine being in this much pain for the rest of time. I lie on the solid steps and begin to rock to-and-fro whimpering uncontrollably.

There's a noise in the gloom ahead. Someone is walking towards me, and I know I should stand and be on guard, but as the shape of the person solidifies out of the shadows it is all I can do not to faint from the pain searing through my flesh.

It's a man, no, a boy around the same age as Theron. He is wearing a long robe, his hair is black and his skin is so pale. My stomach flips as I take in his face. He's handsome in a chiselled jaw and cheekbone kind of way, and I'm caught by his eyes, which are the bluest eyes I have ever seen; they shine like the ocean on a clear day, like the sky in midsummer.

I begin to open my mouth as he takes another step forward and the glowing light of nearby torches suddenly blazes. I flinch as I think of the fire, and when I look back at him and the light shining on the double-ended staff in his hand, his bident, my stomach drops. I realize who he is.

When he speaks, his voice is low like his gaze, and his words are soft and slow as if he has all the time in the world, which I guess he does. "I am Hades," he says.

I swallow and reply, "And I am dead."

He smiles. It's a small flicker at the corner of his lips, playful and shy. "Not quite." His blue eyes dance for a moment and then look upwards.

Following his gaze up into the gloom, I realize something huge is looming over me. My mind fills the shape with that of a huge three-headed dog, with fiery red eyes and large fearsome teeth. But as I continue looking and my eyes adjust, I realize that it is not a dog at all but something infinitely more terrifying.

I look back at Hades and he raises a hand, the light from the torches brightening, filling the chamber, and when I look again I can see it clearly. A massive scorpion, its tail pulled up in an arc, the sting looking deadly in the flickering torchlight. And beyond the huge statue of my sign, I see the dusky sky and the stars of Scorpio glinting down at me.

"It is much worse than death, Ara; you are my token for The Immortal Games," he says.

If the relentless throbbing in my burnt skin would cease I'm sure my tears would be those of joy. I'm in the Games; I have a chance to avenge my sister, to kill Zeus.

But the pain of the burns is overwhelming. I bite my lip to save from crying out as I lower myself flat on the cool stone steps and look up at the statue and the constellation of stars beyond it, whimpering with every beat of my heart.

Hades is kneeling beside me, his intense eyes sweeping over me, his face serious as he reaches out a hand towards my burnt flesh.

I flinch back and cry out, pain erupting from my skin as my red and blistered flesh tightens as I move.

He holds his hands out. "I'm not going to hurt you," he says. And I think about disagreeing with him, but his voice is still low and soft and strangely comforting.

I lie perfectly still as he reaches out again. As he touches my arm and sweeps across the burnt skin, I feel a wave of serenity pass over me, the pain leaving my body as I look down and see my flesh restored. Pushing myself up on my elbows, I watch as Hades gently runs a hand from my ankle to the top of my leg, and I sigh with the relief. Everywhere his hands touch, my body responds, healing instantly.

Then he cups my face and brushes my cheeks with his fingers, his eyes tracing his progress. It is only after he has moved his hand down my neck, over my collarbone and rests it on my shoulder, that he looks me in the eye. That small, shy smile is back, tugging at the left corner of his mouth. I suddenly feel light-headed.

I have never experienced a look so intense before, or the sensation of gentle calm as he heals my wounds. Slowly, gently, he pulls me up so I am sitting. He then runs his hands down my back, healing the burns there. My head falls against his chest. As the last of the pain leaves my body, I breathe in deeply; he smells of the deep rich soil warmed on a hot summer's day.

Hades shifts, moving away from me, supporting me still but at arm's length.

"How do you feel, Ara?" he asks. I'm surprised that he knows my name and that it falls so naturally from his lips, his low voice making it sound like a deep sigh.

"Better." I remember that I'm speaking to a God and wonder if I should add something godly and gratifying, but I don't know what to say so I say nothing.

He tips his head to the side slightly, his eyes running over every inch of me in a way that his hands had not.

"I can't heal you once the Games begin, but I can make sure that you start it injury free. Is there anywhere I've missed?" he asks.

I shake my head and feel the warmth in my cheeks. "No, no, I'm fine, thank you." It's true. Unfortunately I feel no more pain in my body, but then a sudden jolt runs through my heart.

"My mother, is she OK, my father, and Theron too?" I blurt out as I make to stand. Something in me needs to be standing when I hear what he has to say.

Hades is still crouching and looks up at me, then his eyes get a faraway look as if he's concentrating on something just beyond me. "None of them are in my realm," he says.

I let my shoulders drop as a sigh I didn't know I was holding escapes my lips with a "Thank the Gods!" Then I laugh as I look down at him. "Thank *you*, I guess."

He stands and despite me being on the step above him he still towers over me. I crane my neck to look at him and guess he must be at least a head taller than Theron, although his frame is not as muscular, then I check myself and turn away.

"Ara." He sighs my name and I look up into his too-blue eyes. "They are not in my realm, but you should be." He says it gently, so gently that I almost miss the gravity of his words.

"Me, I … I am dead then?"

He shakes his head, that secret smile slipping back. "No,

you are very much alive. For now." The smile drifts away, and I feel a pang in my chest.

"For now?" I repeat, and then I remember that Hades has never won the Immortal Games.

"You should have died in that fire as you saved your mother," he tells me, and I know it's true. "But the Fates chose you as they do all my tokens for the Games."

He holds out his hand and in his palm I see a token similar to the one around my neck. A scorpion is embossed in the circular copper metal and around the edge it reads ARA TOKEN OF HADES.

"My realm is full of many souls; I don't like to add to the total if I can help it, and if by playing the Games a soul will live for longer on the earth then I think that is a good thing."

I listen and don't tell him that the extra time will probably be filled with unimaginable horrors.

"I always choose a token from those who are about to join me in the underworld in the hope that they might win the Games and live longer under the light of the sun." He has a wistful look upon his face and, for a brief second, he closes his eyes as if remembering what it was like to feel the rays of the sun on his pale skin.

I don't want to break that blissful look by pointing out that so far none of his tokens has ever won and very few survive the Games, but who am I to disappoint a God?

"Here." He reaches out to pass me the token and I extend my fingers, brushing his palm as I take it.

Holding the token tight in my hand, I feel a warmth pass over me. I glance down and see that my scorched dress has been replaced by a black tunic, which is covered in gold stars that mark out the constellation of Scorpio. A wide belt with a scorpion on the buckle circles the tunic and on my feet are new sandals. I flex my toes and sigh as the shoes bite my skin.

Hades looks at me quizzically. "Is something wrong?"

"I … I just prefer my old sandals; I've broken them in and they're comfortable." I shrug, feeling foolish.

"I see," he says. The tug on his lips is back and I feel my cheeks blush as this God laughs at me.

I feel a stirring in the air around my feet and look down to see my old sandals back. I smile up at him and as I catch his eye I see a spark in it, like a falling star lighting up the night. He holds my gaze and I feel a strange warmth passing over me, which remains even though he suddenly looks away as if his attention has been diverted.

"We don't have long before the Games begin and the quest is announced," Hades says, looking back at me. "Hermes is the quest master for these Games; he will outline the rules after the initial trial."

"The initial trial, what is it?" I ask.

Hades shakes his head, sweeping his black hair back into place when it flops forward. "We Gods are not privy to everything," he tells me with a rise of his eyebrows so small I'm not sure that it was there at all. "It is against the rules for any but the quest master to know of the quest or its trials before they are disclosed in the Games. There is always an initial trial before the quest is announced," he continues. "Throughout the quest you will face many trials; before each one I will be given the chance to roll a die, which will decide on what action I can perform to help you or not!"

"Not?" I say.

Hades reaches out his hand to show me a twelve-sided die, each side engraved with a symbol of the zodiac. "If I roll an earth sign then you get an advantage, a fire sign then you'll be in an attack position, air is defence, and if I roll a water sign then you'll be at a disadvantage in some way."

I nod as I take this information in. I really am just a flesh and blood playing piece.

He places the die in the folds of his robes and fixes me with a serious stare. "I promise you I will do all I can to help you, but just as you have your own free will and can use it as you wish, I have mine and I will not use it to go against any of the things that I believe in, like the preservation and sanctity of life and living. I will not give you any gifts that are intended to hurt or kill another living thing."

It takes me way longer than a minute to process what it is that Hades, God of the underworld, receiver of the dead, has just said.

"But what about the preservation and sanctity of my life?" I say, hearing the incredulity in my voice.

"This is why I only ever choose a token who was going to perish anyway. I don't believe in violence, not any more, and I can't be responsible for adding to the halls of my land. I have seen the lamenting that the spirits of the dead go through, the loss and sadness, the regret at not living longer, and not living well. I can't be responsible for that."

I look up at him and I can feel my mouth hanging open in shock, surprise and disgust.

"But you are the God of the dead!" I lift my hands up in exasperation.

That sad smile is tugging on his lip again as he nods slowly then looks at me with those large seriously blue eyes.

"I am the God of the dead, but I am not the God of death; that honour and burden goes to another. Nor am I my nephew Ares, God of war, who delights in the death of those he crushes. I live with the spirits of the dead, I care for and punish them as the judges of the dead, Rhadamanthys, Minos and Aeacus feel fit, and during my duties I listen to them. I know how precious this mortal life is to them, and it is important to me too."

I think about how hard I've worked for this moment, to be chosen as a token to the Gods, to win and claim my prize, to take my revenge. But how can I win with Hades as my God? How can I avenge Estella? Everything I have worked towards, all the training, all the pain, for this.

I feel a sickness rising inside me, and I think I might throw up, or cry, or both, and then I remember what Hades said earlier, that he chose me because I should have died in the fire. I remember the flames and the heat, the smoke and the falling column. I look down at my skin not red and blistered as it was and I realize that this is a second chance. Hades is my second chance.

"What type of gifts are you going to give me?" I ask.

"Useful things, I assure you," he says. "Actually, I get to give you a gift now, before the initial trial."

I raise an eyebrow, not knowing what to expect from this *useful* gift. He reaches out a hand and as if plucked out of thin air, he is holding the strap of a leather bag. The strap is long and will easily cross my body. He reaches out a little further, just as he did with the token. He looks so pleased with himself. I take the bag and place the strap over my head, the pouch resting at my hip. The protective flap covering the opening is embossed with the same scorpion symbol as my token.

"Thank you," I say slowly as I glance up and see that he still has that same pleased look. All I can think is that *I'm about to go into the Immortal Games with a new accessory for the tunic I'm wearing.*

This might have come across on my face because Hades drops the small smile and his eyes become big and a little worried as he says, "It's a Trojan bag, made from the hide of a Trojan horse."

I look at him, my face blank. I have no idea what he is talking about.

"You can put anything in the bag, anything at all, and it will fit. You could put me in it if you wanted and carry me about all day, all year, even, and you wouldn't feel a thing. The bag wouldn't get heavy at all, and then when you pulled me out it would be as if I have experienced no passing of time, I'd be exactly the same as I was when I went in. Whenever you want to retrieve something from the bag all you need to do is place your hand inside and think of the item, and it will come to you."

I'm tempted to hold the bag open and ask him for a demonstration but I don't, mainly because by the look on his face, I think he would gladly climb inside the bag and I'm not entirely sure that I'd call him back out.

Instead, I settle for: "I see, thank you." Actually, I *can* see how the bag might be useful.

Hades looks up, like a startled puppy, as if there is something in the air, beyond my hearing, and I guess there is, because he turns to look at me and says, "The initial trial is about to begin."

I feel a knot of fear rise within and I exhale slowly, trying to calm myself. I've trained for this. I'm ready. It's quite literally now or never.

Hades raises a hand and guides me up the stairs past the statue of the massive scorpion and to a large door at the back of the chamber.

"Once you pass through this door the trial will start," says Hades. "I hope the Fates are on your side and that you pass the first trial, but if not, I will see you soon either way, in this realm or my own."

Strangely, a part of me feels reassured that I will see

him again, but a bigger part of me is looking at him with a raised eyebrow. He just underestimated me and my abilities; he has no idea who I am or what I am capable of.

"I'll see you when I pass this trial," I tell him and walk forward, placing a hand on the door and pushing it open into darkness.

THE INITIAL TRIAL

It's suffocatingly black beyond the door. I can feel the ground beneath my sandals, firm and smooth, covered in a thin dusting of grit. I feel the small grains pop and crunch as I tentatively investigate the darkness. I shudder as I think of all the creatures that could be crouching in the shadows. I bet they don't have the same attitudes towards violence as Hades does.

I reach out my arms on either side, but I'm only greeted by emptiness. So, I blink several times to try and adjust my eyes, but it's impenetrable.

"Hey, Hades!"

It feels wrong to say his name out loud, it's such a taboo. No one says his name aloud in case he hears and turns his eye on you. But I've seen his eyes and the blueness of them. I smile in the darkness as I start talking to my God.

"So, I remember hearing once that you are the lord of darkness or night-time or something. I'm going to put night and dark together as one because they're pretty similar, right?" I can almost see him poised to correct me. "Anyway, it's pretty dark in here and I'm going to try and not freak out because, well, this is your dominion, right? And we're like a team or something."

I latch on to that idea of us being a team as I imagine him smiling at me in that small way, his mouth tugging shyly to one side as if amused. I reckon I'm being pretty amusing right now, standing in the dark, talking to an absent God, while I keep my arms out wide and slide my feet along the floor, inching to one side trying to find the edge of the room I'm in. For a moment I wonder if there is no edge, if it is just an open nothingness; my belly drops.

I freeze as a voice fills the void, not the voice I had been hoping to hear. This voice is higher in pitch, more sing-song and cheery, reminding me of the swifts in summer whooping to each other as they soar through the blue sky.

"Tokens, I am Hermes, quest master of these Games. You have each been selected by your God so that you may pay tribute to them with your skills in playing the Immortal Games." He pauses for what I can only assume is dramatic effect. "Before the quest begins you must find your way through … the gauntlet."

As Hermes says this, a soft light suddenly shines from above me. I look up into a dark sky, darker than any winter evening and clearer too, as it's full of stars, each point of light blazing brightly, from white to blue, yellow through to red. Despite the very edge of the universe shining down upon me I am unable to see much of the gauntlet ahead, except the walls that mark the sides of it. I'm glad to see one wall is close to my outstretched hand and, suddenly conscious of them, I lower my arms.

I know that a long thin passageway of unseen terrors awaits, and this unnerves me, which I guess is the point. I continue to stare up at the stars; I marvel at them, eyes wide and mouth open. If this is the last thing I ever see, then it is pretty spectacular.

I push that thought from my mind, but it's too late, my heart rate has shot up. Hermes' voice rings out again.

"The gauntlet is marked with many threats, traps and tricks. All are designed to stop you if they can. This is the first trial of the Games, designed to weed out the unworthy tokens early on. If you are worthy of your God's favour, then you will make it through. If not, your stars will burn in your zodiac sign for all eternity, but not so brightly that you will be remembered forever."

Hades will remember them, I think to myself as I remember the way the God of the underworld had talked about the spirits of the dead. He was not what I had been expecting, not that I had been expecting him at all. But I had thought that when I was selected to be a token I would have feared the God that chose me. Hades, well, I should be more scared of him than any other God, but there is something deep and serious, but playful and sincere, about him. I have to respect his attitude towards violence; if the stories of the Gods are to be taken as true then they are all too quick to

73

bring terror. I try to remember stories of Hades, but my head is too full of the invisible threats ahead of me.

"Come on now, Hades, this is it. The start of the Games. You roll your die then I move, and you move with me. That's how it goes, right?" I whisper into the darkness, feeling my heart rate come down and my breathing stabilize. I don't need him to answer me; I am used to talking to those who aren't there.

The light from the stars above gets a little brighter, or perhaps my eyes become more accustomed to the gloom; the gauntlet lies before me like a long passageway, and I can see the first obstacle now – a thin balance beam of rock with a seemingly endless fall on either side flagged by the walls of the gauntlet. I squint and realize that this is followed by a large expanse of nothing, although in the walls, there are a series of holes. I stare at those holes for a moment and decide that whatever lurks in them cannot be good.

I'm just about to look for the obstacle beyond that when Hermes calls, "Let the Games begin!"

A rumbling sound fills the air from above and without stopping to think, I run.

The beam of rock is narrower than the palm of my hand and smooth. There's no dust to help the bottom of my sandals grip the surface and I am so glad that Hades gave me back my old ones, their tough soles giving me purchase as I race along the beam with as much speed as I feel is safe, my arms out to the side to steady me, the Trojan bag clinging weightlessly to my side. Once over the beam

I don't hesitate or break my run, I lean forward and sprint full pelt through that section of the gauntlet with the holes in the wall. As I run, I hear swift swoops behind me and risk a glance into one of the holes as I pass and see the deadly shine of a knife's blade winking out at me.

I hear a scream from close by and I'm hit by the realization that the other tokens are each running their own gauntlets. I wonder if they are all facing the same obstacles as me.

I think of the blades flying out of the wall behind me and the scream that came somewhere from my left. I turn it up a notch and feel my muscles burning as the knife blades continue to dart out from the walls. Their sinister whooshing stops but I continue running, looking for the next threat, but it doesn't come from in front of me. The ground suddenly shakes violently and I stumble, falling to my hands and knees on the floor of the gauntlet. As I push myself up, I glance behind to see a giant boulder rolling towards me. I curse again. Then start running forward, still glancing over my shoulder as the huge boulder just keeps coming.

I turn my head just in time to see a sharp blade pendulum across my path. I jump back and stand stock still as another joins it, then a third, fourth, fifth. A line of blades all swinging at different times and me standing still, losing valuable time, while the boulder rumbles closer. I dart forward as the first one passes and manage to run straight through the second one too, but my timing is off on the third and I have to pause again; the fourth is swinging up and I lunge out of the way as I run forward, but I'm not quite quick enough and it catches the back of my left arm as it swings down on to me.

I let out a gasp of pain but don't look back. I can feel blood dripping down to my elbow and can hear the boulder just behind me as it collides with the first pendulum. Ahead of me is a short run and then a gaping void, except it's not a void, it's a pit and the bottom of it is littered with spikes. The gap is at least twice my height lengthways and I don't think I've ever jumped that far, but I can't let myself doubt because the boulder is on my heels and two strides later, I've run out of ground and I'm leaping in the air, willing my body to stretch and push towards the other side.

I realize my feet aren't going to make it and reach forward with my torso, my elbows and forearms hitting the edge as my body slams into the side of the void. I feel myself slip and dig my fingertips into the hard ground, my fingernails breaking.

I twist my head and see the boulder tumble into the gap, crushing the spikes as if they were toothpicks as its momentum carries it on towards me. I pull with my arms and dig my toes into the side of the void, scrambling up as quickly as I can and just heaving myself on to the ground as it shakes with the force of the boulder hitting the side of the pit. I roll on to my back and lie on the ground for a moment, looking up at the stars and counting all of my lucky ones. Then I hear a crack underneath me.

"You've got to be kidding!" I cry as I push myself up

and start running again, the ground below my feet opening up and giving way, crumbling in on itself. Just ahead of me is an open doorway. I can feel my feet slipping, the falling ground is faster than I am, so I leap to the doorway, diving through it and landing face down on a hard mosaic floor.

I don't stay down; I get up fast and I'm about to start running again when I look up to see Hades standing in front of me.

"We did it, I did it! Go team Hades!" I say out loud then feel like a fool.

"Yes, we did, well you did most of the heavy lifting, all I did was roll a die," Hades says, that smile tugging on the side of his lips. "The Fates chose well," he adds as he looks at me approvingly.

"Yay, Fates!" I say as I brush the dirt from my robe and start to take in my grazed knees and the gash on the back of my arm that is now bleeding down to my wrist.

Hades takes the edge of his robes and wipes the blood away, before applying pressure to the wound. "I can't heal your injuries, but I can give you a gift for passing the first trial. Place your hand into the Trojan bag and call your gift to you." He is still holding his robes on my arm.

I look at him, his too-blue eyes locking with mine, and raise an eyebrow.

"Fine!" I mutter and place my right hand in the bag, thinking of a gift. I feel something in my hand as if someone has placed it there, and I instantly know it's not the gift I was thinking of.

"Rope!" I pull the length of coiled rope from the bag. "Are you sure you don't want to give me a sword or a bow or a shield or something?"

"I'm sure, Ara," Hades says, releasing my arm which has stopped bleeding. There is an edge to his voice as sharp as a blade as if this is final, and it feels like I can't press him on it, not right now anyway.

Hades reaches for the rope and pulls it away from me. It runs through my fingers smoothly and as it trails it shimmers, its fine silver strands catching the light of the small room we are standing in.

"This rope is made of seven strands of starlight, each one weaved by one of the seven Pleiades sisters. The rope is unbreakable, it will never fray or rot and it will grow and shrink at your command. It will give you hope when you have need of it, just as the glowing of the stars do."

"It's beautiful," I say and it's true, I'm mesmerized by it. "Thank you," I tell him and I mean it.

The God of the underworld looks embarrassed; if alabaster was capable of blushing, then I would have thought that his cheeks had turned a little pink. He wraps the rope in a coil and hands it to me. My fingers brush his hand as I take the rope and he lets go quickly, turning away and walking over the mosaic pattern of the scorpion as he calls back over his shoulder.

"Come, Hermes is about to announce the quest. We will see what we are up against."

THE TOKENS AND THEIR GODS

As I follow Hades through the door beyond the mosaic, I throw my hand up to shield my eyes from the brilliant sunlight. He does the same and I notice that even after my eyes have adjusted to the light, he still squints heavily and raises his hand from time to time.

"An amphitheatre?" I ask as I look around. The door, now closed behind us, is below the rows of curved seats that all look upon the stage in front of us. It is beautiful with high arches and a large performing area.

Hades nods. "Hermes is fond of public oration! No doubt he will treat us to a speech before too long." That small smile is back; I find it infectious and realize that I'm smiling too. But my smile soon fades as I turn towards one of the other doorways. I smell salt on a fresh breeze and my eyes grow wide as I take in the God before me.

I look at Poseidon and I feel it, the awe and terror that I should, but don't, feel when I look at Hades. Poseidon is wearing a small robe tucked around his waist, a thin cape made of net around his shoulders, and in his hand he holds his three-pronged trident. Sun-kissed skin covers long muscles, and although his head is smooth and hairless, he has a long, flowing beard. I can feel myself tremble at the power of this God. When I glance over at Hades, he's looking at me quizzically.

"What?" I say.

He shakes his head, that amused look back on his face. "Nothing." He scarcely raises his eyebrow, but I know the motion is there as he leaves my side and walks to Poseidon.

I wonder if I feel differently towards Hades than I do to Poseidon because he is my God for the Games, because he chose me and we're a team. Perhaps it's part of the Games, making the tokens feel at ease with their Gods so that they perform well together, or perhaps it's just Hades?

"Brother," the God of the sea booms and his voice sounds like waves crashing on the shore.

The two of them embrace and I can see the family resemblance: they are both tall and strong, and their eyes shine with the same intensity although Poseidon's are sea-green. He appears to be much older than Hades, nearly as old as my father I would say at a guess.

It's then that I notice the beautiful girl standing next to Poseidon. Her hair is the colour of golden sands, long and flowing, her face, delicate with full lips, like a marble carving. She is wearing a short robe similar to mine, the same green as Poseidon's eyes, but most of it is covered by silver armour – the design of a fish, the symbol of Pisces,

80

on the breastplate – and in her hand she holds a silver trident, a mirror of Poseidon's, only smaller, although it looks just as deadly.

The Gods talk as the two of us assess one another. She looks scared, and I can't blame her. We have been plucked from our lives to be confronted by a God and given the task of being their token. We just had to run for our lives and are about to set off on a quest that will no doubt get us killed.

The girl is looking at Hades and I realize that most of the fear that she is showing belongs to him. I look at my God. He is listening intently to Poseidon, his face full of attention and concentration. I wonder if she is feeling the same way about Hades as I do about Poseidon, and I just can't understand how this girl can see anything that would bring her fear.

As if he senses me looking, Hades turns towards me and I feel a little gasp leave me, as if I've been hit on the training grounds and winded.

"This is Ara," Hades says, introducing me to Poseidon.

The God of the sea looks at me and gives a gentle chuckle that sounds like the lapping of a rock pool. "What death did you save this one from?" he asks Hades, while slapping his brother on the back.

Hades offers a small smile. "A hot one!"

The rock pool laughter babbles louder. "This is my token, Danae. I've had my eye on her for a few Games now; she will be a worthy playing piece."

I bristle as I hear Poseidon talk of Danae as nothing more than a possession for him to use and wonder if Hades feels the same way about me. I look at the beautiful young woman and see that she is avoiding looking at Poseidon. Does she feel the awe for him that I did, an awe that has faded since he began talking?

"I'm glad the Fates gave me her symbol this time; she would have been too old to play by the next Blood Moon."

I feel a burning coursing through my veins and decide right there and then that if I can help Danae in any way during these Games then I will.

"Brother, are we still twelve?" Poseidon asks Hades.

"Not quite. I feel one outside my gate. Thanatos has been swift in collecting him."

"Was it Zeus' token?" Poseidon asks, a note of anxiety in his voice.

"It was a boy named Philco; he was but thirteen," Hades says. "He enjoyed playing the lute, and was quite skilled at it by all accounts, and he could sing well too; people travelled far to hear his songs."

"It doesn't sound like a token of Zeus." Poseidon's voice is edged with disappointment.

All of a sudden the amphitheatre feels too small, and I realize that while I've been concentrating on Poseidon, other Gods and their tokens have arrived.

My eyes widen as I take in the pantheon of Gods. My heart rate rises as I see Aphrodite, who is so beautiful that I do not have the words to describe how she looks or how

I feel when I look upon her. At her side is her husband Hephaestus, his arms full of rippling muscles, his hand clutching a hammer so large I know I would never be able to lift it let alone shape metal with it.

I wonder how many of the tokens will be wearing armour made by him and, looking around, I see that only two others are without this protection, a girl with a helm and a spear standing close to Ares, and Hephaestus' own token who is holding a hammer similar to his God's and wears a belt from which hangs a burning torch of blue fire. The flames almost seem to lick the edge of his deep blue tunic covered in bronze arrows, the sign of Sagittarius, but I realize he has no burns at all; he doesn't even give the flame at his hip a second look. I rub my hands over my arms, remembering the burns from the temple.

I turn to scour the crowd.

"Looking for someone?" Hades asks, stepping closer to me.

I almost tell him Zeus but instead I say, "Just taking in the competition." And then I can't help adding on, "I see they all have weapons."

"So they all do," Hades says, as if it is an odd thing for a token to have. "You know, they don't have to be your competition, your actions are what make them so."

I notice him glance towards Poseidon, who in turn is looking across the amphitheatre. I follow Poseidon's gaze and see Zeus.

For a second, I am glad that Hades never gave me a

weapon. If he had I'm not sure I could have stayed still; I would have run across the gravelled ground and sunk whatever metal I had into the God. I imagine what it would have felt like to have had a trident like Danae's and to have sunk it into Zeus' chest. How surprised he would have been when I pulled it from his body and told him, "That is for Estella." Would he even remember who she was?

Hades touches my arm, pulling me back to myself. Fists clenched, jaw set, I realize that I'm crying. I quickly wipe my tears on the back of my hand as he lowers his head towards my ear and asks, so quietly it may have been carried on a dying breath, "Are you all right, Ara?"

I close my eyes, not just because I don't want to see Zeus but because Hades said my name in that soft sigh that makes my whole being tingle. I feel myself relax as it flows through me and open my eyes, planning on turning to look at him. But the first thing I see is Zeus' token.

"Theron!" I call out and he snaps his head towards me. I run in his direction and he does the same.

His grey robes are covered in golden armour with his Capricorn symbol blazing on it, a sword hanging from his belt, and when we reach each other I collide into his solid breastplate. We hold each other tightly, so, so tightly. He is a chink of normality within this theatre of the Gods and I am so glad to see him it takes me by surprise.

When he pulls away from me, he moves a hand to my cheek, and I remember how he held my face like that under the Blood Moon just before he kissed me. And

84

for a moment I think about kissing him again. Instead, I release him and take a step back as I realize that everyone is looking at us.

"Ah, young love." Aphrodite's voice is sweet and melodious and carrying. I feel my cheeks blush and I look down at the ground.

Zeus is beside Theron before I realize. Being this close to him I feel a torment running through me. He is magnetic, his whole being radiating power and strength, and I want to please him, I want to be seen by him and for him to turn his favour upon me; but I also want to reach for the sword at Theron's belt and run Zeus through.

I say nothing when he nudges Theron and leans towards him, saying in a loud whisper, "All the world's a game, lad. Don't do anything I wouldn't."

This time, I act on instinct and lunge forwards, reaching for Theron's sword, but Hades has me by the wrist and pulls me so that I'm knocked off balance. It looks as if I swoon, and he catches me.

Zeus laughs. "Ah, Hades. Trust you, brother, to pick the delicate one; she is probably overcome with emotion for my young champion here." Zeus lifts Theron's arm and I watch as my friend smiles with glee.

Hades is still holding me in his arms and he scoops me off the ground, looking at Theron with an expression so cold and still that for a moment I think the pale God really has turned to stone.

"She is delicate," Hades says, his voice as sombre as the

grave and his arms tight around me. I very much doubt that the expression on my face says delicate as I stare at him.

"Maybe you should put her down, Hades, I think you are embarrassing the mortal." Zeus chuckles as he turns, along with everyone else, to watch Hermes the messenger God flying into the amphitheatre.

Hades places me down at the back of the crowd as the Gods and tokens move to surround Hermes, but he keeps hold of my arm. "What was that?" he says in a whisper so deadly that my blood freezes.

For a second I think about lying to him, but instead I just straighten up and raise my chin.

"Revenge," I whisper back in a voice just as detached.

He looks at me with the expression he had earlier, as if he is searching beyond at the things that others cannot see. His face falls and I feel a pain at how sad he suddenly looks, how disappointed he is, disappointed with me.

"I see." He looks away from me, releasing my arm. "I am the God of many things, Ara. Of the underworld, of the dead and the darkness, of dreaming and of the unknown; except to me the unknown is known when I seek it out, and I know what you hold in your heart." He looks down at me, his eyes measuring me and pitying me. I feel the chill on my skin as he moves away from me and towards the knot of Gods and tokens that have gathered around Hermes.

I follow him but at a distance. He is still a God after

all, their wrath is legendary, and I did just attempt to kill his brother.

Hermes floats above the stage, his winged sandals flapping continually, keeping him in the air. Pointing his caduceus, the long-winged staff surrounded by two twisting snakes, at each God in turn, he begins to count them. "Eleven, we are all here, well, those of us who are still playing!"

Some of the Gods laugh, Zeus booms with merriment, but Hades remains quiet.

I glance at him and see that faraway look slip back on to his face for a moment. I wonder if he is thinking of the token who had perished, the boy, Philco, seeking him out at the gates of his realm the way he did earlier, the way he had searched when I asked if my parents and Theron were dead. Or if he is thinking of me and what he has just found out about my intentions in the Games. But Hades looks across at Theron and I follow his gaze.

Theron is standing close to Zeus, his chest out, his hand resting on his sword; he looks handsome in his golden armour and grey tunic, and I realize that this is his chance to fulfil his destiny. I study Zeus, his white-gold hair curling, his beard short and his handsome face beaming, his light blue eyes the colour of a washed-out sky. He looks younger than Poseidon but older than Hades, and as I look at the ruler of the sky, the God of all the Gods, I realize that just like Theron this is my chance at destiny too.

I wish I hadn't reacted the way I did, that I hadn't let

Hades know what was in my heart. I've kept my plans a secret for this long, and in one move Hades has discovered me. If I had been chosen by any other God, I'm sure that the contents of my heart would have been safe.

THE QUEST

Hermes is still floating above the crowd and after a final spin he holds his hands out and talks to us; well, not all of us, I notice, just the Gods.

"Now, I hope that you have all bestowed your initial favours before I announce the quest." He pauses for dramatic tension; the Gods are impatient for his announcement. "This quest will take your tokens to little-travelled lands, through great perils and tough trials, but the prize is a worthy one … the Crown of the North!"

The Gods let out oohs and ahhs of appreciation. I look to Hades, but his face is impassive, his eyes low in concentration.

"The constellation that was cast by our own Dionysus as a symbol of the love he had for Ariadne, a symbol of their marriage, their union." Hermes gestures towards the God, who is a beautiful young man; his dark skin shines with a deep lustre and his whole being radiates confidence and certainty. The boy by his side wears a tunic as red as the wine Dionysus is famed for, and he seems to have a confident air about him too.

Hermes continues, "I have taken the crown from the stars and I have hidden it. Your quest is to retrieve it. The winner will be the one whose token wears the crown."

There's a pause and then light chattering begins.

"Where will we find this crown?" a bold girl says. She is wearing the marks of Aquarius and I realize she is the token of Ares, God of war, that I noticed earlier, her spear in her hand, her helm now under her arm.

Hermes looks at her with indignation then turns his gaze to Ares. "Does your token speak for you?" he asks with a light laugh that is anything but as it ripples through the other Gods.

"No mortal speaks for me." Ares' voice is as sharp as his blade. The girl shrinks a little, moving a step away from the God of war.

"Tokens, I feel it is time for me to tell you of your rules." Hermes opens his arms and beckons as if trying to call us mortal tokens to him like small children. I guess to the immortal God that is just what we seem to be.

I look up at Hades and he gives a small nod so, like the other tokens, I dutifully make my way towards Hermes. He has come to land on the stage now, and we stand below him like a groundling audience.

"Twelve of you entered the Temple of the Zodiakos and only eleven of you have proven yourselves worthy of the quest," Hermes says with a raise of a single eyebrow.

"Philco of the sign of Libra, token of Apollo, has fallen in the first trial. I hope that the other Gods have chosen more worthy tokens for these Games that I have devised; it would be a sad day in Olympus if the festivities were to draw to a close too soon."

I feel a little sick at the thought of our deaths inconveniencing the entertainment of the Gods.

"The first rule you need to follow is that all favours from the Gods belong to the token to whom they are given. When a token dies their godly gifts cannot be taken by another token, but while still alive a token can share their gifts … if they choose to. We added that rule after one token amassed a great armoury of magical weapons; the competition was very one-sided after that, and distinctly predictable." Hermes gives a theatrical yawn.

"The second rule is that a token must pledge their full allegiance to the God that chose them; no alliances or bargains are to be made between tokens and any other Gods but their own." Hermes looks seriously around the tokens. "And while the double-crossing and deception is fun, it leads to more drama than even I can deal with! So you have to say I swear my allegiance to – and then name your God! Swear it now."

I turn my head to look at Hades. He looks so out of place standing next to the other Gods, but I can't quite figure out why. He has just as much presence as they do, just as much gravitas and might about him, but there is something that sets him apart.

"I swear my allegiance to you, Hades," I say, and while the other Gods stand still listening to the cacophony of voices filling the air, all just out of time of each other, I am sure that I see Hades' lips move as he says, *"And I to you, Ara."*

"And the third rule: no mortal token may wittingly draw the blood of another; instant disqualification will be bestowed upon the token and their God, and great punishment will be given. The Games are over far too soon when you all start killing each other!"

Yeah, it's far more fun when you eek it out and devise the killing yourself, I think as I glare at Hermes and the melodramatic look he is giving us.

In an instant he slaps a smile on his face, large and false with a strangely sinister edge to it.

"Get to know your fellow tokens, they may be the key to your success. We Gods do so love to see the forging of alliances and the cooperation between the tokens as they face the perils in front of them, it's so … mortal. And provides us a lot to speculate over once you all start to turn on one another."

He has a wistful look of longing on his face before he turns to a boy standing near the front of the stage and points at him. "Solon, sign of Aries, token of Dionysus." He then gestures to a beautiful girl next to him. "Kassandra, sign of Taurus, token of Aphrodite." Then another. "Heli, sign of Gemini, token of Athena. Ajax, sign of Cancer, token of Artemis. Thalia, sign of Leo, token of Hera. Acastus, sign of Virgo, token of Demeter." Then he is pointing at me, smiling in the same delighted way he has greeted all the others. "Ara, sign of Scorpio, token of Hades. Nestor, sign of Sagittarius, token of Hephaestus. Theron, sign of Capricorn, token of Zeus. Xenia, sign of Aquarius, token of Ares. And, last but not least, Danae, sign of Pisces, token of Poseidon! Phew!" He gives an over-exaggerated wipe of his brow.

"You are all part of the Immortal Games; from the moment you were taken during the Blood Moon your destinies have been entwined with that of your Gods. While they will live forever, so a small memory of you will live with them; regardless of whether you win or not you will be remembered among the stars of your constellation, how brightly you will shine will be determined by the skill with which you play the Games." Hermes pauses and tips his head to one side, raising the back of his hand to his lower cheek in dramatic contemplation.

"Although, you won't be playing alone! Remember, as well as providing you with rewards for the trials you face, your God will roll their die to help or hinder you along your way! This adds an element of chance and surprise and fun that keeps us all on our toes." Hermes' eyes glint.

"To the winner will go much acclaim, and you may ask one favour of the Gods! The only thing you cannot ask for is to become a God – the Games don't work like that; if they did we would need to build a second Olympus!" Hermes laughs again and the Gods join him. "But anything else your heart desires – riches, fame, an army, a lover – it will be given to the victor." He opens his arms wide as if surveying the gifts on offer, then he claps his hands together and faces the tokens.

"I have given you all the rules and you know the object of the quest – to wear the crown; now it is up to you to find its whereabouts. How you get there and tackle the trials you will face along the way, and the favours bestowed upon you for success, are up to your Gods. May the best God and their token win."

With that, Hermes holds his caduceus aloft and flies into the heavens.

I turn to roll my eyes at Hades, expecting to share a small smile at Hermes' theatrics, but he's not there; none of the Gods are. I feel a little bereft.

"They've all gone," Solon says, the sign of the ram on his deep wine-red tunic ripples as he lets out a large sigh of relief.

I make my way to Theron. The pinch of tears is back but I'm determined not to cry. He smiles at me, and he looks so familiar among all of this unfamiliarity, I quicken my pace just as he rushes to me. I don't hold him as close as I did earlier, but just as tightly. I can smell the training grounds on him and know then that he is really here in this weird dream-like situation.

"I thought … the fire, you…!"

"It would appear that death is on my side," I say, as I point to the copper token that is now hanging over the top of my tunic, resting on the one hidden beneath the black fabric. ARA TOKEN OF HADES.

Theron grimaces. "Yes, I saw him. He was younger than I had imagined, taller too."

I laugh as I realize that I'd thought the same things when I first saw him. "And you, the token of Zeus. I see he has given you some pretty favours!" I gesture to his armour and sword, and he delights in showing me both. I look at the exquisite craftmanship and try to keep my face passive while thinking of Zeus – I can't let him take Theron from me too.

"What did Hades give you?" he asks.

I lift the bag. "Accessories!" I say, with a rise of my eyebrows.

Theron shakes his head. "That's ... rubbish!"

I can't help but let out another laugh. "It seems that the God of the underworld is not too fond of weapons or violence."

"Really? Sounds to me like he's just trying to get you killed. But don't worry, despite all Hades' best intentions, I don't plan on allowing him to take you to his realm." He looks at me in that way he did on the training grounds under the moon, and I feel the warm tingle spread over me again.

I'm so glad that we are here together. I reach out and squeeze his hand as I smile at him. I'm just about to tell Theron that I can handle Hades, when Thalia, Hera's token, calls out.

"Does anyone know where we are?" She's standing on the stage above the rest of us, close to where Hermes was, her black hair shining in a halo of curls, her golden tunic marked with the lions of Leo.

"I think I do," Ajax says, as he comes running down from the stepped seats of the amphitheatre, his white tunic making his bronzed skin look darker. "I think we are in the kingdom of Thessaly; we are probably in the amphitheatre of Larissa."

"Excellent," Thalia calls. "We know where we are and we know what we want, the Crown of the North, now we just need to figure out where it is and how to get there."

Thalia is certainly a go-getter, and I know that some of that energy is going to be essential in the days to come.

"It wouldn't be far to travel to the capital; we can ask for assistance there," Theron says as he moves away from me and joins Thalia on the stage. "It should be a day's walk north."

"Yes, or we could travel west to the Marshes of Ambracia," Heli adds. She looks to be the youngest of us all, thirteen or fourteen, her large brown eyes and soft curled hair reminding me of Estella, with whom she also shares a sign. "I come from a small village in Acarnania, and in my homeland there was once an oracle of great skill, Melia. Many would travel from far and wide to hear what she had to say. Once, Zeus visited her as he wanted to know what would be the fate of one of his lovers, but what the oracle told Zeus was not to his liking so to punish her he banished her to the Swamps of Sadness, somewhere around the lakes of Ambracia."

"Sounds like a cheery place, and exactly how long will it take us to get there?" Theron asks.

Heli shrugs, looking a little unsure of herself, which might have something to do with the edge in Theron's voice. "A couple of days, three maybe?"

"So, you think we should go to see this oracle, Melia, and ask her where the Crown of the North is?" Thalia asks.

"Yeah, I do," Heli says, sounding more determined as she turns her small face up to look at Theron on the stage. "That's what I'm going to do. You don't have to come with me; you can go to the capital if you choose. I'm sure that you will find your way; if you are fated for the crown then it will not pass you by."

I can feel the tension rolling from Theron, his stubborn-headed nature kicking in.

"Heli, I think this oracle of yours is exactly what we need. I'll travel with you," I say, taking a step towards her.

Theron gives me a look I know so well; he's challenging me, trying to get me to change my mind. "Are you sure?" he asks, his eyes focused and intense.

I smile sweetly up at him, knowing it will infuriate him. I tip my head to the side slightly and say, "Oh yes, I'm sure, Theron." I move closer till I'm standing next to Heli. "Athena, the Goddess of wisdom, chose Heli as her token so if she says that visiting an oracle will help us on the quest then I'm going to have to agree with her."

"I would also like to see this oracle," Ajax says, and I smile at him.

"We can't all split up this early on in the Games. All the research that I have done shows that the Games with the most survivors were the ones where they all work together," Thalia says.

I see Theron thinking this through. Like me, he's heard the recounting of the past Immortal Games from the instructors, as well as the strategies that are most likely to succeed. He knows that Thalia is right.

Theron drops his icy look and smiles, then sheepishly leans his head to one side. "We should stay as one, at least for a while," he declares, jumping off the stage and approaching me and Heli. "I will follow you to your oracle." He offers a slight bow to Heli and a raise of his eyebrows to me.

The young girl nods back and picks up the lance that Athena gave her, then walks towards the exit of the amphitheatre. I follow after her, with Theron by my side and the other tokens close behind us. After a while we fall into a familiar pattern, our steps matching each other's perfectly.

13

THE ROLLING OF THE DIE

Zeus is jovial as he places his token down on the board. "Ah, Hades, I see your token is another saved soul."

"Yes, brother, I am not about to change the way that I play the Games just because the outcome of it has shifted."

Zeus laughs. "Nor I, brother, nor I." He raises his eyebrows and takes a long draught from his cup.

Hades pulls the small figurine of Ara from within the folds of his dark robes. He notices that the small Ara is a perfect representation in every way, from the ink black tunic of her sign, to the deep brown hair pulled into a flowing braided ponytail. He holds the figure gently and rubs a thumb over her face, across the white scar he had seen on her cheek, just under her eye, rich and warm. The face is a mixture of determination and wary surprise.

Hades reluctantly places the piece on the table and takes the seat next to Artemis, Apollo sitting on his other side. He regrets his placement immediately.

The twinned bodies are as competitive with one

another as he and his brothers had been in the past, and when the two of them start bickering around him, he is glad that he mostly escapes to his underworld leaving the Gods to their own devices and derisions.

Battles between Poseidon and Zeus are always stormy, but he knows from past experience that if he himself were to join them then the earth itself would quake with his wrath. However, unlike his brothers, it was always Hades who had to look upon the unfortunate souls who passed through his gates after being caught up in the battles of the brothers.

"I like the look of your token," Demeter says to Athena, across the board from Hades.

"Why, thank you," Athena replies to the Goddess of the grain. "I have had my eye on her for some time; she is quite exceptional this Gemini. And your young man is quite … ripe for the harvest!" The two of them laugh, the air filling with a perfume of joy.

Hermes calls for attention from his seat at the head of the board. As master of the quest he has ultimate power over the Games and all the Gods look to him as they play. Hermes enjoys the deference.

"Have you all placed your tokens on the board?" he asks, looking around the table, before stopping at Apollo. "All those who are still in the game that is." He gestures to a plinth of white marble in one of the twelve alcoves around the room, on which reads, THE TOKEN OF APOLLO.

At the foot of the plinth lies golden armour and floating

above it is a young boy of thirteen. His eyes are open, his mouth too in shock, one hand is at his throat as is a golden dagger. His curls are dark but not as dark as the blood that covers his green tunic. Suspended in the moment of his death, his last breath still waiting to escape his body, his soul waiting at the gates of the underworld, Philco adorns the game room. He will be the first but not the last to do so in these Immortal Games.

Hades knows that this is how he will stay for the duration, as will all tokens that perish in the quest, caught in the moment between life and death until Hermes calls the Games to a close. At which moment they will release their dying breaths, their bodies will be returned to their families and their spirits, untethered, will pass through Hades' gates and into the underworld.

Apollo looks daggers at the dead boy, sharp enough to kill him again. The God of the sun and truth doesn't like what he sees before him and sulks.

Hermes claps his hands, and the pieces all move to one place on the board.

Hades watches as the miniature Ara walks across the map of the world from where he placed her to join the others.

They are in the amphitheatre at Larissa, where the Gods left them. Hermes waves his caduceus in the air and above the table an apparition of the tokens appears.

Hades looks for Ara.

"Ah, young Theron, taking charge I see," Zeus says, as Theron leaps up on to the stage next to Thalia.

"I think you'll find, husband, that my token was on the stage first," Hera says.

"Yes, my dear, she was making a good show of it," Zeus says.

A light ripple of laughter spills out from the Gods and Hades feels a headache coming on.

"Ahh, it looks like Athena's young Gemini is the true leader here," Hermes says.

All the Gods, including Hades, listen to the token.

"The Oracle of Acarnania! They'll find nothing of value there," Zeus bawls. "They should have listened to my token."

"Just because the oracle gave you the truth and you didn't like it, doesn't mean that the tokens will not like the truths they hear," Poseidon tells his brother as he raises a cup.

Hades watches him and thinks of the twisting in the tapestry of the world and the truths that are being hidden around this table as these Gods play the Games, and he and his brothers play a far greater and more dangerous one.

How could he have ever agreed to such a wager? His brothers make him foolish; the old Hades of war and strife rears his helm when his brothers don their armour. Now his realm is in peril, as is Ara.

He watches as the figures shift and the board moves.

"Hermes," Hera calls out, "this isn't going to be one of those long Games where the tokens have to travel far to get to the object of their quest, is it?" There is a note of warning in Hera's voice and Hermes hears it.

"Yes and no. I am the God of travellers after all. But don't worry, I will keep the travelling light and swift," he says.

Aphrodite lets out a little laugh. "Oh, not too swift, Hermes. I feel an attachment growing between two of our tokens, and a few boring nights on the road are just what they need to find each other."

"No doubt you mean my token and that pretty little lost soul of Hades," Zeus says.

Hades looks up, taking in the idle chatter that he was not paying attention to.

"What is my Ara doing?" he asks.

"Theron," Zeus says with a chuckle, and the rest of the Gods join in.

"Wrong, dear brother. It is my token, Acastus, and Aphrodite's bull that are getting to know one another better," Demeter says.

Athena leans forward and in a loud whisper says, "I told you, ripe!" The Goddesses laugh again, and Hades sits back in his chair.

"Now, I have a trial in store for you that will test your tokens' resolve," Hermes says with a smile, taking command of the room. "The swamps that surround the new home of the oracle are full of dangers that most mortals would never face; your tokens are not most mortals. Chosen by Gods and armed with their favours they will face these dangers with their skills and wits, but also a roll of the die."

Hermes holds out a twelve-sided die.

He hands it to Dionysus, who takes it and rolls it on the board.

"Advantage!" Hermes calls, as the die lands on the sign of Taurus. "A great start!"

The die then makes its way around the table, the Gods in play rolling for an advantage, attack, defence or…

"Disadvantage!" Hermes calls, as Hades' roll of the die comes to a stop on the sign of the crab.

"Not to worry, brother. I'll keep the fires of the underworld warm," Zeus goads.

Hades sets his jaw almost imperceptibly and looks at the playing piece that represents Ara on the board. He feels a pang of anguish for not doing better by her already; she said they were a team, he and her playing the Games together. But he feels that he is losing, and it has only just begun.

14

THE SWAMPS OF SADNESS

Apollo has ridden the sun hard across the sky again today and twilight feels like it will descend upon us too soon as we reach the Swamps of Sadness. I had hoped that we would arrive under the safety of the sun, the bright hours of the day casting their light, chasing away all of the spectres conjured by the name of the place. I can't help but think that Apollo's haste might have something to do with Philco's death and early exit from the Games.

The ground beneath my sandals is becoming softer with every step. I look down and see that my legs are splattered with small clots of thick dark mud. Theron is close by; I see him just ahead as he picks his steps through the deepening swamp. His attention is on the front of the pack as we eleven tokens press onwards, into the gloom and the gathering dusk. Thalia is leading the way, Heli beside her; I've come to know them both a little better on our travels from the amphitheatre. I've come to know them all better and I can't help but think that might not be wise; even if we are drawn together through the pressures of the Games, we're not all going to make it.

The trees are becoming more twisted and numerous, their leafless branches a weird bone white. Around patches of firm ground and narrow paths of deep brown earth are swampy pools which are completely black and look more like thick soup than water. The twilight birdsong is fading with the greenery, and everything is becoming encased in the same colours of misery: dank brown, impossible black, bone white.

I reach into the Trojan bag that Hades gave me and think about the apple I placed in there this morning after we'd passed a grove full of ripe fruit.

I have the hang of how the bag works now. At first it felt odd, unnatural, which I guess it is, but now I hardly register what I'm doing as I place a hand inside and think about whatever I need to retrieve.

I take a big bite and the apple crunches loudly in the near silence of the eerie marshes. Juice runs down my chin and as I wipe it away with the back of my hand, Theron looks back over his shoulder and shushes me.

I look straight at him and take another bite.

"Don't mind him," Acastus says from beside me. "He thinks he's in charge of us all just because he is Zeus' token!"

I almost tell him that it wouldn't matter who his God was, Theron would still take charge.

"Leading and being in charge are two very different things," I tell Acastus instead, and he gives a little ha, as he tips his head to one side, his long hair swishing.

"Yeah, I guess they are." He claps me on the shoulder. I offer him the half-eaten apple and he takes it, munching loudly.

I like Acastus. Outside of the Games I feel we could be good friends, and that makes me worry, because the chances of us both getting through are slim. I know I shouldn't be getting attached to anyone; it's bad enough that I've come into these Games with one firm attachment, a deepening friendship that if we had been left together on the training field might have been something else by now.

I watch Theron as he walks ahead, and I suddenly realize that since Estella died, he has been my only friend; the only one who understood me and shared my need to be chosen. I've been cutting myself off from people for so long and working hard towards this, towards the Games, and now that I'm here, with the other tokens, I feel like I have something in common with them, something that bonds us and makes me want to connect with them. I guess that's one of the reasons why Theron and I are so close: we both have a common goal. Theron moves away from me through the swamp, and I can't help but remember his kiss. We are close, very close, too close for these Games.

"Besides," Acastus says, pulling me from my blushing memories, "I'm happy for Theron, or anyone really, to go ahead. Who knows what's lurking in these marshes and if it gets one of them first then it means we'll have more time to get away."

I nod. "Smart thinking!" I say, as I start to evaluate that

information and wonder if my feelings of friendship and familiarity are futile and foolish.

"Where's your friend Kassandra?" I ask Acastus, with a raise of my eyebrows. "The two of you look like you're getting to know each other better."

Acastus blushes as he pushes his hair to one side and smiles. "Is it that obvious?"

"Well, you did keep half the camp awake last night," Ajax says, clapping Acastus on the shoulder from behind, and joining the two of us. His white tunic is covered in red armour, a giant black crab on the breast, and over his shoulder is a bow and arrows. I wouldn't have expected anything else from Artemis, Goddess of the hunt.

"You know, there is a lot to be said for relationships started in such conditions," Ajax says with a big grin on his round boyish face. "I think it's wonderful that the two of you have created such a deep and emotional bond in the midst of all this uncertainty."

I chuckle. "There is nothing deep or emotional between Acastus and Kassandra, but they deserve connection, and I'm happy for them. However, I'd be even happier if they were quieter when connecting," I add with a wiggle of my eyebrows.

"What, you don't think that young Acastus here is serious about the beautiful and fierce Kassandra?" Ajax holds out his hand to Kassandra, who is flicking some mud off her pale green tunic with the edge of her sword. Then she reaches back to take Solon's hand, pulling him out of the quagmire in which his foot is stuck. She looks up and smiles sweetly over at us, and Acastus grins back soppily, waving at her.

I don't know how but Ajax and I manage not to laugh.

Acastus looks from Ajax to me and rolls his eyes. "We can't all have the childhood romance that Theron and you have, Ara," he says.

"It's not like that!" I punch him on the arm and glance over to see if Theron heard, but he's too far ahead now.

"Well, someone should tell Theron that," Ajax says. "I've seen the way he looks at you."

"You have?" A part of me wants to ask him exactly how Theron looks at me, but another part remembers how Hades looks at me and I suddenly feel confused and shake my head. "You must be mistaken; Theron and I are ... friends."

"Sure, whatever you say, Ara!" Ajax says. "And Kassandra and Acastus are just hanging out!"

I glance at Acastus as he looks back over at Kassandra and smiles.

The ground becomes harder to walk on, my feet sinking a little deeper and sticking fast with every third or fourth step. Ajax, Acastus and I work together, pulling each other along when needed. I glance at Theron up ahead beside Thalia, Nestor and Heli. The Gemini is still pointing the way even though she confessed hours ago to not knowing where exactly in the swampy marshes the oracle lives.

"Look, a banner!" Solon shouts from a little behind and to the east of where I am.

He's pointing up ahead of us and there, hanging in a dead tree, is a frayed and faded banner. What colour it had once been I can't quite decide, but on it is the symbol of the all-seeing-eye.

"We must be getting close!" Heli calls out, and I can hear the relief in the young girl's voice. The banner has come just when I, and probably Heli herself, was beginning to feel that this was a very bad idea. I wonder how long it would have been before Theron started saying, *I told you so.*

A screech fills the air. Ajax reaches for his spear and Acastus his sword, while I reach for my bag and roll my eyes.

"Honestly, Hades." I plunge in my hand and pull out the length of rope. It shines in the gloom, and I feel a warm feeling of hope spread over me as I hold it. But a bit of rope and a warm fuzzy feeling isn't going to save me from whatever just made that noise.

I look down for something to use, anything, and see a sharp, jagged rock about the size of my fist. I tie it to the end of the rope, knotting it securely, then I let the rope hang loose in my hand and swing it a few times, testing the weight of the rock and the way that it makes the rope spin. It's not ideal, not exactly a weapon, but it might give me a chance, and a chance is all I need.

Another cry fills the air, but this one is different. It comes again. "Help!"

It's coming from somewhere off to the right and it's more desperate and sad than the original urgent and terrifying screech. I move in the direction of the cry, Ajax and Acastus following me. As we clear a small overgrowth of thorny bushes, we see Danae stuck in the mud, almost waist deep, tears running down her face as she holds her trident above her head.

"Are you OK?" I ask. As I reach the edge of the dry safe ground, I can see the change in the colour as the sticky mud starts to become swamp water.

Danae doesn't answer me; she's still crying big tears and silent heaves come from deep in her chest. I know what it feels like to cry like that. I go to throw my rope to her, but she reaches the end of the trident towards me instead. I grasp the smooth pole as she holds on to the end with the sharp barbs. I tug, but nothing happens. I tug again and Danae begins to rock herself forward, releasing some of the suction that holds her in place.

Acastus joins me, his large hands wrapping over mine as he reaches around from behind me. He smells good, a deep earthy scent that reminds me of Hades. He gives me a winning smile and a wink. I shake my head and smirk at him in good humour, but all I can think about is Hades. I find myself wondering what it would feel like to have his arms wrapped around me and I feel a thrill run inside me that I push down as quickly as it rises. He is a God and even if he wasn't, I am going to kill his brother.

"Ready, Ara? Now!" Acastus says and we pull. "Now,"

and we pull again. Danae is inching forward, her body squelching with every movement and her tears reducing as she becomes calmer.

As soon as we've pulled her close enough for Ajax to grab her hand, he pulls her to him. The mud is around her ankles now and as the last of it relinquishes her, she topples forward, landing on top of him and covering him in the stinking sludge. They both lie there for a moment panting as Acastus uncurls his arms from me and I release the trident.

Acastus looks at me, concerned, before he turns back to Danae and I move away and help her to her feet. "Thank you," she says, her voice small and quiet, not confident and direct as I have come to expect.

As I extend a hand to Ajax, I hear Acastus ask, "What were you doing all the way over here on your own?"

Danae looks out over the shiny mud, her eyes wide and her bottom lip trembling. "I thought I saw someone out there, someone I knew."

"Who?" I ask automatically.

"My mother..." Danae shakes her head. "It doesn't matter, it can't have been her; she drowned when I was little. I'd been playing by the riverbank and fell in, and she jumped in to save me. The river was fast flowing, with a stony bed, and I kept tumbling in the water, round and round. I thought I was on my way to greet Hades, until I felt her hands grab me. She got me out, used the last of her strength to do it and..." She falters. "But I was sure that it was her, that I saw her."

Acastus suddenly drops the trident and stands up straight. "Can you hear that?" he asks.

"Hear what?" I reply.

"Singing, it sounds like." The colour suddenly drains from Acastus' handsome face as he casts his head around. "Elektra!" he shouts, and starts to move off through the marsh at a pace.

I scoop up the trident and pass it to Danae as Ajax jumps up, and the three of us go off in pursuit of Acastus.

"Who's Elektra?" Ajax shouts to Acastus when we catch him up.

"A girl from my village. Her father is a great warrior and we're … we're betrothed."

"Oh… oh!" Ajax says, pulling an awkward face as he looks over at me. "And does Kassandra know about this sweet singing Elektra?" he jokes. Then he stops dead, with a faraway look on his face that reminds me of Hades, and starts sniffing the air. "Can you smell that?" he asks, looking from me to Danae.

"Smell what?" she asks.

"Lavender bread. My grandmother used to make it when I was little. I would always steal a roll while they were cooling, and she would always pretend not to look."

"Something strange is happening." Suddenly I realize that the four of us are on our own. I can't see Theron and the others who were in front of us, or Kassandra and Solon who were behind. I spin around, taking in the bleak swamp, the gathering gloom making it all merge into one endless landscape of dead trees and grey skies, dark black mud and "Estella!"

My heart forgets to beat for a moment and all reason leaves me as I run towards her. She's standing deeper in the swamp, and looks exactly as she did on the morning of the Blood Moon that claimed her.

"Estella!" I scream.

Behind me I hear Danae call, "Ara."

But I need to get to my sister; she's moving away from me, through the dead woods of the swamp, and then she's gone.

I cry out to her as I spin in a circle trying to see her, but she's no longer there. The shrill cry I heard earlier fills the air and I look up. There is something in the tree above me, something that for a second is wearing Estella's face but then it fades to reveal a flat dark-grey face with uncommonly large eyes, all black pupil, and a wide mouth with razor-sharp teeth.

I drop the rock end of the rope and start to swing it back and forth as the creature scuttles along the branch at speed. Its long arms and legs have claw-like fingers and toes that bite into the barren branches, giving the creature purchase as it races in my direction.

Retreating backwards, I move my head from side to side, and realize that I'm alone, but not alone in my torment.

The eerie silence of the swamp is suddenly alive with cries, not the sharp screeches of these scuttling creatures, but the cries of my fellow tokens. I turn in what I hope is the direction of Ajax, Danae and Acastus. The rope is still swinging in my hand as I run, and I can hear the creature tracking me through the trees above.

In the gathering gloom I see a flash of sea green and head towards it. Acastus, in his brown tunic, is standing back-to-back with Danae, both of them attacking as four of the creatures circle them. I swing out my rope and strike one of the creatures in the skull with the jagged rock, the crunch that rings through the marshes making me feel sick, and the creature falls to one side with a black ooze dripping from its head. Another of the creatures scurries forward and grabs it, pulling it back into the soft ground and dragging it down into the sodden marshes.

Acastus and Danae each attack one of the two remaining creatures. I advance to help them and in the second that I feel the claw pierce my skin I remember the creature that had been following me through the trees. Its claw digs deep into my left shoulder blade like a meat hook, it tugs me to the ground and then drags me away. I scream and kick my legs, trying to stop the creature from pulling me away into the swamp, its claw cutting a little deeper, a little further into me as it drags me away from the others. I can feel the ground moistening around me; if the creature pulls me into the muddy water, I might not ever come out.

The rope is still in my hand and, as we pass a tree, I throw it out with as much strength as I can muster. The rock flies around the trunk twice then hooks over the rope, fixing it fast. I hold tight and brace myself as the rope pulls taut and the creature jolts forward, ripping its claw out of me. I scream in anguish, and I can't help but think how similar my cries are to the ones these creatures make.

I roll on to all fours and force myself up. The creature crouches in front of me; its dark eyes reflect a shadowy image of my face back at me. It opens its mouth and row after row of sharp teeth glare at me. The rope is still in my hand; I lash it out at the creature, striking it around the face, hard enough to knock it off balance and into the foot of a tree. I advance on it, swinging the soft end of the rope around.

But it scuttles back on all fours and straight into the murky mud of the swamp. And that's when I see Theron, or at least I see a bit of him, as even though the edge of his grey tunic is almost the same colour as the creatures, I glimpse his light brown hair and golden armour as he slips beneath the dark waters.

"Theron!" I scream out and, ignoring the pain in my back, I run for the swamp. The rope is still in my hand and I wait for it to pull taut, but it never does, and then I remember what Hades said about the rope, that it will grow and shrink as I have need of it. I pull it around me, tying the rope around my waist as I plunge into the muddy waters. Cold spreads up my legs and when it hits my waist, I take a deep breath and plunge in head first.

I open my eyes to the darkness only to close them as I feel the sting. I force myself to reopen them, to look for Theron. I aim for where I think I last saw him, and I'm rewarded as I see his foot. I grab it and start to pull my way up Theron's floating body, my hands climbing up his strong leg muscles. All of a sudden, I can feel us both being pulled through the water. My hands grip Theron's thigh as long grey arms are wrapped around his torso. The powerful legs of the creature kick out as it drags us through the depths: down, down.

I pull my way up to Theron's belt and I can see his sword is still in the scabbard. With one hand holding tight to the belt, I release the sword and strike out with it, hitting the creature. We instantly stop moving and the dark waters become a deeper shade of midnight as the creature's blood spills around us. I pull Theron to me, keeping the sword out for protection as I see the creature writhing in the dark bloom; then it sees me, it's large orb-like eyes fixed on me and its mouth open in a soundless scream.

I feel my heart race. There's no way I can hold Theron, defend us both from this creature and pull us along the rope to safety. Besides, the burning in my lungs would force me to open my mouth and breathe in this putrid water long before we got to shore. Then I look down and see the rope still glowing in the gloom and I wonder if it works the same way as the bag. As I form the thought, I feel a pulling from behind me as the rope begins to shorten, pulling us through the water at a terrific rate, leaving the creature behind writhing in the murky depths of the swamp. Water gushes around me as we break the surface and I pull air into my lungs.

The rope doesn't stop shrinking till we are on the firmer land near the tree that it is tied to. As soon as we stop, I let go of Theron and turn him on his back. His face is pale, his eyes closed, mouth open.

"No, no, no, no, no," I chant, as I smooth his hair and the dirt from his face then put my ear to his chest. Nothing.

"Theron!" I shake his shoulders and I remember how my father had told me once of a fisherman whom he had seen drown and revive. I hope that it wasn't just another of his tales of war and conquest. Before Estella, he had told many of them and I was never sure if they were all true. I hope against the odds as I tilt Theron's head back and pinch his nose before breathing into his mouth, my lips on his in an almost familiar motion, but this time I don't pull away. Then I rip his armour from his torso and climb on top of him, one leg either side of his hips. I pull my hands together tight and bring them down hard on his chest again and again.

I look out into the fast-gathering dark, the sun already set, the moon rising, and I call out, "Hades, if he's at your gate, send him back, send him back!"

Then I breathe into his mouth again and on the fourth breath he splutters up at me. I climb off him and roll him on to his side as dark dirty water spills from him on to the ground. His whole body shakes, I rub his back and say a quiet thank you to Hades.

15

THE ORACLE

"Ara!"

"Here, we're over here, Ajax!" I shout, and when he crashes through the twisted black thorny bushes, holding a torch aloft, the light falling on his face, I don't think I've ever been so glad to see anyone.

He crouches next to me and holds the flame above Theron, the fire a strange blue-green colour that makes Theron's pale skin look translucent.

"Where did you get that from?" I ask, nodding towards the torch, but it's not Ajax who answers.

Nestor has joined us, followed by Thalia, Heli and Solon. "It's Promethean fire. Hephaestus gave it to me as my first gift. I thought it was pretty lame at the time, but the ... whatever they are... they're scared of it," Nestor says.

Ajax helps me get Theron to his feet and while he's holding him, I remove the rope that's still around my waist and untie the other end from the tree. The rock is covered in black sticky blood so I wipe it on the ground. Then I wind up the rope and put it back in the bag, whispering to Hades, "Thank you, I guess your gift is not entirely useless." I smile as I imagine the look Hades might give me if he was here, that ever so slight lift of his eyebrows.

I go back to helping Theron and turn to Ajax, "Where are Danae and Acastus?" I look around. "Kassandra and Xenia are missing too."

"Kassandra's gone … one of those creatures – I couldn't stop it," Solon says.

"No one's seen Xenia, but I found the helm that Ares gave her next to the water." Ajax holds up the helmet, his voice hard, and I feel a little lump in my throat.

"We should find somewhere to camp for the night, set up watches so we can rest," Thalia says as she leads everyone on.

"Can you walk?" I ask Theron. "I can probably carry you in my bag if not." I smile, only half joking; I think it would probably work.

"I can manage," Theron says, eyeing the bag with contempt and pushing away from me. I let go of him, but stay within arm's reach. He walks a couple of steps before I'm back at his side supporting him. He groans but doesn't argue and lets me help him, which for Theron is a huge deal. Ajax walks behind us, his bow in his hand, the Promethean fire held high, casting a large circle of light around us.

"I think this is where I last saw Danae and Acastus," I say. I look around at the ground and see signs of the struggle we had been in, the dark blood on the muddy bank smeared into the waters as the other creature pulled in its fallen comrade.

"There are more tracks over here," Solon says. "Three of them." He holds his torch aloft.

"Maybe they found Xenia?" Thalia adds.

"Maybe." I hope.

"We should follow the track and see if we can find them," Nestor says. He joins Solon scanning the footprints that lead off to the left, his Promethean fire flickering on the end of a small torch that I remember him having at his waist when Hermes revealed the quest. It looks strange seeing such a big muscular boy hold such a small thing. Like Hephaestus, Nestor is strong and powerful, but I wonder how quick he is or if his bulk slows him down.

"What if it leads us into a trap; what if there are more of those creatures?" Heli says. It's the first time she's said anything since we regrouped, and her voice is small and timid. I guess she's feeling guilty about leading us all here, but we all decided to come; it's not her fault that these creatures were lurking in the swamp, but I realize the others might not all see it that way, especially Theron.

"Don't worry, Heli. We have the Promethean fire and, besides, we're together and I'm sure that the tokens of the Gods are more than a match for a band of swamp creatures," I say.

I see a glint of a smile pass over her face.

But Theron is recovering fast. He steps away from me and pipes up. "I'm not sure that finding shelter is the best thing to do, we'd be sitting ducks if those creatures found us. We need to keep going, find the oracle and get on with this quest."

"Do you think that's wise, Theron?" I say to him. "You just drowned, you narrowly escaped Hades' gate, you need to rest."

"I'll be fine," he snaps at me, and it stings like a slap.

I've seen him like this before, on the training ground, when his pride is pricked. I resolve to keep my distance till he calms down. I've found that the best way to soothe him is at arm's length, but part of me is too angry at him to even think about trying to offer him solace. I risked my life to save his and he's lashing out at me for caring about him.

"Look, another banner!" Thalia calls out, as she holds her light aloft. "The footprints lead that way too."

Theron doesn't say anything as he moves away from me. He crouches with Thalia, looking at the ground. I can see the sheen of sweat on his brow as I hear the two of them whispering before Thalia gives the signal for us to move out.

I find myself next to Ajax in the middle of the pack, with Heli in front of us and Nestor and Solon behind. Everyone has their weapons drawn, even Theron has his sword at the ready now, his golden armour back in place. I feel foolish, like a sitting target, but I don't want to pull the rope from my bag, as it just feels pathetic when the others all have the means to defend themselves properly.

But then I think about how the rope saved me and Theron, and I guess if Hades had given me a weapon, I would have only sunk it into Zeus when I saw him in the amphitheatre; and I wouldn't be here now if that had happened.

I find my mind wandering back to Zeus again, to how he looked, and I feel more than a little sick at the way that I wanted him to notice me, to see me. I try to imagine how things might have played out if I'd had a bow like Ajax. I see myself nock the arrow and loose it towards the king of the Gods, but before it reaches its target, I see Hades step in front of his brother. I'm shocked from my daydream and look about me in the dark. I don't want to hurt Hades, but I wonder if I would if that was the only way to kill Zeus.

Soon we pass another banner and then the light from the Promethean torches falls upon a small hovel, little more than a hole in a rocky outcrop. But there is a glow from within and a whisper of smoke rising above the outcrop from somewhere inside.

"Danae, Acastus?" Thalia calls out. I can see her spear in ready anticipation.

"We're here! Xenia too!" Danae calls out as she exits the hovel, a gaping hole where the door should be. "We found the oracle. Acastus is injured and she's helping him." Danae beckons us all forward.

"Have you asked her about the crown?" Theron asks, as we draw near.

"No, I had a few more pressing concerns," Danae said, and I can hear the edge in her voice. She is much more like herself than the girl we rescued from the swamp, as she glares at Theron and grips her trident.

Then she sees me and Ajax and rushes forward, pulling me into a big hug. "You're OK! I thought that thing had killed you for sure." She leans away, looking me over and noting the large cut on my shoulder.

Then she pulls Ajax to her. "You look completely untouched!" she tells him.

He shrugs and smiles. "I'm lucky like that." I hope that his luck lasts.

The cave is large and warm and dry; a huge fire burns at the centre, and with the torchlight it feels almost as light as day.

"How bad is Acastus?" I ask Danae and she turns and gives me a peculiar smile.

"Oh, it's so bad," she says, holding back a laugh as she takes my hand and leads me deeper into the cave.

There are alcoves cut into the solid rock walls and in one of them on a low bed lies Acastus. He's face down, his tunic off, his body covered with cuts and scratches; a woman is tending him, running her fingers over his flesh and applying ointment to the wounds.

My eyes run over his naked muscular body in a way that the woman's fingers do not. I should look away; I should but I don't.

Danae, next to me, says, "See, very, very bad." She smiles again, and I join her.

"Did the creatures do this?" I ask.

Danae shakes her head, a small smile on her lips. "No, he fell into one of the spiky bushes and couldn't get out.

The thorns lodged in his flesh and she's pulling them out; by all accounts they can be quite poisonous if you leave them in for any length of time."

Acastus looks over his shoulder. "Apparently I'm going to live," he says.

"That's good, I'd hate for this to be the last I saw of you," Danae says, and I feel my cheeks blush.

"Ah, so you found your friends," the woman calls out over her shoulder to Danae, her voice playful and warm.

"I'm not sure they would call themselves my friends, well, not all of them." Danae glances in my direction with a smile. "But yes, I found the other tokens ... those that are left." She looks around trying to count us.

I realize that we're ten now not the eleven that we had been a few short hours ago.

Theron has followed us deeper into the cave. I hear him clear his throat and I feel myself recoil slightly when he speaks with ridged formality. "Oracle. We have come..."

"I know why you have come, young Theron."

"You do?"

"I wouldn't be much of an oracle if I didn't!" She continues to pull thorns from Acastus. "Call me Melia."

Danae moves closer to the oracle. "Melia, could you take a look at Ara? She was injured by one of those things."

"Those *things* are the Children of Sadness; they are those who got lost in the swamp and succumbed to the feelings of sadness and the remembrance of loss that the vapors of the dark waters give off."

I remember how, just before the Children attacked, before I reached for the starlight rope, I had felt that sadness seeping into me and I am sure that the others had too.

Melia turns towards me, the torchlight shining on her face. She is young, barely a wrinkle on her forehead, and her eyes are like two moons, orbs of white looking out but not seeing. She is filthy, dirt smeared across her face and clumped into her long hair.

"Ara, I can tend to you, but unfortunately I cannot look at you for I am blind till the morning."

"Till the morning?" I ask, not quite following her meaning.

"Zeus not only banished me from the city I loved so well, but he torments me day after day. Each morning as the sun rises, I am greeted not only by its rays but by a flock of stymphalian birds, their beaks tipped with brass; they have but one purpose – to seek me out, and when they do, they pluck out my eyes." She reaches up to touch her sightless orbs. "During the day my eyes grow back; as night descends, I start to see shapes in the darkness and as the rays of the new day dawn, my sight is returned. Then the birds attack and I am left bereft and in pain, to stumble in this world, knowing that I will only glimpse it for a moment before it is taken from me once more."

"That is so cruel." I feel my hands ball into fists at the injustice.

"The Gods are cruel, all of them in their way. Never forget that, Ara. You being here is evidence of the spite and contempt they hold for mortals. They want us to love and adore them and yet they treat us like this." A thunderclap rings out above the cave.

"Yes, you can shout all you like, you'll not change my mind that way, Zeus," Melia calls out, and I feel my chest swell with admiration for her boldness.

"Now, I know why the ten of you are here, I know what it is that you seek and I know where you might find it, but I will not tell you where the Crown of the North is unless you do something for me first. I want you to destroy the feathered beasts that cause my daily ruin, that is my price."

The thunder rumbles again, louder this time.

"I think we can do that," I say, before any of the others have a chance to comment, and I extend a hand towards Melia.

Theron grasps it instead. "Wait, we should discuss this. Zeus is not a God I nor any of us should want to displease."

Heli moves forward. "But if we don't find out where the crown is being kept then we will displease him in a different way, will we not?"

I can see Theron thinking this through.

"Let us take a vote," Thalia suggests. "All those in favour of meeting Melia's demands?"

Only Theron and Solon keep their hands down.

"Well, if we're going to do this, we're going to need more information so that we can come up with a plan. Melia, tell us more about these birds," Thalia says.

16

THE GOD OF THE DREAMING

I'm not in the cave any more. I'm in Oropusa, in the woodland at the back of our villa, running along the river much like I had done on the morning of the Blood Moon. My body feels strong and clean, and as I look down I realize I'm wearing the green dress from the night of the choosing, except it isn't burnt and charred as it was when I saw it last.

I'm conscious and aware but I know that this, right here and now, is not real. I hit a familiar curve in the river, and it opens on to an unfamiliar landscape. Everything has shifted; there is a different quality to the trees on this part of the river, the light shining through the leaves glows with an intensity I've never seen before. The river sounds different too, with a deep, more melodious tone.

I stop running and look around, taking in more shifts. I have never before seen the golden yellow flowers that line the banks, nor the meadow at the end of the path. I start to cross it, taking in the blue sky and the wildflowers as I head towards a small grove of olive trees.

And there, lying in the middle of the trees, face turned towards the sky, is Hades. I walk over and stand above him, my shadow casting itself long and lean over his body. He smiles up at me, his eyes closed.

"Ara." I smile as he sighs my name on to the light breeze that sweeps over the meadow, making the flowers bow their heads to the ground.

"Hades." I sit down beside him, my hand resting next to his as I tip my head back and look up into the blue sky. Big white clouds are scuttling across, and he reaches out a hand and points to one.

"That one looks like a scorpion!" he says.

"So it does." The cloud looks exactly like the small scorpion on my token. "Did you do that?"

That small smile tugs on the side of his mouth and he turns his head towards me. "Of course."

I smile as I realize that not only did he do it but he did it for me.

We sit in silence as the cloud scorpion crawls across the sky. The quiet feels full and natural. I lie back on the ground next to Hades and join him in looking up, enjoying the feeling of being close to him. I wonder again if this is a God thing, the feelings of connection that are running through me, through us.

"Where are we?" I eventually ask.

"In a part of my realm called the dreaming. Just as you can talk to me in the darkness and the night, you can talk to me in the dreaming; it's easier for me to communicate back to you here because it is part of my dominion, whereas the dark and the night fall on the earth and sea from the sky and I am not the master of those lands."

"So this is a dream?" I ask.

"It is a type of dream, yes." He rolls on to one side and props his head up with his arm. "There are many different varieties of dreams; I am sure I will introduce you to many of them."

I glance up at him, his dark hair glinting in the light, his alabaster skin pale but healthy. I focus on his lips; I didn't notice before how full they are, a light pink like the colour of peonies. They remind me of the one that I placed at Estella's feet in the crypt. And I pluck up the courage to ask Hades something that I've been thinking of from the moment I first realized who he was.

"Hades, you're the lord of the underworld."

"Yes, that hasn't escaped my attention, Ara," he says with that small playful smile, and I just about manage not to roll my eyes at him.

"As the lord of the underworld, would you be able to let me see my sister?" The words tumble out of me one after the other in a fearful rush. "Maybe as a gift, instead of a favour?" I add.

Hades looks at me thoughtfully and I see a little shadow of sadness pass over his face.

"It is not uncommon for mortals from time to time to see the spirits of those who have passed. Estella has been in my realm for five years now, and she is changed from how you might remember her; are you sure that you would want to see her?"

"Yes!" I can't believe that he is even asking that.

"I will make you no promises, Ara, but I will see what I can do. You know that you will see her ... one day. Although, I hope that day is many, many years from now."

"At the way these Games are going I wouldn't count on it," I say, and unconsciously reach for the wound I gained in the swamp.

"How's your shoulder?" he asks.

"Painful." I remember the rip in my back where the creature had pierced its claw through me. Melia used her ointment on it, but it's starting to hurt; even though I know this is a dream it's as if I can feel the wound, really feel it.

I sit up and Hades does the same, moving close to me. "May I?" he asks.

I nod and keep very still as he moves my hair from my shoulder and pulls the strap of my green dress down my arm, examining the wound closely. I feel his touch on my skin, his warm breath on my neck and I close my eyes as a pull rises in me.

"Well, it's not going to kill you," he says, and I guess that he should know. "The oracle has done well."

He gently pulls my strap back up and releases my hair.

"Here." He reaches out and gives me a water skein.

I look at it wearily. "It's your prize," he says.

"Of course it is," I say with a sigh. "A water skein, not a dagger or a lance."

He raises an eyebrow at me.

"The water inside is from the Eridanos, the mighty river captured in the stars; the waters will never run dry, and they are restorative. If you're feeling depleted it will revive you and if you are wounded it will help to bring comfort. It won't heal you at all, but the pain will be less for a time." He takes the skein and pulling my hair aside again, he pours some of the water on to my back.

I instantly feel better, the pain subsiding, the burning sensation fading, and sigh in relief. "Ahh, that feels good." I take the skein and swallow a big refreshing gulp.

"Can you tell me anything about these birds that we are to face?" I ask him. He sighs as he leans back in the tall grass again, then he waves a hand across the sky and a cloud in the shape of a fierce-looking bird appears.

"Stymphalian birds act as a flock and are relentless; if you are going to kill them then you need to kill them all. I have none of them in my realm, but I guess that will change if you are successful. Once upon a time they were but a simple flock of crows till Zeus charged Hephaestus with fashioning them metal beaks for the eternal torment of Melia."

"Sounds about right." I think of Zeus and his penchant for creating misery.

"My brother has his reasons for his actions," Hades says.

"That may be, but it doesn't make them right, does it?"

We're quiet for a while. I wonder if he is thinking about the way I lunged at Zeus, about what he knows I plan to do if I win the Games. This is what is running through my mind in that moment. As I lie next to him, a small worry creeps over me that he might be disappointed.

"It was very brave, what you did there in the swamp, with Theron." Hades speaks softly.

I wasn't expecting him to say that. I run through all that happened in my head, every image in clear detail within the dreaming. Above me the clouds are shifting and I see one that looks like Theron.

"Did you hear me, when I called out to you in the darkness of the marshes?" I ask.

"Yes," he replies.

"Did you send Theron back?"

"I didn't need to, not that I could have even if I had wanted to. You plucked him from the clutches of Thanatos yourself, Ara. I've seen it done a few times; each time is always impressive. I'm sure that the Fates have a hand in it somewhere too."

"He looks ill, and he's stubborn – he won't rest. Will he live?" I ask.

"For now, Ara. All mortals get to live for now. It amazes me that you don't make more of it. Now passes so swiftly and then it is gone."

I lie back in the grass, nearer to him this time. I can sense his shoulder close to mine, his arm running alongside my own, our hands just out of reach, and even though there is no contact I can feel a tingle all along my arm and hand, the anticipation of his closeness, his touch.

"Now doesn't pass quickly for you," I say.

He turns his head and looks at me, his too-blue eyes fixing on mine. "Right now, it's passing far too quickly for my liking."

Something about the way he's looking at me and the way that he says it makes me feel hot inside. I'm sure that I'm blushing. I look away, gazing back up at the sky, at the clouds, which now all look like me. I laugh and turn back to face him. He's still giving me that look, and my insides feel like they are full of butterflies as I slowly reach out my fingers and touch his. He doesn't move away, instead he extends his fingers and entwines them around mine.

"Ara," he says, except it's not him, it's not his soft voice; it's harsh and jarring and I feel my shoulder being shaken.

17

THE STYMPHALIAN BIRDS

"Ara."

My eyes snap open and I'm in Melia's cave. Theron is above me, shaking me awake. I want to hit him, thump him hard for breaking my dream, and I lash out at him with the water skein that I'm holding.

"Hey! What was that for?" he says.

"I was sleeping, you … you startled me!"

I couldn't well say I was having a nice dream, a dream that made my heart sing, a dream that I was … I don't know, perhaps I was being foolish? I feel foolish now as I stand looking at Theron. I feel my cheeks heat as I hold the water skein, the softness of it reminding me of the softness of Hades' touch. I run a finger over the skein and I find the stamp of my symbol on it. My fingers are still tingling, the butterflies still fluttering inside me, but this feeling slowly fades as reality seeps in.

Something about Theron's expression makes me feel defensive. "Why did you wake me?" I ask him. He still looks a little pale. I pass him the skein and he eyes it before taking a drink. One small sip, then another, followed by a big guzzle and a huge sigh.

"Are you feeling OK?" I can hear the edge in my voice. I'm not just angry with him for waking me, I'm angry at myself. Hades might not affect me the way the other Gods did when I met them at the amphitheatre – there is none of that childlike awe with him, none of that power dynamic – but I think the way I'm starting to feel about him might be something slightly more terrifying and exquisite at the same time.

"Sure, why wouldn't I be fine?" Theron says. He juts out his jaw.

"Oh, I don't know, because yesterday you got dragged into the swamp by a monster and I only just saved you from becoming the latest inhabitant of the underworld."

He looks at me fiercely, and then his face softens and he moves closer so he's right beside me, looking at me intensely, and I feel a ripple of annoyance. He scoops up my free hand in his.

"Ara, you know how hard it is for me to be … vulnerable, to show any kind of weakness. It's not in my nature." He raises a hand to my face; it's warm and familiar and, closing my eyes, I can almost imagine that I'm back in Oropusa in front of the temple. "Thank you, for saving me, for bringing me back, for not letting Hades take me. I won't let him take you, either." His gaze makes me feel hot and cold at the same time and I feel guilty about all of the feelings that are running through my body.

He leans closer to me and runs his thumb over my bottom lip. "I remember your lips on mine as I was pulled back to life. It's the first memory I have after the blackness of the underworld. You, Ara, your touch, your kiss." And he leans towards me and I towards him.

"Hey there, sleepyhead," Acastus calls, as he walks into the nook of the cave where I had been sleeping. Theron quickly drops his hand and turns away from me.

"Oh, sorry, didn't realize I was ... interrupting," Acastus mumbles as he turns to leave.

"It's fine," Theron says abruptly. He looks at me and I feel foolish and confused again, twice in one morning. "I should go and check on the others anyway, it's almost sunrise." He doesn't even glance back at me as he makes his way past Acastus and into the main area of the cave.

"Sorry," Acastus says again, pulling an awkward face before looking over his shoulder at Theron, then back at me with a roguish grin and a raise of his eyebrows.

"Don't," I warn him.

"I have no opinion on this." He shrugs. "I mean, he's handsome and he has that whole macho brooding thing going on – I can see what you find appealing."

I don't mean to smile quite as broadly as I do, then I feel the water in the skein jostle as I move my hand and a wave washes over me, not of guilt, I realize, but more of

137

longing, and I can't quite think straight for a moment. So, I focus on Acastus.

"What's that?" I point to the golden horn that's hanging across his body on a leather strap.

"Demeter visited me late last night and gave me a cornucopia. All I have to do is ask it for food and it will provide. Here, hold up your hands, what would you like for breakfast?"

"Um … berries," I say.

Acastus holds the cornucopia above my hands and commands, "Berries."

Fresh, ripe wild strawberries, raspberries and other fruits I don't know spill into my cupped hands.

"Ha! That's amazing. Hades gave me something similar, a water skein that will never run dry."

"OK, I'm starting to think that maybe Poseidon needs to give me more practical gifts," Danae says, as she comes up behind Acastus to steal one of the berries, popping it in her mouth. "He gave me a net, which Theron and Thalia immediately commandeered for their plan."

I look around, realizing Theron has left the cave. "Where are they?"

Danae shrugs.

"Outside!" Ajax calls, as he wanders over and also steals a berry. "The pair of them have this weird leadership contest going on."

"Thalia is winning," Danae says, as she takes another berry and I try to move them away from her.

"I can't wait for you to ask the cornucopia for a roasted hog with all the trimmings!" Ajax says with a smile.

"What did you get from your God?" Acastus asks him.

"I have to say I was surprised by what Artemis gave me!" He points to the golden band around his neck.

"Jewellery!" Danae says, with a small snigger.

"It almost goes with my bag," I add with a smile.

"Apparently, it will always keep my head above the water. I think the swamps might have spooked her, which is a little counterproductive if you ask me, planning a prevention for something that's already happened. But to be honest I was too struck by her" – he waves his hands around and makes a strange sound – "to ask any questions."

"By her what?" I ask.

Acastus nods, his eyes wide. "Oh, yeah, I know. The God factor! I feel completely foolish whenever Demeter is near. It's like I'm a child again and my mother is chastising me for not behaving in front of company, but also giving me sweets at the same time."

"Oh good, so it's not just me then," Ajax says. "I am honestly terrified every time I see Artemis and I feel so utterly pointless and pathetic."

"And desperately unworthy," Danae adds with a nod.

"But so grateful to be in their presence," Acastus agrees.

"So grateful, it's like I want to impress Artemis, I want her to see that I am brilliant."

"She already does see that," Danae says. "Remember, she chose you. That's what I keep clinging to every time

Poseidon talks to me. It's like a massive tidal wave of emotions ready to lift me up and carry me off: elation and fear all mixed together. But I keep reminding myself I must be worthy because he chose me. I bet it's worse for you, Ara, the intense Godliness! Is Hades really terrifying? I think if I was the token to the God of the underworld, I wouldn't be able to even look at him."

"I know what you mean. I took a peek in his direction after the gauntlet and it felt as if an arrow of emptiness had hit the very middle of my soul; his eyes must be like bottomless pits." Acastus shivers. "Maybe that's why so many of his tokens die," he adds. "What is he like?"

The three of them look at me expectantly. But I'm in shock. I'd been thinking that all of the tokens had the same deep connection that I did with Hades, but I was wrong, so very wrong.

"He's definitely not what I was expecting," I say. "He's deep, thoughtful, kind even, but he has this hard shell of an exterior that at first seems almost impenetrable but when you get to know him you find a way in, and his eyes … well, they're more like the empty expanse of space and time than a bottomless pit."

The others look at me and then laugh.

"Kind and thoughtful, yeah, right, Ara," Acastus says.

"I don't know, I think a kind God of the underworld would be pretty terrifying actually," Theron says from behind me, and for some reason I feel tense at the thought of Theron having heard what I said about Hades.

I turn around to see he is giving me a hard look, like I've seen him use on the training grounds right before he tears down an opponent.

"It's almost time," he says, and walks away from me without a second look; I feel the blow.

As we move towards the opening of the cave, Melia calls out, "I can see you all – you're still a little hazy around the edges, but my sight is almost returned, the birds will be here soon."

Thalia appears from the cave entrance. "Theron and Nestor, you know what to do?"

"Climb up the outside of the cave and wait for your signal, then drop the net and light it," Nestor says in a slightly irritated voice; Thalia has been going over and over the plan with us all since last night. "Solon, Acastus, Heli, Ajax and I will be ready to fight the birds. Xenia and Ara, you're to guard Melia and get her to safety, while Danae…"

"Yeah, yeah, I know." Danae lifts one of Melia's long robes and twists it around her, pulling the hood over her head, hiding her face. "I'm bait."

"Wait, what am I doing again?" Ajax asks, and I swear I see a blood vessel in Thalia's forehead bulge. Ajax smiles. "Only joking! I know what I'm doing."

I lean over to him and whisper, "You might want to stay clear of Thalia. I think she might strike you down while you are fighting the birds."

"Lucky for me one of the rules is no causing intended harm!"

I shake my head at him. "This way, Melia," I call to the oracle as I take her hand and lead her towards the back of the cave as Danae gets into position.

Melia pauses and lifts her hands to Danae's face as she passes. "You are very brave." I can't help but agree as pride for my friend fills me. "Remember, the birds can sense where I am," Melia says. "It's so they can always find me. If I'm outside of the cave they will just head straight for me and your plan would never work, so both you and I need to be in the cave when the birds arrive. But as soon as all the birds are in the cave and the net has dropped to trap them in, I will leave you here as the only Melia." The oracle kisses Danae on the head then on each of her eyes.

I lead Melia away from Danae. She reaches out and touches my cheek. "I can see your face; no wonder he is in love with you." She smiles, and I feel my heart skip a beat.

At that moment a screeching fills the air, a screeching that tears through me, as if my bones are grating together.

I hurry to the back of the cave, keeping hold of Melia's hand. As the first of the birds fly in and begin to circle, I pull back a tattered tapestry hanging over the wall of the cave. Behind it, a narrow gap leads to an almost vertical shaft: our way out.

I hear Solon, Acastus, Ajax and Heli fighting the birds, protecting Danae. Then one of the birds flies towards us. Xenia cuts it down. I remember what Hades said, that they must all die for Melia to be safe and for that to happen they all have to be inside the cave before Theron and Nestor can drop the net to trap them.

A few more birds realize that Danae is a decoy and fly towards Melia. Xenia defends us as I draw Melia in, holding her face against my shoulder, protecting her eyes.

Ajax is close by and grabs two arrows from his quiver and uses them like small spears, his bow too large to use in the small space at the back of the cave. I can barely see the main entrance to the cave, let alone Solon, Acastus and Heli, who are standing between it and Danae. There are so many birds flying around and around; they swoop and attack like a cyclone of bronzed beaks and black feathers.

"Thalia!" I hear Acastus call out. She's outside watching to make sure all of the birds are inside; if they're not, well, I'm not sure we can wait much longer. The birds are overpowering us. They are attacking me as I hold on to Melia, pecking my hands and arms as I hold her close, their blade-like beaks slicing through my skin, and I can't imagine the agony that Melia must have gone through each morning as they pecked out her eyes.

Finally, Thalia runs into the cave, her sword raised against the birds.

"Quickly," I call to Xenia, who has a small litter of dead birds around her feet. She moves away from Ajax as he continues to strike them down.

Xenia slips past me and into the narrow passage, taking Melia's hand and guiding her as I drop the tapestry behind us. I don't think it will be long before the birds rip through the twisted threads with their razor-sharp beaks.

There are small holes in the sides of the vertical shaft, making it easy to climb, but in the darkness of the tunnel and the dusk of the early dawn I have to feel my way up. Melia is finding it easier than both Xenia and I to navigate the dark passage, moving with practised ease. The walls are tight, I feel them grazing both my shoulders as I struggle to climb; it feels so claustrophobic and reminds me of an underground tomb. I try to push the thought from me as I feel my panic rising, and struggle to focus on something else, something good and hopeful, as we slowly climb further away from the battle below and the cawing of the birds.

I think of Hades, of his blue eyes and that slip of a smile, and I whisper to him in the dark, because I know he can hear me.

"I hope you rolled an advantage, because if I get trapped in this tiny tunnel, I'm not going to be happy."

I imagine that ever so slight smile of his and him saying, "I did my best, and now it's up to you." I smile and climb more confidently towards a chink of light I now see above us.

Nestor is waiting by the hole; he reaches down a hand and helps to pull me out. I squint then shield my eyes, waiting for them to adjust. The sun is above the horizon and casts a golden glow over the world. I look across the rocky outcrop that the cave is carved into.

"Where's Theron? He's supposed to be here. Is he OK?" I can hear the panic in my voice.

"He's fine. He didn't want to miss out on proving himself a worthy hero, so he snuck into the cave after we dropped the net and before I lit it with Promethean fire to stop the birds from escaping. Speaking of which, give me a hand, Ara."

Nestor and I move closer to a large boulder that he, Danae and I had found towards the part of the outcrop that gives way to more of the twisting white trees that litter the forest. We had rolled it as far as the hole last night and now we remove the braces securing it in place and tip it inside, blocking the escape route so none of the birds can break through.

"Look at it," Melia calls out, her arms wide as she stands on top of the rocky outcrop. "It is so beautiful." Tears stream down her cheeks, her deep brown eyes taking in every detail of the swamp.

"Yeah, it's great," Xenia says, raising her eyebrows.

And I get what she means, but I try to see the beauty that Melia sees, glimpsing it in the twisting spires of the dead trees, bone white and silk smooth as they reach like fingers into the bluebird sky; in the sunrise, orange and gold, to the east; in a flock of black birds to the west, moving like shadow puppets across the sky towards us, the light of the rising sun catching on their beaks so they sparkle like stars.

My smile fades as I realize what they are a second before their screeching caws fill the air.

"Push back the boulder! Get Melia inside!" Nestor shouts, as he and I try to grab the boulder, but it's too far down the hole for us to reach and likely jammed in place even if we could.

I plunge my hand into my bag and pull out the rope; the stone from the swamp is still tied to the end and drops to the ground. It gives me an idea.

As the birds flock ever closer I rush to the oracle.

"Melia, I need you to trust me," I tell her.

She turns and looks at me calmly and nods as she leans towards me and whispers, "I trust you, Ara, you who will bring a God to his knees."

I pull back and look at her, my eyes wide, and think of Zeus on his knees in front of me as I hold a thunderbolt above him, then I blink as I see how close the flock of birds is. I swiftly hold the bag open and move it through the air, pulling it over her head and down her body so that she disappears inside it.

"What did you just do to the oracle? We need her," Xenia says.

"It's OK, she's safe, I think." I hope, but I don't say that out loud. I've never put anything alive in the bag before.

The birds circle around us, cawing as if they sense that Melia is there even though they can't find her. I wonder how long it will be before they get frustrated and attack us.

Not long at all, it would seem.

I spin the rope, lashing the rock towards whichever bird is closest. There must be at least thirty of them, far fewer than in the cave, but these ones have the advantage of being able to fly away, and we need to get every single one of them if Melia is to be free of her curse and tell us what we need to know about our quest.

They peck at us with every opportunity, those sharp deadly beaks glinting in the sunrise.

Xenia's armour protects her, as does Nestor's. "See," I say to Hades, not sure if he will hear me at all. "Armour, that would be nice; it's not a weapon, it's protection. Maybe we can negotiate on that one." I feel every scratch of talon and peck of beak.

I swing wide with the rope as a stymphalian bird changes direction mid-flight and I miss it. The rope continues in its arc and passes through Nestor's Prometheus torch, alight at his waist.

The moment the rope touches the blue flame it catches, the fire eating its way up the rope and stopping just before my hand. I swing the rope wide, and it creates a fiery shield as it revolves around; any bird that dares to get too close is caught by the flames, their feathers instantly blazing and burning to ash.

I see Xenia light her arrows from Nestor's torch before firing them like meteors into the sky, taking out the birds on the edge of the flock.

Nestor uses the flame to light the blade of his sword, which he sweeps in a fiery arc in the direction of the birds.

I change the spinning of the rope and begin throwing it out towards the remaining birds like a lasso. I think of how the rope grew and shrank as I needed it to in the swamp and watch as it does the same now, reaching and pulling back to hit its mark every time. As the black dust of the charred birds gathers around me, I hear Xenia scream and Nestor call out.

I turn my head to see that Xenia is no longer on the top of the outcrop and Nestor is looking over the edge. The last few birds are making their escape beyond him. I throw out the rope, which extends to follow the retreating birds, striking the one furthest away, then I flick my wrist and the rope twists back to strike another one. I then pull the rope in a large flaming arc to hit the last remaining bird as it caws a sad pathetic war cry and charges towards me. The rope hits it, bursting it into flames and then ash.

"Xenia!" I call, as the rope shrinks and I rush to Nestor, who is looking down. Xenia is lying at the bottom of the drop, leg twisted under her, her helm broken and blood flowing from beneath it as she looks up into the sky, her eyes seeing nothing.

"Xenia," I say again, and I feel a lump rise in my throat as I remember Estella, lying in our bed looking just as broken. I feel the injustice of it all, the wrongness of us tokens dying for the pleasure of the Gods, for their entertainment and satisfaction.

"Look after her, Hades," I whisper. And then I realize that he is part of this too. He might be trying to play the Games in a way that soothes his conscience, but he is still playing, and that confuses me.

"What's happening to her?" Nestor asks, as Xenia's body begins to shimmer and fade.

"I guess she's going back home, to her family," I say.

"That happens?"

"It does."

Nestor takes in a deep breath and shakes his head. "Promise me, Ara, that if I die, you'll close my eyes and fix me up before I'm sent back. I don't want my parents to see me like that. My sisters, they shouldn't see me like that." He shakes his head.

It fills me with sadness to hear the tenderness towards his family. I hadn't really thought about the ones that will be left behind; the ones like me. I feel angry and sorry for Nestor's sisters should one of them be the first to find him. I wouldn't want that for anyone. We must all have people waiting at home, those we don't want to have to bear our loss.

I think of my parents, and I realize that they will not be able to bear it, not again.

I reach out and touch Nestor's arm. "I promise, and I know you'll do the same for me if the time comes."

Nestor nods. Then he lifts his torch to my rope and the fire leaps back into the flame of the torch, leaving the rope with no sign it had just been burning.

THE TIGHTENING OF THE KNOT

Ares sits brooding at the table, his eyes fixed on the body of Xenia that floats above her plinth, her helm broken and blood pooling around it in a red halo, her leg twisted behind her and bent arms out to her side. Her eyes stare unseeingly at the God who chose her.

Hades can feel her outside his gate, her spirit and body still connected as each one is suspended in the moment of death, her body in Olympus caught on the cusp of its last heartbeat and her spirit cast into the darkness just outside his door. She is not alone; Philco and Kassandra are there too, waiting for the Immortal Games to end, and with it their lives.

Zeus joins Ares at the table. As the other Gods make idle chatter about the Games, the two of them watch the stymphalian bird attack play out again.

"When the Games are over, I will visit this abomination of a place, this Swamp of Sadness and it will be sad no more," Demeter says with a wave of her hand towards the vision that hangs above the board. "Where my feet tread, firm ground and flowers will spring, and where I sing, the winds shall blow sweet with the seeds of blossoms, and where I dance, the birds and bees and small creatures of the earth will come and make their homes."

"That sounds wonderful, Auntie," Athena says from her seat beside Hades. "How gracious of you to show it your favour; I am sure it will be a relief to the land after all of these years of desolation and darkness."

Demeter smiles and leans across the corner of the board to grasp the hand of Athena. "Thank you, Niece, I am sure my favour will be most appreciated. I will tell the others of my plan."

Hades leans in close to Athena. "And I thought you were the Goddess of truth and wisdom."

"Yes, well, I have learnt a thing or two about truth from the mortals, who are more aware of the fluidity of it and of the flexibility of wisdom and how the vessel through which both are seen is of the utmost importance. I told Demeter the truth she wanted to hear, and it was true for some but not for many. The Children of Sadness who live in the marshes, who feed off its decay and darkness, will not thank her for her wandering, nor will the plants that she deposits there, for although she may add to the land, the waters of the marshes are still stagnant and plentiful. It will be beautiful for a season – I will make sure that I hunt there – but when the rains return it will be washed away and restored as it now is." Athena looks over at her father,

Zeus, his jaw set and eyes low as he watches the visions of the tokens play out above the board.

"Change can only happen when it is deep, when it is entangled in the fabric of the loom of living, and when it is desired by those who must cultivate and grow it. You see change, making things better, is an immortal task that requires time, strength, diligence and foresight. Demeter lacks all but one of these and even that she fritters away."

"Remind me never to ask you to examine me in this way," Hades says, with a small smile and a pinch of worry.

"Oh, I cannot. I have tried, and I am unable to understand you at all, Uncle. You play the best game of all of us, you know. Never showing us your hand."

Hades smiles, although Athena doesn't see it.

"This is bad form, Hermes!" Zeus erupts as he brings a fist down on the table, threatening to topple all of the playing pieces. "Melia's punishment was mine to give and not yours to take!"

The room is in a state of silent wariness as all eyes focus on Zeus. Hermes holds his hands up, the golden snakes circling his caduceus glinting. "It was not me, mighty Zeus, it was the tokens! Their free will chose this path; it is part of the Games after all – the element of surprise that adds to the entertainment."

Hades sighs. He knows where this is going; he has seen his brother's wrath enough times to know what happens next.

"Brother," he says, leaning towards Zeus, "can we not

chalk this one up to the Games? Yes, the stymphalian birds have been vanquished and now reside in my realm, where they are being put to good use in Tartarus, I assure you, and Melia is free of her torment, her punishment – but Theron has shone, has he not?" Hades lifts a hand and the visons above the table show Theron releasing the net with Nestor before climbing down the outcrop and entering the cave moments before the fire engulfs the net, and then drawing his sword to begin cutting down the birds.

"He is a fine token," Hera says, touching Zeus' arm. "He honours you with both his bravery and his skill." Hera is used to calming her husband's temper.

"He *is* a fine token," Zeus agrees.

"And just look at how he deals with those birds," Hermes adds.

Poseidon takes a big gulp from his glass and Hades looks at him. They both know that now is not the time to press Zeus, his mood has been on the edge ever since Ara saved Theron from the swamps. For Zeus there is no challenge to be made over the worthiness of his token, his judgement is always sound and good in his eyes and any challenge to that is not only unacceptable but wrong.

Hades tries to remember if Zeus was always like this, definitely for as long as he has known his brother, but they both had such different upbringings. Zeus was raised in the knowledge that all would be his eventually, Hades in the darkness of his father's hubris. Things that grow in the dark are often more aware of the shadows within; Zeus has only ever known the light of his own importance.

"Theron is a token of note. It was he who agreed that they should travel to the swamp and then led them valiantly through it. He was even at your gates for a moment, was he not, Hades? And yet he overcame death. I guess if young Theron is to kill a few birds and free a few oracles on his quest to greatness, then so be it!" Zeus proclaims.

All the Gods relax a little, although Ares is still glaring at Xenia.

Hades glances over again at Poseidon. The Games are young and already the tempers are fraying. The Fates are right, the stakes have never been higher, and even though Zeus and Poseidon are unaware of the knot they have caused in the world, Hades can see the tension of it resting on them.

He curses the Fates for laying the responsibility of unpicking this situation with him. But he knows that if it were left up to his brothers the knot would only grow.

It fills him with a deep sadness that aches in the bones of the earth he inhabits, to think of how it used to be, how the Gods of Olympus were once the guiding stars for the mortals, how they lived to make the world better. Now they exist only to find pleasure and self-gratification in the world.

Hades thinks of the vison he and his brothers once held, a vision he still tries to uphold in the lands of Elysium.

"What merriment do we have now?" Zeus calls. "What

trials are there for young Theron? I am sure that he will meet all that are on the board and off it." Zeus smiles in Hades' direction. "Only a matter of time before he takes the crown and, no doubt, the heart of Hades' token with it."

Some of the Gods murmur in agreement, but Hades watches Aphrodite from the corner of his eye and sees that she tilts her head to one side and glances in his direction; she, it seems, is not so sure about that.

Hades is not so sure either. There is something about Ara that is causing him turmoil. He would reach for her in an instant if he thought it was what she wanted, but he has seen in her heart and he knows that she means to kill his brother if she can.

The knot pulls a little tighter. To unpick it he and Ara must win the Games, but by winning she will have the opportunity to fulfil her revenge. It is a fine thread that Hades walks upon, one that he wishes had never been stitched for him.

19

THE DECEIVER OF WINGS

Nestor and I climb down from the outcrop and make our way to the cave entrance. I can see the others moving like shadows in the quiet cave beyond the flaming net. Nestor touches the torch to the flames and, just as it had with my rope, the fire retreats from the net back into the torch.

I hesitate before I reach for the net, expecting it to be hot after the fire, but it's cool to the touch and completely unmarked. Nestor and I start to pull the net back so that we can slip over the threshold of thick ash that we find at the entrance, and into the cave.

"Is everyone all right?" I call out, as my eyes swiftly adjust to the gloom.

Theron is by my side in moments, pulling me close and hugging me, just as he did when we first saw each other in the amphitheatre. I feel a rush of relief flood over me that he's safe, but instead of hugging him in return, I pull back and look at him. His face and arms are covered in thin papercut-like scratches, just like mine. I run a hand over his arm, the thin red lines of blood smearing under my fingertips.

I look behind him at the others. "Are they all gone? The birds?"

"Most of them tried to fly back out after you left the cave, but they flew straight into the fire and died," Theron says, as he scuffs up the band of black ash with his sandal.

"What happened to you?" Thalia asks, pointing to my cuts.

"Not all of the birds were in the cave when we dropped the net," Nestor says. "A small flock of them attacked us. But we got them all."

"Where's Xenia?" Solon asks.

I look over at Nestor; I don't have to be an oracle to know that he is thinking of Xenia after her fall. I shake my head and the others become still and silent. I cast my eyes around each of the tokens, the realization that the same fate could befall any of us in a moment is sinking in, but also that we are all one trial closer to the crown. That's when I realize that Ajax and Danae are missing, and I fear the worst; Danae had the most dangerous part to play in the plan.

"It's all right," Theron says, when I ask where they are, my voice high and panicked. He places a hand on my shoulder. "They're at the back of the cave. Danae is injured, though; the birds thought that she was Melia and they started to peck out her eyes."

"What?" I push past him and deeper into the cave to

find Danae lying on the floor writhing in agony, while Ajax tries to put the lotion that Melia had used for Acastus on Danae's eyes.

I crouch down behind Danae and reach out to her, pulling her towards me, placing her head into my lap. I stroke her hair and whisper into her ear, "Oh, Danae, it's OK. It's going to be OK." She whimpers in my arms.

Nestor has followed me. "Ara, what can I do to help?"

"Lights, Nestor, we need some light to see by."

He uses his Promethean flame to light the lanterns in Melia's cave and they burn brightly, white-blue with no flickering.

I smooth back Danae's golden hair and I can see that around both of her eyes, the sockets and the lids, there are angry red, bleeding scratches. She opens her left eye but her right remains shut, the eyelid falling back inside the socket where her eyeball used to be.

Ajax is poised with the ointment, but I reach into my bag and pull out the water skein. "We need to wash it first," I tell him. "Find me some cloth."

He jumps up and starts searching but Thalia steps closer, ripping a piece of material from her tunic and holding it out for me. I douse it with water and Thalia kneels in front of Danae and gently washes her eyes and cleans all her wounds. Danae sobs but doesn't flinch.

Thalia talks to Danae as she cleans. "At home, when our warriors fight in an epic battle such as this, such as you have, and they distinguish themselves through their courage and valour, it is customary for them to receive an epithet. So, as my father has bestowed many a name to a warrior, I will give one to you, Danae, token of Poseidon, Deceiver of Wings."

Danae stops crying, the refreshing waters of Eridanos calming the pain enough for Ajax to then spread the ointment over her cuts.

"It … it doesn't hurt any more," Danae says, her voice quiet. As she looks up at me with her one eye, large and full of watery tears, she looks so young, much younger than her eighteen years.

"That's good," I tell her, stroking her golden hair. "That's really good."

"It's looking better already," Thalia tells her with a kind smile.

"It's going to look very badass when it heals," Ajax says. "Scars worthy of a hero! Worthy of Danae, Deceiver of Wings," he adds with a small smile.

Danae lets out a little laugh that quickly turns into gentle crying. Ajax pulls her up on to his lap, holding her to him, and my heart feels like a little bit of it has broken off. Philco, Kassandra and Xenia have gone, Theron almost died, Danae has lost her eye – and we've only just begun the quest. I'm not sure that I can take the loss that is in front of me.

Theron comes raging into the cave. "Melia's gone, I can't find her anywhere. She cheated us."

"What?" Thalia says sharply, as I stand up and shift my bag around me.

"She's not here, I've searched everywhere. She got what she wanted, and she left before telling us where the crown is. She tricked us, she used us! We travelled all the way here and now we're in the middle of nowhere and have no idea where the crown is!" Theron glares at Heli, who shrinks away a little.

"Calm down, she's right here," I say, standing up to face him.

"Obviously not, I just told you I searched everywhere!" He growls as he rounds on me, his face full of anger.

I'm used to his flares of passion, and I feel myself getting defensive and stick out my chin as I turn away from him and place my bag on the floor. I lift the flap and think of Melia as I place my hand inside. I feel her slender fingers entwine with mine and pull her up; hand, arm, head, body appear and then she steps out of the bag, looking around in wonder.

"What happened? Where did I go?"

"I put you in my bag," I tell her. Realizing how weird that sounds, I add, "Hades gave it to me; he called it a Trojan bag." I lift it from the ground. "Stuff goes in, and the bag keeps it safe."

Melia takes it in her hand then looks inside. I know what she can see, nothing!

"It was darker in there than when I was sightless. How long was I in there for, it felt like a fraction of forever."

"You weren't in there for long. And you were safe," I say, even though I know that I had no idea when I put her in there if she would be, or if I could retrieve her again. Then a thought whips across my mind and I feel a little guilty, as I realize that if I had died like Xenia, Melia might have been lost in the bag forever. But then I think of Hades; if Melia was in the darkness, he would have found her and restored her to the light.

Melia looks around the cave. "I don't want to be in here right now. Come out into the day with me so that I can see you all better."

We follow her outside, Ajax still holding Danae close to him. The nine of us that are remaining gather around Melia and she looks at each of us in turn, as if she is seeing beyond our flesh and into our very souls. I feel as if I have been examined under her gaze, a little like when I was a child and my mother would know all the things that I had been up to just by looking at me. Like the time I had taken the honeycomb from the pantry and eaten it all without asking.

I think we all feel something similar, as I look at the others and take in their childlike expressions. I glance over at Theron, and it is as if he is ten again and late for training.

"You have done me an enormous service," Melia says to us all, breaking the spell. Theron is back to being grown up again, his face full of that seriousness he's been wearing since the night of the Blood Moon. "You have freed me from my torment and given me back my sight. Now I will reward you with that which you seek. You are nine who are soon to become seven. I can see your journey, the fallen among you, the friendships, and betrayals. The crown you seek is in the Forgotten Isles, the lands at the very end of the world, where many have travelled to, but none have returned from. You will need a vessel of worth which you will find in Gythion. In Gythion, look for the symbol of Hermes, his caduceus; below this sign there will be a trial to face and, if you pass, you will be granted access to the worthy vessel."

"Gythion!" Theron says. "That's weeks away by horse and boat, months on foot."

I look over at him harshly, then turn to Melia. "Thank you for your wisdom."

"Will you come with us?" Acastus asks Melia, his handsome face still with an impish childlike look as he gazes at the oracle.

"No, I will stay here … for a time," Melia says with a smile. "I have a feeling that this place is going to bloom soon, and it is going to become quite spectacular. I would like to see that."

I look about the swamp, its twisting branches and murky quagmires, and wonder what signs Melia can see that an alteration is soon coming. But then I see her smile and her eyes glint, and I realize that just like when she looks at each of us and sees more, she is looking at the swamp and seeing more too.

"We should get going," Thalia says, collecting her sword.

I feel reluctant to leave Melia. The threat to her has passed, I know she'll be safe, but I guess I'm worried that leaving her behind, leaving the swamp and travelling into the unknown, is only going to hold more dangers.

I look around at my fellow tokens as we make our way south, the sun rising steadily above us, our shadows shortening with every passing moment. I wonder how many of us are going to make it through the quest, how many of us will join Hades? I think of Xenia and then my thoughts leap to Estella. However many of us make it to the crown, I have to be one of them; I have to win and avenge not only my sister, but Xenia, Kassandra, Philco and anyone else that we lose along the way.

I glance over at Theron and feel a pull deep in my stomach. I don't think I could bear losing him. Then I look around at the others and realize that I don't want to lose any of them either.

THE OATH

The sun is high and hot, the soft ground of the swamp far behind us, as my sandals kick up the dry ground. Out of the marshes, we quickly found a trader's path south over the low mountains, not that we have seen any traders. "I've travelled this way many times with my uncle and cousins," Solon told us when we stumbled across it a few hours after leaving Melia.

"My uncle is a cloth merchant, and twice a year we make a trip to gather silks from the port at Chalcis. We are usually part of a larger caravan of traders all travelling in the same direction – there are many dangers on the path, and not all of them are sent by the Gods!" he says with a raise of an eyebrow, before telling us tales of vicious sandstorms and attacking bandits.

As the unrelenting sun beats upon me, I half think that a sandstorm might bring some welcome relief. If Solon is right, we have weeks of travel ahead of us. I look down at my dust-covered legs and pull my sticking tunic away from my body.

I'm so relieved when the murmurs of stopping and resting become overwhelming and Theron and Thalia, who have become the leaders of our little band of tokens, suggest that we find some shelter just off the path and rest from the midday sun. The earth may be dry here, but I can see the tops of lush, dense forests in the distance, and scattered in this rockier terrain are small islands of thick bush and small trees.

We head towards a thicket, its shade a welcome relief. Thalia suggests that we can make up time by walking into the night when it's not so hot, but I don't mention it to Acastus as we sit together, his cape hoisted above us as if we are children making camp.

I share my water among the group and Acastus uses his cornucopia to feed everyone. I realize that if the two of us were to perish then the others would have to fend for themselves when it came to provisions, but they are happy enough to take from our favours and we are happy enough to share.

Heli sits close by us; she's holding a small golden trinket in her hand and watching as the sunlight makes it shine. "What's that?" I ask her.

She looks round at me, her eyes wide. "They're the scales of truth; Athena was just here and gave them to me. Didn't you see her?" She holds the small set of golden scales up to the light. The scales are on a chain around her neck, and I see that one of the plates has a brass heart on it, and the other a copper feather.

Acastus and I both look around us. "We didn't see her, but I don't think that's how it works; I don't think we can see each other's Gods," he says.

"That makes sense," Nestor says. "And I think the way that they visit is linked to their power somehow, all of the things that they have control over. Hephaestus always visits me in fire or light, he kind of takes me into it, but I'm not sure that I physically go anywhere."

I find myself nodding as I think about the dream I had of Hades the previous night, and remember his blue eyes and the way he looked at me.

"Yeah, it's like our spirits commune with them. Not surprisingly, Poseidon always calls to me when I'm looking at water," Danae adds, and she's obviously been to see him recently because she is wearing a golden eyepatch over her empty socket. I wonder for a moment if it has any special properties, as I think about Poseidon and his powers.

This is when I realize that Hades might hear me in the dark, but when he gave me the water skein, I was asleep. Hades is the God of the underworld, of darkness, of the unseen, and of dreams.

The heat is still beaming down on me, and I can't shake the image of water from my mind. I feel a deep longing for the river that runs along the back of my home, to dive into its deep chilly waters. I close my eyes and imagine the river, how the light splits through the canopy of trees that run either side of it, then glints off the water that flows in soft currents at this time of year. My daydream takes hold and I imagine the freshness of the green shadows, the softness of the earth as I sit on the grass by the bank and slip off my sandals, dipping my toes into the water. I can almost feel the tranquil coolness running over my hot dusty feet. I look up at the trees and through their leaves I can see the blue of the sky, deeper and softer than it is here, and the smell of the baked and broken earth around me is replaced by the scent of the water and the delicate perfume of flowering trees.

I know that Hades is here, I don't need to turn my head to see him. He's sitting next to me in my daydream; I can feel his presence wash over me in the same way that the river is cooling and cleansing my feet. I let out a deep sigh of contentment and feel a smile creep over my lips as I turn my head away from the sky to face him.

"Another dream?" I ask.

"Of a sort," he says, as he looks straight at me, straight into me. "It is a waking dream, a daydream of a kind, and it is happening in the space between two heartbeats as you breathe in and breathe out; when the dreaming is done it will feel like no time has passed at all, but whole lifetimes can be lived in that small space between the beats of life."

I am mesmerized by him. I can't get over the pull that I feel towards him, his eyes, his smile, his surprisingly kind and gentle manner, the almost poetic way that he looks at the world. I realize that I covet that and feel sorry for him for it at the same time.

"I've come to reward you for facing the stymphalian

birds. That was some quick thinking with the bag." He smiles as he looks up at the trees then reaches to pull a fresh red apple from the branches.

"I didn't know if it would work, if she would be alive when she came out," I admit to him, feeling a little foolish.

"I'll be honest with you: I was not sure, either." His smile deepens and he looks at me sheepishly. "I've never tried to put anything living in there before." He extends the apple to me, and I hesitate before taking it.

"Is this my gift?" I ask, turning it in my hands.

He lets out a short deep laugh that sounds like the very earth rumbling in merriment. His eyes sparkle with mischief under the dappled light of the glade and I feel defensive, as if he's laughing at me; I tilt my head to the side, my look stern, and he holds his hands up in surrender to me.

"No, it is not your gift," Hades says, shaking his head. "I just thought you looked as if you were in need of refreshment."

I look away at the water. "Thank you." I bite into the sweetness of the apple and wipe my chin as the juice runs down from my lips. Looking at my hand, I realize how dirty I am; the miles of walking have covered my whole body and clothes in a layer of fine brown dirt.

I lift the bag from me and place the apple on top of it before slipping into the deep waters of the river, fully clothed. I feel instantly refreshed as I dunk my head under the surface. I dive down and swim a little against the current and then I see something dark flash just behind me. I spin around in the water and realize it's my cape twisting around in the stream, but it's enough to remind me of the creatures from the swamp and I feel spooked. When I come up for breath, I see that Hades is standing on the bank, watching me.

I unhook the cape from my shoulders, heavy with the weight of the water. I throw it up on to the bank where it lands in a twisted sodden mass.

Hades lifts it over a tree branch, pulling it out so it can dry.

"Come on in," I call to him.

I see him hesitate for a moment and then he kicks off his sandals and starts to pull at the looping fabric of his robes till he is standing almost naked. My eyes quickly run over his body: muscular, toned, lean, and almost as white as the perizoma covering his loins. He looks self-conscious for a moment and, as he dives in, I look away, feeling as if the temperature of the water has risen by a few degrees.

Just when I'm beginning to worry and I'm thinking of diving deep to look for him, he surfaces just in front of me. He gasps for air and wipes the water from his face before pushing his hair back, although the water pulls it forward again and I like the way it flops in front of his eyes. That small smile is back, and I suddenly feel like I'm in a river full of rapids and currents that I can't see.

I tread water furiously as I move a little closer to him.

"I thought this place was the river that runs along the

back of my family's villa, but it's too deep and wide for that, the waters move differently, and we don't have the same fruit trees growing there. Where is this place?" I ask.

"Nowhere," he says, as he looks around. "This place isn't real; it is part of my imagination and part of yours. In the east of Elysium there is a glade that looks very similar to the one beyond the bank, with a deep stream running through it, but that stream flows faster and the waters are dangerous."

So are these, I think to myself.

"Elysium, is it as beautiful as they say?" I ask.

"It depends on who it is that says." I can hear the smile in Hades' voice. It's infectious and I join him, my smile broad for a moment, but then it falters.

"I guess I'll see for myself one day, one day soon no doubt."

I see a flickering in his eyes, "Oh Ara, I hope not. Death changes a person, both when you take a life and when you slip from it." He has that faraway look again, as if he's seeing things that I will never be able to comprehend, that I will never know exist.

"How?" I ask, intrigued but also worried about Estella, has death changed her?

"When you are all spirit, the world is a very different place, and in Elysium there are none of the pressures that you find in the mortal realm. Souls expand; they become lighter and more. That changes a person, Ara. Their essence is still the same, but they are changed through their experience.

And then there is the slow unwinding that happens over time, the forgetting of your former life till it is as distant as the light from a far-off star." Then he looks at me earnestly. "To take a life is to mark your spirit, to restrict your soul with a band of penance that is almost unbreakable."

"Almost?" I say.

"There are times, such as saving others or yourself, when the mark on the soul is lighter, the band thinner, but the heaviness carried is still the same and it can take eons for a soul to recover."

I know that he is trying to warn me in his own way, to prepare me for when I slip from my life and when I take Zeus' life from him.

"Ara, I hope that it is a very long time until you see the fields and meadows, mountains and springs of Elysium, but when that time comes, I … I would like to show you the full splendour of that land." Hades sounds serious, hopeful.

"I would find that comforting," I tell him. "I think that dying would not be so bad. I mean, I'd see my sister again and if this is but a shade of Elysium then I will be happy there, and you'll be there too." I'm closer to him now. I can feel the river around him shifting as he treads water, and if I extend my hands a little further out then I could touch him.

"But if I were to go to Elysium before I have fulfilled the promise that I gave to my sister then you might as well lock me in Tartarus for it will be agony for me to see her, to exist beyond, and know that I never avenged her."

I watch as a knowing suddenly falls into place and Hades' brows knot together for a moment before his face becomes smooth and hard as stone.

"So you do mean to punish the Gods for what happened to her? I had hoped that I was wrong, that the flash of what I saw in you was but a passing fancy. Many mortals have wanted to punish us Gods," he says, and the way he says, *us Gods* firmly places him alongside his brother. I feel a fear rising in me, not a fear of him, but the way that he looks at me makes me feel I've wronged him in some way.

"I do not mean to punish all the Gods, only one," I answer. I can feel Estella's token against my skin as my own pushes down on the fabric between them.

"I see, well, if it is this God that you mean to punish then know that I am in torment." He looks at me then swims away to the bank.

As he climbs out and begins to wrap his dark cloth around him, his back to me, I follow him, calling, "I … no, I do not want to torment you in any way. I don't ever want to cause you pain." And it's true.

"And yet, you do." He turns towards me as I pull myself out of the river and stand in front of him, dripping all over the bank. I feel a lump in my throat and a flutter in my chest as he raises a hand to my face and cups my cheek. I feel my breath catch at the lightness of his touch and I watch as a single tear runs from his blue eyes and down his perfect cheek. He lowers his head, his face so close to mine, and he says in a voice as low as the night,

"You torment me by wanting to kill my brother; you torment me by the thought of the fate that would give you. To even try to kill a God is no small thing; your punishment would be long and brutal, and it would be I that would deliver that punishment to you for all eternity. I would be charged with punishing you, Ara, every moment of every day, and that would torment me more than you can imagine."

I feel a tightness in my chest as I realize what he is saying is true. If I kill Zeus then Hades will have no option but to take me to Tartarus, to lock me up and hand out my punishment personally. A crime of that magnitude requires that great a punishment.

I lift my hand to his and he lowers his forehead to mine. Our eyes meet and I feel as if all the fires of the underworld have been lit within me. "I don't want to hurt you, but I could never live with myself if I did not fulfil my oath to Estella." My voice is quiet but strong; despite what I'm feeling, despite the way that Hades makes me feel, I must think of my sister first.

"I understand," he says, dropping his hand and pulling away from me. I instantly feel cold, standing in the shadow of his discontent.

"Our time in the dreaming is drawing to a close," he says, his voice holding a formality that I have never heard before. "Come, it is time for you to go back." He holds out his hand to me and I feel a jolt in my heart as I reach out and take it and allow him to guide me up the bank. He takes my now dry cape and drapes it around my shoulders, fastening it in place.

"I'll be watching over you," he tells me, no smile on his lips, no glint in his eye.

"Will you try and stop me, deter me from my revenge?" I ask.

He shakes his head, then takes up my hand and starts walking with me along the riverbank. "Your revenge is your own, Ara. I could no sooner take it from you as I could anything else that is yours by right, yours to keep, and yours to give away."

I let my shoulders drop, and I wish it was different. I wish I didn't have this between us. I look at him and I feel the spark that had been growing between us gutter and die. He places something into my hand and then lets go of it, lets go of me.

Then he leans close and whispers in my ear, "Wake up, Ara." I hear the sigh of my name echo as I jolt into my body and open my eyes.

No time has passed; the others are as I left them both seconds and hours ago. The sun is beating down on us relentlessly and the taste of dust is back in my mouth. I could almost believe that none of it had happened except my hair is damp and my tunic fresh and clean from the river. I look down at my hand and see a compass made of brass and silver; a disc of pearl studded with small chips of jet mark the stars of my constellation and form the compass rose. It glints in the sun, reminding me of the dappled light from the trees that shone down on the river. The way that it glistened off Hades' alabaster skin and how his jet black hair flopped over his face when wet. His smile, his eyes, his touch, and his disappointment.

I turn away from the others, holding the compass close and wiping the tears as I try to forget both of the ways he had looked at me.

21

THE WEAVING OF THE WORLD

Hades shakes the water from his hair as he moves into the rainbow-filled cave.

He is surprised to find the three Fates standing as one before the tapestry of life, backs to him, their voices reaching him before they realize that he is there.

"He has a decision to make, a decision that will either break the world or break his heart," Atropos says.

"If it were any other God I would shudder for the world," Lachesis declares.

"Now, sister, do not be so hasty in thinking that he won't choose love," Clotho adds, as she plucks a thread on the tapestry then lets it fall. "It is after all what we all want and need, he more than most. And besides, it is what we all deserve, and again he deserves it more than many do."

"I know that; I have seen it in the pattern of this thread since it was first spun, and I hope he can have the love he deserves; but will we all deserve the sacrifice that comes with it?" Atropos muses.

"Maybe he will get to have both?" Lachesis suggests.

"When is the weaving ever so smooth?" Clotho asks.

"Maybe the choice will be made by another?" Lachesis says.

"I do wish we could see into the knot!" Atropos' voice sounds like the tearing of fabric.

As Hades nears the Fates, he can see the threads of the loom and that small twisting that he had seen on his last visit, except it is no longer small. The knot has spun like a whirlpool, pulling into it all the coloured strands of the weaving, which are now spiralling in towards the dark convergence of the threads.

"In all my years I do not think I have ever seen the three of you idle."

"Ah, Hades, we were not expecting you, forgive us!" Lachesis says.

"Now I know that something truly is wrong; you always know what is occurring before it is occurring."

"Not any more," Atropos says, with a shake in her voice that makes the God worry. "This knot in the fabric, it is growing bolder, pulling tighter on the strands of life, and twisting them in its own pattern. We cannot trace the threads as we have grown accustomed to."

"I see," Hades says. "And this is still to do with the wager?"

"Yes, with the wager and the games, not just the one that is being played this Blood Moon, but the one that is always being played: the rivalry of foolish gods, with no written rules, where some are fair, though most are foul, and a few endless," Clotho says.

"A challenge of being and all the complexities that that contains," Lachesis adds.

"What if I break this wager with my brothers; what if I tell them that I take back my word? It would pain me, but not as much as the pain of seeing the threads of life snapped."

Atropos looks at him, her bright eyes wide. "We fear that if you did that then it would break the knot immediately, snapping the threads and leaving a hole in the weaving of the world. No, the knot must be picked undone by the deeds of all those contained within it. You, Hades, are at the centre of it along with your brothers, Zeus and Poseidon, but all the other Gods have a part to play."

"And your tokens too, those mortals are most important, especially Ara," Clotho says, staring at Hades intently and making him feel uncomfortable.

"Should I tell my brothers of this?" Hades asks.

"And what do you think they would do if they knew about it?" Clotho's soft grey eyes are still holding his.

"Nothing. I do not think that they care much for the lives of the mortals and if I were to try to explain to them that the golden threads of the Gods were part of the weaving, threads to be pulled and sewn just as the mortals' threads are, I don't think that they would believe me."

"Yes, we once tried to show Zeus how his golden thread snagged and puckered on the lives of the mortals that he loved, those whom he had taken to bedly conquest and … interacted with, how their patterns altered and often frayed, their colours fading as they began circling, disappearing, ending. But he only drew attention to the threads of the heroes that his golden presence altered, leaving their threads brighter and their patterns bolder. It is hard to see the small sufferings when one is only looking at all that shines."

"Zeus would never see his influence as anything other than a tremendous favour towards a mortal," Hades says with a sigh. "So, this game is to play out and we are to be at the centre of it, Ara and I." He shakes his head. "I do hate being at the centre of things, the underworld is beneath everything for a reason."

"Yes, to support all that is built upon it!" Atropos says with a smile.

Hades brings his brows together. "No," he says. "It is so that it remains outside of everything, so that I don't have to be drawn into the sport of the other Gods, save for the Games."

Clotho lets out a laugh that sounds like the soft click-clack of the loom. "You and your realm are the sphere that contains all of this, all of the experience of life and living. It starts in darkness and mystery and returns to it."

Atropos places a hand on Hades' shoulder. "Everything returns to you in the end."

Hades stares at the knot. He can feel it twisting inside him, pulling at all of the strings of his being, tugging him away from what he thought he had known about his place in the golden scheme of things. He realizes that he knows nothing of how the world works, and for the first time he wonders if there is something greater than the Gods playing its own game, weaving its own pattern.

"What must I do?" Hades asks. "What pattern must my thread take to undo this mess?"

"Even if we could see through this jumbled tangle of lives, we could not tell you. Fate is hard to see once you Gods get involved," Lachesis says. "But we know this much: if the knot becomes too big, if it consumes the tapestry of life, it won't just be the threads of the humans that are broken, it would also be the threads of the Gods. We will all be lost, and the underworld would be full forever."

Hades feels an emptiness pulling at the edges of himself far deeper than any he has ever experienced. As he remembers the conversation he was not meant to hear, he wonders if he would ever break the world for love, for Ara. He worries that he might.

22

THE PSAMMOPHIS-HYDRAS

Thalia is true to her word. Artemis is pulling the moon across the heavens, a waning gibbous three-quarters full, and as I look at the nine of us, walking side by side in the dark, I can't help thinking that we are three-quarters of the tokens selected when the moon was full and red.

The night sky is crystal clear, the stars are solid steady points of light seemingly unmoving in their path across the sky, but I know that's not true; their slow progress is not to be mistaken for no progress at all. That's how we get things done, slow and steady like the stars; we set our course and move towards our horizons, and although we don't think that we've moved much, before we know it, we meet the dawn.

Darkness lies to the east; Apollo won't be up for hours. I wonder if I will see the sunrise and if I do, will I get to live through it? I've been tirelessly preparing for this moment, for the chance to put things right, to avenge Estella, but in my mind all I can see is Hades' face, his sorrow and disappointment, and all I can feel in my heart is mine. I can't help but wonder if I may have been wrong; what if putting things right, avenging my sister, is actually the wrong thing to do? I shake my head; it's not wrong for Estella, she can't make Zeus pay for what he has done to her, but I can.

I wipe a hand over my face and stifle a yawn. The night is cooler to walk in, but I feel so tired. Next to me Acastus stumbles and I just about catch him.

"You OK?" I ask.

"Yep, fine, I just didn't see that rock, that's all." He stifles a yawn of his own.

Theron is near the front; I wouldn't expect to find him anywhere else. He's alongside Danae, whose eyepatch has some interesting abilities, one being that it lets her see clearly in the darkness and she leads the way. Theron's barely spoken to me since the cave, since he touched my face and tried to thank me for saving him in the swamps. I know how difficult that must have been for him, but part of me realizes that he didn't manage it, what he said wasn't enough, and I wonder if Theron will ever be enough for me. I move up the line of tokens to his side.

"Do you think we should make camp soon?" I ask, although it's really more of a suggestion.

"Soon," he says to me. Then adds, "What did the God of kindness, Hades, give you after the last trial?"

I ignore the tone in his voice and pull out the compass to show him. He takes it, studying it carefully.

"What did Zeus give you?" I ask, lightly as I always do when I say the name of the God who murdered my sister.

Theron pulls a golden shield from his back, holding it out in front of him, and calls, "Helios." A wide beam of pure sunlight shoots from the shield, lighting up the night brighter than any warning beacon.

"That's impressive," I say.

Ajax is nearby and scoffs a little as he pulls out a locket on a chain from inside his tunic.

"More jewellery!" I feel my eyebrows rise.

"What can I say, she's a God who loves her bling!" Ajax rolls his eyes, but as he opens the locket a soft silvery light fills the night. "Moonlight." He shrugs, and I smile.

It makes sense that Artemis would give him that. He leaves the pendant open for a while, bathing us all in the comfort of the soft light, and when he closes it I involuntarily shiver. The night feels too strong, too oppressive, and then I remember that Hades is in the darkness but when I reach for him, I am greeted by an abyss of emptiness.

Theron nudges me with the compass in his hand and a smile on his face. "It's broken," he tells me, extending his hand to the heavens and pointing at Polaris, the north star, and then down at the compass that is very definitely pointing east. His smile shifts to one of arrogance and I feel a twist of annoyance inside me. Theron has never been gracious, but this feels like more than just bravado. I look back up at the stars and see the moon and remember when it was full and starting to turn red and how he had kissed me, and I blush with anger at my past self.

I sigh as I reach out a hand and take the compass from him, then when I look down, I see the needle has moved; it's still not pointing north, but now due south.

As I put the compass away, Thalia drops back to join us, leaving Heli and Solon out front with Danae.

"What is it?" Theron asks her. I realize that it's always business between the two of them.

Thalia walks smoothly: she's straight and tall where the rest of us nearly always slouch; even now she looks as if she is about to be presented to Zeus.

"We need to rethink how we get to the port at Gythion," Thalia says. "It's going to take us weeks to get there, and with every day that passes we will suffer trials and get weaker and there will be more … fatalities." She looks around at the tokens.

I follow her gaze and in between them all I see the tokens that are no longer with us: Philco, Kassandra, Xenia. Hades will be looking after them and I try to comfort myself with that thought, but it's not as comforting as it once was.

"Do you think many of us will make it to the end?" I ask.

"I hope so. I don't think any of us deserve to die," Thalia says.

I'd never for a moment thought that any of us did, but the way that she says it sounds like we are being punished for something that we haven't done, or maybe, in my case, just haven't done yet.

"The quests where the most people survive are usually the ones where they all work together," I add.

Theron nods. He keeps turning the lance in his hands. "But what do we do when we get to the crown? There can only be one wearer, one winner of the quest. Even if we all were to survive."

I can hear it again in Theron's voice, that ambition, and it sends a chill down my spine because if it comes to it, if it is between the two of us, he won't hold back and neither will I.

Thalia sighs and says, "I guess we work that out when the time comes. Either we choose someone or we all go for it and see who comes out on top. I mean, we might not even have any control over it; you know what the Gods are like, they enjoy this – they get a kick out of watching us suffer and die. I'm pretty sure that when it comes to it, Hermes has a trial up his sleeve that will mean only one of us can win."

Theron nods again, the lance still turning. "Yeah, I guess you're right."

"You know, there are worse things than not claiming the crown," I tell him, not because I believe it – for me there is only the crown – but because I want to see how he reacts.

He lets out a hollow laugh. "Honestly, I'd rather die than go home having survived but not won. I couldn't live with myself, I won't." He throws the lance at the sandy ground, and it sinks in.

"I know you can't, Theron. I'm sure it will be fine," I say, as I watch him pull the lance from the ground, but part of me knows that it won't be fine, he won't be fine unless he wins it all.

"Hey, did you see that?" Nestor says loudly from behind us, and I turn to see him pointing out into the darkness of the sandy scrubland, the low bushes and trees littering the rocky dry landscape, the moon weakly shining down on them. Ajax clicks his locket open, and the world gets a little brighter.

We've all stopped now, all on the lookout, following the direction of Nestor's outstretched hand. My hand is already in the bag; letting go of the compass, I call forth my rope.

"What did you see, Nestor?" Acastus asks, holding his sharp sickle at the ready.

I see nothing in the darkness, and after a long moment I start to feel everyone relax.

Then a rasping hiss drifts in on the wind from behind us and we all shift around, back on guard.

"Something is definitely out there," Danae says, as she stares in the direction that Nestor pointed. "Something big."

Ajax moves towards Danae, nocking an arrow into his bow and aiming into the night.

"Another trial?" I ask Theron. He's standing close to me, almost protective with his shield close and his sword ready.

"Probably," he says. "Put out the fires."

Nestor makes the flame on his torch die down and Ajax closes his locket. I realize how much light both were giving off and the darkness leaves me feeling vulnerable, as if a layer of protection has been removed. It doesn't help that the second the fire is out the hissing rips through the air again, closer this time and on the move.

We all take up defensive positions and without speaking we form a ring facing outwards. Acastus stands on one side of me, Solon on the other. Another hiss sounds closer, louder.

"Two of them!" Heli says. "I can't see them, but it sounds as if they're circling us."

"There," I shout and point. "The sandy ground, it's moving, can you see it?"

"Yes," Danae shouts out, her voice full of revelation.

"Oh no! Giant psammophis-hydras," Acastus calls, as he holds his sickle high, tracking the shifting sands with its point. "Triple-headed sand snakes. Their bites are venomous and they can eat a person whole! But the good news is that they don't like—"

Acastus' next words are stifled in a scream as the sand in front of him explodes, pushing Solon and I away. We tumble in the sand as the psammophis-hydra rises into the air, its three heads hovering above Acastus for a moment before it sinks down at him, each of the heads biting into his body, straight through his armour; it lifts him off the ground into the air.

"Acastus!" I scream, as I run towards him. Theron grabs me, wrapping his arm around my waist, his shield pinning me to him. Thalia is there. She slices her sword through one of the heads and it drops to the sand with Acastus. The other two heads scream out in pain. On the other side of our fractured circle, another psammophis-hydra breaks through the sand, then a third.

Theron turns towards the nearest giant snake, letting me go as he advances on it, shield up, sword slashing. I run to Acastus; the jaws of the psammophis-hydra are still wrapped around his body, the teeth deep in his chest, blood pouring from the corner of his lips.

"Acastus," I call again, as I kneel and pull the jaws of the sand snake open. The second I do, the blood gushes out of Acastus, collecting under his body like a dark puddle.

"Ara," he gargles through his own blood.

I grab his hand. "I'm here, Acastus, I'm here." I push his hair back from his handsome face.

"You need the fire, the light, they're scared of it," he says between rasping breaths.

I remember how the psammophis-hydra only attacked after Nestor quelled the fire and Ajax the moonlight from his locket.

"Acastus, hold on, we'll get help, OK," I tell him, squeezing his hand.

"Ara, leave me. Go, light the fires." I shake my head as he raises a bloody hand to my face. "I don't want to greet Hades knowing that I didn't do all I could to save his token." He gives a huge smile tinged with desperation, and as I hold his hand, I see the light fade in his eyes.

"Acastus!" I say numbly, as I squeeze his limp and lifeless hand. I lean over and kiss the top of his head, my tears mixing with the blood on his face.

"Please look after him, Hades," I say to the darkness, as I push myself on to my feet and search for Nestor.

Just as I see him, standing close to Heli and Danae fighting one of the giant serpents, I feel the ground shift and the sand next to me fall aside as the psammophis-hydra that killed Acastus pushes its two remaining heads out of the ground, covering me in sand and sending me rolling to one side, the rope catching under me as I come to a stop. I feel hands on my shoulders pulling me up and Ajax is next to me. We both look up as the snake towers above us, hissing loudly. When the two heads rear up, I grab Ajax's moonlight locket and open it. The soft glow fills the night and the psammophis-hydra pulls back, not wanting to cross from the shadows into the soft glow of the moonlight.

I pull the rope and lash it around one of the creature's throats, the starlight strands glowing as they touch its skin, and the monster lets out a deafening hiss of pain as I pull with the rope and think of it becoming shorter; it tightens and slices through the creature with ease, cutting the head from its body. I hear Ajax loose his bow, once, twice, three times in short succession, each arrow finding its target; the psammophis-hydra falls to the sand, its remaining head writhing in pain.

Ajax looks down at the moonlight pendant and starlight rope. "Theron's shield," we both say at once, and run towards him.

Theron, Thalia and Solon already have one head down of the psammophis-hydra they're fighting: it's still attached to the body of the giant sand snake and is being pulled limply across the ground. One of the remaining heads is homing in on Thalia and Solon, the other on Theron, who is crouching under his shield, his sword and lance nowhere to be seen. The head of the psammophis-hydra crashes down repeatedly on the golden shield.

Ajax lets another rally of arrows fly, as I call out, "Theron, use the light of your shield!"

He looks at me blankly for a second and then the bright ray of light shoots from his shield up to the sky, straight through the head of the psammophis-hydra. It bursts into small particles like the fine sand around us; the remaining head shrieks and rears back as Thalia leaps towards it, but Theron's there, twisting his shield and shining the light on the giant sand snake's remaining head. Thalia pulls back, shielding herself from the heat of the light.

Nestor, Heli and Danae are a little way from us, and they have all three heads of the last psammophis-hydra caught under Danae's net.

I glance at Theron and see the look of jubilation on his face as he swivels his shield to face the monster.

"Look out!" I scream, as the ray of sunlight cuts through the darkness.

Danae hits the sand, the intense beam passing over her head, Heli jumps back and scrambles on the sand, but Nestor isn't quick enough. He screams out as the ray passes over him quickly before it rests on the psammophis-hydra. The creature writhes in the net for a moment then explodes.

The beam of sunlight ends, and Theron is looking down at the shield with a strange look of power on his face.

Nestor is screaming out in pain and Heli is next to him, kneeling in the sand.

"You should have been more careful!" I snap at Theron as I take off towards Nestor.

"I just saved us all!" Theron shouts after me. I can hear the menace in his voice.

When I get to Nestor I try not to yell out. One side of his body is burnt from heel to head, the burns deeper than those Hades healed from my body. Nestor is writhing in agony, and I don't know how to help him. I reach inside my bag and pull out the water skein, then pour it over his body. Steam covers him and as it clears, he lies still, completely still, his eyes open and his face in anguish.

"Nestor," I say softly, but I know that just like Acastus – Acastus who laughs and jokes and raises the spirit, Acastus with his easy smile and warm heart – Nestor too has gone.

I feel an energy buzzing through me like lightning and I want to release it all at the heartless Gods. The world suddenly feels much bigger and emptier without Nestor and Acastus in it.

As I stand, Nestor's body takes on that strange shimmering that we had both seen with Xenia, and I quickly reach forward and close his eyes. I think about his parents, his sisters and how they will find him and how I made a promise to him that I can't keep.

I look over to where Acastus fell but his body has already gone. All that's left is a pool of blood darkening the sandy earth under the head of the psammophis-hydra, its teeth bared as if it were smiling.

I stand up and coil my rope over my hands as I walk.

"Ara," Theron reaches out to me, but I shake him off and walk straight past him. I know it's not his fault, it was an accident; if there had been any intent, Hermes would have disqualified Theron for his actions. I wonder if Theron could ever do something like that on purpose, and I don't like the answer I come up with.

As I walk away, the others move behind me and I say the names of those we are missing to myself; Hades won't be the only one to remember them: Philco, Kassandra, Xenia, Acastus, Nestor.

23

THE PTERIPPI

I sleep uneasily that night. Theron is beside me, but I can't get the visions of Nestor and Acastus dying out of my head. I look for Hades in my dreaming. I call to him as I walk through a land I've never seen before, one full of sand and shadows and fallen temples. But he doesn't answer, and when Ajax shakes me awake, I feel the deep loss of everything rush in at me with the soft light of predawn.

I start to complain to Ajax, but he moves a finger to his lips to hush me, then takes my hand and pulls me up. As he does, I catch a glimpse of my hand and the ring that wasn't on it when I fell asleep: a small gold sun and silver moon, each sitting on a band of copper. It must be from Hades. I feel sad that he gave it to me this way, and I worry that I might not see him again, well, not while I'm alive anyway.

The others are still asleep around the makeshift camp in the denser forest area that we headed to after the psammophis-hydras attacked. As Ajax pulls me through the foliage of the trees, I see that to the left is a large pool. A thin silver river flows into and out of it, with long grasses lining the waterway. I can smell the wild fennel in the air, like aniseed, mixing with the thyme from the bushes that litter the river, fresh and welcoming.

We are on a raised bank overlooking the lake and the trees and meadow around it. It reminds me a little of the meadow in the dreaming where Hades and I lay side by side and looked up at the clouds.

Ajax sinks down on to his stomach and crawls along the rise till he is looking over at the short curve in the river. I lie alongside, my eyes widening in surprise.

"Flying horses, pterippi?" I whisper.

"Yeah, just like Pegasus!"

I feel the smile spreading across my face as I watch the herd of flying horses drink from the stream, their silver manes shimmering in the predawn only a shade darker than their silvery pelts. A few more land gracefully and rush to join the herd and soon there are ten. They are all of a similar size, as large as my father's horse, bigger than anything I've ever ridden before, and their beauty is mesmerizing. The newcomers nuzzle at the grazing pterippi who are pulling up and chewing on the vegetation that lines the water.

I've only ever seen paintings and mosaics of them before, only heard tales of the parts they have played in the quests of heroes, and I wonder if they are here to aid us.

I can't pull myself away from them as I try to commit

every detail to memory: the way their wings extend from just behind their front legs, folding back along their sides; the shimmer from their pelts; the way that they move so gracefully.

"They're magnificent," Ajax whispers.

"Just look at how fast they are!" I say, as I point towards the sky. Two more are swooping in, their wings extended as they glide soundlessly to the ground before their hooves hit, kicking up a little cloud of dust around their long, sleek legs. As they trot towards the river, slowing, they fold their wings back against the sides of their bodies.

I lean across to Ajax. "I've got an idea." I tug him back down the hill to camp.

"You want us to do what?" Thalia says, as she stands with one hand on her spear, the other on her hip.

"Wait, wait, I think Ara's on to something," Theron says.

"Look, it's going to take us weeks to get to Gythion at the rate we're going; you were saying just last night that we needed to find another way, Thalia. Well, on a winged horse we could probably be there by sunset tomorrow!" I say.

"What if they stampede? I can't see them being happy about us trying to ride them, can you?" Thalia says.

Heli gives a little ha, then says, "How many of you have ever seen a flying horse?" No one answers. "Exactly, and I don't know anyone who has ever seen one, either. My point is, I don't think they're here at random – they're here as part of the quest!"

"Yeah, of course, Hermes has instructed them to find us," Solon adds.

"Right! I mean there are twelve flying horses and there were twelve of us. That can't be a coincidence!" Ajax agrees.

Thalia shifts her hand from her hip. "OK, let's say they are part of the quest, we've still got to capture them."

"I've got this," Danae says, holding up her net.

"And I've got my rope," I add.

"One rope between seven of us!" Thalia says. "I guess we could link them all together and form a chain of flying horses!"

I hold out the rope. "It's made of seven strands." I start to pull one of the strands away from the others. "And the rope has a calming influence – I felt calm and hopeful as soon as I touched the rope when I was in the swamps. I'm sure if we use the strands from the rope to harness the flying horses, it would calm them enough for us to ride them all the way to Gythion."

"Fly them you mean!" Ajax says, with a grin as big as the moon.

"Let's take a look, see what we're up against," Theron says, and I can tell that he is positively chomping at the bit to see the pterippi. Thalia shoots him an incredulous look. "Come on, I'm not about to pass up the opportunity to ride on a flying horse!"

Ajax leads the way up the hill, Theron close behind him, Thalia way behind us all. As we make it to the top of the rise, we all look down over the river and I hear a collective gasp from the others. The flying horses have settled down, bunched tightly together in the shade of the trees, deep in the tall grasses. They are so peaceful; I could stare at them all day.

"OK, we need to use stealth for this," Theron says, after we've all slid back down to the camp.

"Ara, you're pretty sneaky," he adds, and I can't help but smile and think of the many times when I've caught him out by sneaking up on him. He returns my smile as we share the memory and, for a moment, I deeply miss the people we were before the Blood Moon. "Do you think you can get close to them, maybe slip the ropes around them?"

I shake my head. "I doubt it, not without alerting the whole herd."

Danae pulls her net from her shoulders where she is wearing it like a second cape and lays it on the ground. "What about using this? I can make it big enough to cover the herd, and" – she places her trident on the net then takes a bow shaped from coral and shells, that Poseidon must have recently given her, and adds that too – "if we stand on the top of the rise, maybe we can shoot the net over them?"

"Yes!" Thalia says, throwing her lance into the net too. "With my lance and your trident, we can hold the corners in place. Heli you have a bow, don't you, and Ajax?"

"Yes," Heli says. "And I can make us some wooden pegs to hold the net down, although they might not last long if the pterippi thrash about." She adds her bow to the collection of weapons in the net, and I can't help but feel I have nothing to contribute as Ajax adds his bow too.

"Zeus gave me this after the last trial." Theron pulls a lyre from close to where we were sleeping. "He said that if I play it the strings create a soporific sound."

"Sopo-what?" Ajax asks.

"It will make you sleepy or calm or something," Heli says.

"But if we hear it, won't we fall asleep too?" Thalia asks.

Theron shakes his head. "No, Zeus was very clear that it would only work on beasts."

"That's handy," I say, and something tugs at the back of my mind that I just can't make sense of.

"Do you know how to play it?" Danae asks.

"No, but it's a magical gift from the Gods so I'm guessing that it will work no matter how rubbish I am."

"Let's hope so, otherwise you might just piss the pterippi off!" Danae says and I stifle a laugh.

"Right, this sounds like it's actually going to work," Thalia says, and she doesn't exactly sound happy about it. "But if not, we can just stick to the plan and walk."

I realize that it's not the plan that she's against but what comes after we catch the flying horses. As the others start to sort out what we're going to do next, I manage to team up with her to attach arrows to the net using some of the strands of my rope.

"Have you ridden a horse before?" I ask.

Thalia gives me a withering look. "Yes, of course, many and often."

"Then why are you—"

"Heights, I do not like heights." Thalia's whole body is tense next to me.

I put my hand on hers. "Do you want to ride with me?" She shakes her head with such force that I think it might fall off. "No, there is much in my life I have had to overcome, and this is just another thing to be conquered."

I suddenly realize that I don't know any of the tokens very well, except for Theron. I give Thalia's hand a squeeze. "I'll ride close to you," I tell her. "And you can call out to me if you need to."

Thalia turns and looks at me, her face as serious as ever, but I see a softening in her eyes as she nods at me. "Thank you, Ara."

I give her a small smile back, as I finish attaching the rope to the last arrow.

Before I know it, it's time to put the plan into action and I take up my position next to Theron, holding Danae's trident. It's lighter than I expected, and the triple points of the trident look deadly, like the sharp edges of coral on a reef.

"They're beautiful," Theron whispers to me as we watch the pterippi. He leans his head towards me, I feel his warm breath on my ear, and it sends waves over me that make my skin prickle and my stomach churn like a soft summer swell. "I never thought that I would see one." His eyes are fixed on the pterippi, as mine are fixed on his lips and the memory of the kiss we shared.

I look away and I'm sure that my cheeks are glowing as I remember the way it felt. I close my eyes for a moment and all I can see is Hades looking down at me in the meadow with the clouds behind him. I shake my head and focus on the now, on Theron, who is here, who has always been here.

"Me neither. To be honest I wasn't sure that the pterippi were real when I first saw them," I whisper back.

"Yeah, I've only heard stories of them, but then I'd only heard stories about monsters too and we've seen plenty of them so far."

I shake my head. "Oh, I knew that the monsters existed and that some of them look as beautiful as these winged horses, so don't be deceived into thinking that they're benevolent just because they shimmer and shine."

Theron reaches out a hand and grabs mine. It takes me by surprise and is so achingly familiar in the midst of all this strangeness that I feel the prick of tears in my eyes. "It's all going to be all right, you know. You won't end up like Estella, I won't let that happen to you."

He looks at me and I feel that fizz of attraction between us, just like on the night of the Blood Moon.

He leans closer to me and although I don't move towards him, I don't move away, either. His lips brush mine softly as if he's testing my reaction, like I'm one of the pterippi and he doesn't want to spook me. Once he's sure that I'm not going to bolt, he leans in further and pushes his lips on mine hard just as I hear a light hoot, the signal from Danae that the others are ready, and another hoot sounding back to signal that Thalia and Solon are in place. I pull away.

Theron keeps his eyes on me as he cups his hands and lets out another low hoot. That was the final signal.

The arrows fly over the winged horses, pulling the net behind them.

Theron and I are on our feet running towards the pterippi who are still sitting on the ground, the net over them. Just as they begin to realize what is happening, I pull my arm back and throw Danae's trident hard through the air. I run after it as it soars, hitting the ground with a thud and pinning part of the net down. Theron throws his spear and misses his corner; it never was his strongest weapon. Thalia and Solon are on the other side pegging down the net with their weapons.

I reach where the trident hits and, like Thalia and Solon, I start to use the wooden pegs Heli has made to hold the edges of the net down. Theron reaches for the spear to secure the corner tight, tugging it out of the sandy ground where it has landed.

I realize that one of the pterippi near Theron has its wing out of the net, and in the second before it raises it, I dive on to the net to try and hold it down as the flying horse senses the opportunity for freedom and pushes up, raising the net and creating a gap. The pterippus next to it pushes out of the gap as the first one rises, sending me rolling off the net.

"Play the lyre!" I yell at Theron and, as if he has only just remembered he has it, he starts to pluck the strings.

Thalia takes the spear from him and forces the open section of net to the ground just as a second pterippus makes its bid for freedom. Solon rushes to help, pushing the pegs into the ground as those soporific effects of Theron's lyre start to take.

The second escaped pterippus extends its beautiful wings, ready to take to the air. As it stretches, its feathers graze my legs. I expected them to be soft as air but instead they are sharp as steel. I let out a hiss of pain as I look down and see two red lines form on my shins and blood run down each one, covering my ankles in seconds, as the pterippus flaps its wings once, twice, then takes to the air, running on the wind after its friend.

I stare after it for a long moment then back down at my legs.

The other pterippi, still trapped under the net, are calm and tranquil as the sweet melody from Theron's lyre fills the air and suddenly the world feels calmer, I feel calmer and more secure, and Zeus said it only worked on beasts!

"Did you see them fly?" Danae calls, her voice high, her face turned up to them. I wonder if her golden eyepatch allows her to track them through the heavens, as she, Ajax, and Heli rush towards us.

"That'll be us before we know it, flying among the clouds," Ajax says to her, a boyish smile on his face.

"You're pretty good with that thing," Heli says to Theron.

"Oh, thanks," he replies, and when Heli moves away Theron holds the lyre out towards me. He isn't plucking the strings and yet the sweet melody still plays. He nods in Heli's direction then puts a finger to his lips.

"Cheat!" I whisper at him.

"Hey, it's not my fault that the thing is enchanted, although for all concerned it's a good job that it is!" he tells me in a conspiratorial whisper, and I chuckle, feeling a lightness return to our friendship.

24

THE BROTHERHOOD OF GODS

Hades sits at the table and watches as Ara and the other tokens round up the pterippi. The distance that he is trying to put between his token and himself is a strain. He watches her smile with Theron and wants her to smile at him instead. He closes his eyes and slips into the memory of the dreaming, of her close to him in the water; the feeling of connection that has grown and bloomed from their first meeting has not lessened due to her absence, if anything it has grown bigger and more consuming.

Hades opens his eyes and as he does, he thinks of the Fates, the tapestry and the growing of the knot. Is it his love for Ara that is fuelling the growth, or is it the growing resentment between him and his brothers? Maybe it is both, he realizes, as he remembers overhearing the Fates:

He has a decision to make, a decision that will either break the world or break his heart.

"Studying the board, are you, brother?" Poseidon says, as he returns from the feast of refreshments laid out in the adjoining hall and sits next to Hades. "Or just keeping an eye on that pretty little token of yours?"

Hades feels himself prickle. "What is it that you want, Poseidon?"

"Always to the action, Hades. I guess there is no point in beating around, after all you are the God of the unknown." Poseidon slaps his brother on the back. "Both our tokens are doing well. I'll be honest, I didn't expect you to last this long."

"You thought my kingdom would already be on the table."

"Something like that. My point is, we have two strong tokens and I think that Zeus is feeling the pinch."

Hades looks through the archway at Zeus, who is standing close to Hermes, the two of them in an intense conversation.

"Do you really want to rule over everything?" Hades asks.

Poseidon takes a sip of nectar from his glass. "No, not really. No offence, Hades, but the underworld doesn't interest me at all." He gives a small shiver. "I quite like the idea of ruling over the sky; I like the idea of ruling over Zeus even more." Poseidon gives a wicked smile, like a killer wave before it falls.

"Why?" Hades tips his head a little to the side.

"Do you really want to know?"

"Genuinely."

Poseidon places his cup on the board then turns to his

brother, his sea-green eyes flashing with the foam of angry oceans. "Zeus is always there, always in charge, although he never acts as he should. You can be in charge of a thing without lording it. But he is *always* lording it over me, over us, all of us. And I can't remember when I stopped loving him and started resenting, and in the end even hating him, but I do."

"Do you think that if you win this wager, if you become God of us all, you'll love him again?"

Poseidon laughs. "I think I will love the power I'll have over him, just as he now has power over me. We were supposed to be equals after we defeated our father and the Titans, we were supposed to rule it all, together, but instead…"

"Instead, the two of you conspired to send me to the underworld and once I was gone, Zeus used his ambition to put himself above you too."

Poseidon's face becomes that of a flat, calm sea. "So, you know about that then."

"I wouldn't be doing my duty as the God of the unknown if I didn't, now would I?" Hades barely lifts an eyebrow.

"I guess not." Poseidon rubs his bearded chin, looking apologetically at his brother.

Zeus comes back to the table and sits on the other side of Hades.

"Are you two plotting over which one of you will take my throne?" Zeus asks.

Poseidon opens his mouth, but Hades reaches out a hand and touches his arm.

"We were catching up; it has been an age. And we were reminiscing about the old days, about our father. You should both really come to Tartarus and visit him sometime. The eons and his punishment have not been kind to him, we have not been kind to him, brothers. And how can we call ourselves Gods if we only do so in hate, and war, and anger? A God surely shows himself more brightly in acts of kindness and openness and tolerance."

"I am not a God who forgives the deeds done to him," Zeus says, his voice full of wrath, his eyes blazing in warning.

"And nor am I," Hades says, his voice level and calculated. "You can show kindness while also ensuring a debt is paid or a wrong is righted. Punish the crime, educate and nurture the perpetrator."

"You'll be educating and nurturing me next," Zeus says with a laugh.

"Only if I win our wager," Hades replies, and a little of the merriment leaves Zeus.

"It will be a sad day in Olympus if you beat me. But I'd deserve to give up my throne if that ever happened."

"What sport is this?" Hermes says, as he appears above the board. "Are you three having another wager, maybe on who will fall off their pterippus and die first?" Then he adds in a not so quiet whisper, "My money would be on Hera's token."

Poseidon drains his cup, then leans past Hades towards

Zeus. "I must say, brother, the gifts that you have given to your token these Games have been quite impressive. That lyre was an inspired choice and has proved to be very handy with the pterippi. What made you think of giving it to your token?"

"Oh, it was nothing really. A happy coincidence. Young Theron and I were talking after the psammophis-hydras and he mentioned that he liked music. I was going to give him an enchanted dagger, but instead I thought he might like the lyre."

Hades looks at Zeus and knows he is lying. "Ah yes, the psammophis-hydras. It was a good job your token had his helios shield, I dread to think what might have happened otherwise."

"My token would still be in the Games," Hephaestus booms from behind, the anger in his voice rattling through the halls of Olympus.

"Now, Hephaestus, we've been over this," Hermes says. "Zeus' token did not act with intention; if he had he would have been disqualified and punished. We must make allowances for the mortals, for their imperfect nature and their free will. Zeus has done all that he can by changing the actions of the shield as agreed; it will now only cause destruction to non-human things as well as lighting up the dark and revealing the hidden."

Hades wonders if the free will of the Gods is something that mortals needed to make allowances for, or if it was something they should be rising against.

25

THE FLIGHT TO GYTHION

We work together, while the lyre plays. Each pterippus is released from under the net in turn and secured with one of the strands of the starlight rope in a makeshift tether. Solon then ties them each to a tree nearby and stands talking to them, stroking their necks and comforting them. After the second pterippus is secure Thalia stands with him, and by the time the fifth is secure I see that she is stroking their heads and talking to them too, feeling more at ease with the beast that is about to rise her into the skies.

Once seven of them have been tethered we lift the net off. I make sure that I stand well back as the final three pterippi stand up and trot off, but even though they flex their wings they don't fly away. Instead, they stay close to their tethered friends and the two that had escaped earlier swoop down to land near them.

The way that they keep staring at us and the tethered pterippi makes me think that they might be planning something, and I feel a little anxious. Theron, Ajax and

Heli return from breaking the camp and I try to encourage everyone along.

As I take the rope of one of the flying horses, I'm surprised to see that Thalia is the first of us to mount up, but then I realize that, actually, it's just like Thalia to face her fears and take charge of them.

I lead my pterippus off to one side and plunge a hand into the bag, calling one of the apples that I have stowed there. I hold it flat in my hand and the flying horse sniffs it, then snorts over it, before swiping it from my hand and crunching on it loudly.

"You are quite magnificent!" I tell him, as I stroke his silvery pelt. "We're going to be friends for a little while, you and I." I fish out another apple. "I think you need a name. How do you feel about Timaeus?" I ask. The flying horse snorts and tosses its mane. "OK, no to Timaeus," I say with a laugh. "How about Cletus? My grandfather was called Cletus and he was a good man, always kind and honourable; I loved him very much." I stroke his muzzle. The flying horse nudges into my hand and neighs lightly.

"Cletus it is. Now, we need to get to Gythion and we could walk, but that would take weeks and I know that you can fly me there in a fraction of the time. I don't know if you can understand what I'm saying, but I'm pretty sure that you're here to help us so, if it's OK with you, I'm going to climb up on your back now." I feel nervous as I get closer to the winged horse; my shins have stopped bleeding but the sting from the cuts reminds me of how dangerous these beautiful creatures are.

Cletus stays completely still as I pull on the makeshift reins and lift myself up on to his back then swing my leg over.

I smile as Cletus moves underneath me, smooth and steady and effortlessly graceful. I tug the reins to one side, and he turns that way.

"Brilliant, that's so good," I say, stroking his mane, before tugging the rope to the right. He turns a full circle then extends his wings, taking me by surprise as he shakes them out. I adjust my legs, pulling them away from the lethal feathers. I notice that as Cletus folds his wings back, he holds them a little away from his body so as not to touch me.

Ajax is the last one to mount his pterippus and as he sits on the back of the flying horse I can see the blood running down his legs and arms. The other pterippi and their riders are getting impatient and when I look back at the five that are free, I see them moving slowly towards us.

Heli is the first to spur her winged horse forward. It starts with a run then on the fifth stride it extends its wings and begins to flap them, leaving the ground in a smooth arc, its hooves running as if on unseen rising land.

Danae follows just behind, then Thalia, then Solon and Theron take off.

"Are you ready, Cletus?" I ask, as I lean forward and whisper in his ear. He neighs and shakes his head back in answer before pelting forward.

My stomach lifts as Cletus flaps his wings, lifting into the air. I grasp the rope, my knuckles turning white, as I push my knees into Cletus' sides. I force myself to sit up straight, resisting the urge to lean forward and throw my arms around the neck of the flying horse as it lifts me higher and higher into the sky. The air rushes past me, it whips around my body, pulling on my tunic, the cape drawing out behind me with the loose strands of my dark hair, like a torn banner of threads.

I smile as Cletus soars swiftly upwards and then levels off. He keeps close enough to his fellows that I can hear the whoops of delight from Danae and Solon as well as the cursing from Thalia, who is clinging to the neck of her winged horse and looking a little pale.

"Thalia, you're doing great," I call to her, as we fly alongside each other. She looks over at me and I think for a moment that she's going to be sick.

I don't want to look down, I don't want to know how far away the ground is, not yet anyway, but I do glance behind, and I see the five free pterippi flying behind us like a rear guard.

Up ahead, Ajax is having the time of his life. Where the rest of us are flying in a pack, he is pulling his pterippus off to the side making it soar and then dive as he whoops in delight. It's amazing to watch the flying horse perform, running high above the rest of the herd and then tucking in its wings and holding its hooves still as it dives down at us. On the second dive he narrowly misses Thalia and she threatens to shoot him out of the sky with her spear. After that, Ajax keeps his tomfoolery to outflying the herd.

"Watch you don't tire her out!" Theron calls to him. "We need to get all the way to Gythion."

"Please, Tiliad could fly there and back without a stop in the time it takes your flying horse to get halfway."

"Is that a challenge?" Theron calls.

"Come on, you two, be serious," Heli shouts out. "Just enjoy it. I mean, we're flying!" She laughs with delight, and I start to laugh too. I feel elated, so light, and free and powerful. Defying the ground and flying in the realm of the Gods where only a few have spread their wings and travelled.

I feel the tears on my cheek instantly blown away. I can't remember having ever felt like this before, free of burden. I lift my hand up to my chest and feel Estella's token, and I remind myself that it is I who has placed it there, it is I who has sworn to avenge her. I have chosen it all freely, but what I've never stopped to consider are all of the things that I was not choosing, all of the things I have stopped myself from having, from experiencing. As I look around at the other tokens, I realize that I've not only been spending my days missing my sister, but I've also been missing the kinds of friendships I've found over the last few days; missing me, missing being, missing love.

We fly all day and when the sun drops down behind the horizon, I watch the sky change from blue to red then inky black.

Neither Cletus nor the other pterippi show any sign of fatigue; they continue to fly as the stars take their turn to shine on the world. I trace the constellations of Aquila, Cassiopeia, the great bear – Ursa Major, and I think of their stories.

The great bear Callisto placed in the sky to escape the wrath of a God. Cassiopeia, the vain queen, hung in the sky as punishment by the Gods; she turns endlessly around the fixed star of the north, destined to forever spend half of the year upside down in penance.

The Gods and their spiteful nature are on display for all to see and as the night darkens even more stars become visible. I can't help but think of how and why the Gods had placed people in the stars: warriors rewarded for their valour, women renowned for their beauty or punished for their actions or placed in the sky as sanctuary from the deeds of others. The night sky, so vast and free, and littered with the will of the Gods. As I look up at the stars, I can't help but think of the heavens as a prison.

I see the stars of Scorpio. All those who play in the Immortal Games are said to become part of their constellations when they perish, remembered forever as their stars shine brightly. But I have no intention of being the plaything of the Gods; my sign has a sting in its tail and so do I.

The sun rises with the pinks and peaches of a summer rose in full bloom, and I'm surprised to find that the gentle motion of Cletus' wings and the soft sweeping sound that they make as they cut through the air, kept me sleeping soundly all night, although my dreams were not peaceful.

I searched for Hades in my dreams; I walked for miles and miles, down lanes I knew and streets I did not, as I called for him. Once or twice, I thought I heard him saying my name, but it was only the echoes of the sigh my name makes when he speaks it, and I felt a deep longing for my name not to be the only part of me on his lips.

As the sun rises, the day feels too bright. I drink greedily from the water skein and eat the last of my supply of fruit from my bag, thanking Acastus as I do and hoping that he is in Elysium with Xenia, Philco, Nestor and Kassandra. I smile as I think of him and Kassandra; I hope that they have found one another again.

It is late morning when I catch my first glimpse of the sea, blue and green and all the shades in between, with silver flecks of light as the sun glints off the waves.

The golden coastline curves against the sea, creating a natural harbour of brilliant blue that kisses the land. It is bordered by buildings and temples that look on unabashed.

As I stare at the sight on the horizon, Cletus pitches his wings, and as one the herd of pterippi begin to make a slow descent, gliding to the ground in large circles that swoop gently downwards. I enjoy the sensation of the deep arching decent, then all of a sudden my stomach pitches as Cletus folds his wings in against his side and points his nose forward. I'm not the only one who screams, as I hold tight to Cletus, pressing my face against his neck and feeling the air rush past me in a dizzying stream, pulling my hair back, snapping all the breath into me. Then as suddenly as he had descended, Cletus levels off, flapping his wings and landing on the ground with a firm jolt before running to a halt.

As soon as he stops, I leap from Cletus and stand panting, looking at him wearily. My body feels stiff and sore after being still for over a day, and I stretch up then shake out my legs.

I stroke Cletus. "Thank you," I say, as my hand slips down his silvery coat, which shimmers in the sunlight.

"Well, go on, you're free now." I take a step back from him. But Cletus doesn't move, he just stands still, looking at me.

"Maybe it's the ropes," Solon says from close by as he dismounts. "Maybe they need to be fully free before they leave?"

"Good idea." I swiftly unknot the rope of starlight, as Solon does the same. "Besides, the rope is the only decent gift Hades has given me," I say with a laugh. "I'd like it back."

The moment the rope is off, the flying horse turns away from me, raising his wings and lifting into the air. He doesn't take a run up this time but lifts straight up and kicks out with his hind legs. I throw myself on to the floor, his hooves flying over my head.

"Whoa!" Ajax yells, as he slides from his pterippus and heads towards me before freezing.

Solon has untethered his flying horse but has turned to

watch me; he doesn't see his own pterippus rear back on to its hind legs. I see Solon turn too late, the front hooves of the pterippus driving down on his head with a crack that fills the air.

His eyes grow wide and he crumples to the ground beside me, blood pouring from his skull on to the dried grass of the hillside we've landed on.

I crawl to him and turn him on his back, shaking him by the shoulders. "Solon!"

Theron is beside me; he places his ear on Solon's chest, then looks up at me and shakes his head. "He's dead, Ara." He moves a hand over Solon's face and closes his surprised eyes.

"Another one for Hades," Thalia says from behind Theron.

I let go of Solon's shoulders just as the same shimmering quality that took over the other token's bodies covers him. He disappears, so quickly. One moment he is here and the next he's gone, taking his gifts with him; all that is left is a patch of blood on the earth and my starlight rope, which I pick up and hold in shock.

"Erm … I think we might have a problem," Ajax says as he moves away from his flying horse. I look around and see that Cletus and Solon's pterippus have been joined by the five free flying horses, and they are heading straight for us.

"Untether the others, quickly!" I shout, as I race to Ajax's pterippus. He joins me as we untie the knots.

"I know you like the rope but…"

"It's not about that; they want their friends, they want to be a herd and be free and they'll attack us until they are." I understand exactly how the pterippi feel.

"Theron, play your lyre," I call out, but Theron is busy with his own tether.

"Help, help!" Thalia calls to my left and, as I pull the rope from Ajax's pterippus, I immediately turn to flee and help Thalia, not thinking about the way the flying horse is about to react.

The pterippus spreads its razor-sharp wings and moves them up across my body, slashing my torso, before bringing them down to tear through my back in a giant arc as it lifts into the sky.

I stumble towards Thalia, grabbing hold of the rope and fumbling with the knots as I feel my head swim and my tunic become wet with blood.

As the rope slips from the pterippus I feel myself slipping too, down to the ground. The flying horse rears up on its hind legs, wings open, as I lay on the ground beneath it. I can't move as its hooves come down at me, and then Theron is there covering my body with his and holding his shield up high. He locks eyes with me as the hooves come thundering down on the shield and he holds it in place, bracing himself, protecting me.

The pterippus turns and makes its way towards the herd and as Theron lifts me into his arms, I hear the beating of many wings. As he carries me across the field we've landed in, I see the silvery flying horses ascend behind us.

"You'll be fine, Ara, you'll be fine. Remember, I won't let anything bad happen to you," Theron tells me, as he moves faster.

I don't have the energy or the wherewithal to point out that many bad things have already happened to me.

I see people rushing towards us, hurried voices, but I can't focus on anything as the world gets a little darker around the edges. I try to keep my eyes open, but they feel so heavy and the pain running through my body is so deep and complete that I have no room to do anything but submit to it. I surrender myself into the darkness, my body limp, my arms open, the sensation of falling filling my soul.

26

THE NATURE OF GODS

I can feel Theron's strong arms around me, except they feel different, he feels different: warmer, more comforting than anyone I have ever known, and even before I open my eyes, I know exactly whose embrace I am in.

"Hades." My voice is hoarse and low as I look up at him, his jaw set, a grim and serious look on his face, as he holds me.

"Hush now, Ara. Save your strength."

"Am ... am I dead?" I ask him for the second time.

"No." His voice is ice, and I feel fear creep into me.

"Will I die?" I ask.

He looks down at me and I feel myself fall into his eyes, so deep and blue, scattered with starlight. "I hope not," he says.

He lowers me down on to a bed so soft I'm sure that it's made of clouds. He sits close to me, his hand holding mine, my fingers laced in-between his. And I feel a soft peace drift over me.

He lifts a hand to my brow and runs it over my face. "I can't restore you to health, it's against the rules. I can give you a gift that might help, but I can't ensure that you'll live; you must do that for yourself, Ara. You have to want to survive this for *you*, not for anyone or anything else." He looks at me seriously and moves a stray hair from my face.

"What is it that you want, for you, just you, more than anything in the world?" he asks me.

It should be such a simple question to answer, but it is so full of everything that I've been keeping tightly packed inside me that I can barely breathe. He wipes my tears as they fall and when my breathing has calmed, I tell him what I want.

"I want ... I want to not feel empty any more. When Estella was taken by Zeus, when she became part of the Games, I felt scared, so scared for her that it consumed every part of me. And when I woke that morning to find her next to me in our bed, her body broken and bruised, scarred and shattered, I felt something in me break, something that will never heal. I loved her so much, she was my big sister, she looked out for me and cared for me, and I lost her; she was taken from me and for what? For the sport and folly of you Gods?

"And it wasn't just her that I lost. I lost my mother so completely as she fell into a despair deeper than any person has a right to sink into, so deep that no one can bring her back. I lost my father's smile, his laughter and good humour, it slipped from him, stolen by the thief that is

221

grief, and when he looks upon me all he sees is the memory of the daughter he lost and all the ways that he failed to keep her safe, failed to prepare her for your Games.

"I miss not having the life I would have had if Estella had not been taken, the sister, the parents, the love that has been lost. But most of all I lost myself; I lost all the parts that were happy and carefree and didn't know that such cruelty and spite lived in the world, which, once I had seen, I could not unsee. It overshadows everything. I don't know how to live in the sun any more, my life is a constant twilight because of Estella's death – she was the sun that lit my days. I have wandered in darkness for so long, so alone, and now..." I reach up and touch Hades' face. I lay my open palm on his cheek, and he closes his eyes and leans into it with a sigh.

"Ara." He opens his eyes, and I see them flash with an intensity that ripples through my being. He moves closer to me, cupping my face in his hands. "You are the sun, Ara; you are a guiding star; you can light your own darkness, and you have lit mine."

I feel a thrill radiating through me, soothing the pain from all my wounds, those I can see and those that I cannot.

"If you were to die, I would feel the way that you have felt with the passing of your sister. I have lived in the darkness for so, so long, then the Fates brought you to me. Now I have felt your light I don't want it to go out, not ever."

I stroke his cheek and catch the tears, as I feel my body quiver and stir. I force myself to sit up, reaching for him, folding my arms around him, my lips finally finding his. I was expecting them to be cold, but they are bursting with warmth. As my lips leave his he lets out a soft sigh that sends me straight back.

His arms around me, his chest pushing against mine, I could easily spend the rest of eternity here, locked in his embrace, filled with the delightful bliss that is currently coursing through me.

He pulls himself from me, resting his forehead on mine. I nudge my nose against his, feeling giddy.

"You have your next gift from me, the kiss of death, which is not the curse that many think it is. It is the darkness that will allow you to see the light. Death has kissed you and you have embraced it."

I run my fingers over his lips then up to his temples and through his hair, examining every moment of his face. He smiles at me with that small sideways twitch that pulls on me like a rope around my very being.

I shake my head at him. "You are not at all what I expected. You're making this all so hard for me." My voice sounds harsher than I mean it to.

His gaze is intense, but his voice sounds defeated as he says, "And what do you think you are doing for me. I am a God, Ara, and I am bound to my family and you … you wish to destroy both me and my kind."

I pull back from him a little and he relaxes his arm to

223

give me distance but keeps it around me, supporting me. "I don't wish to destroy you."

He runs a finger down the side of my face to my chin. "If you destroy one of us then you leave the rest of us vulnerable. Of all the Gods I am the one that mortals would want to kill more than any other. I am the God of the underworld; I am the keeper of souls. Those that die live in my realm, and I am their guardian. If I, the keeper of the gates, were to die, then death would die too, all life would be restored, and no one would ever know the suffering pain of loss. Even you, your sister would return to you, her light would shine for you again."

"My sister returned? Is that even possible? Can she be returned?" I ask, eager to hear his response.

"She can, but she might not thank you for it."

"Why?" I ask, and then I remember what Hades said before, that death changes a person.

He shakes his head and looks away. "She has been dead too long. She has lived in the underworld long enough to make a life there, and besides, her body ... it will not be fit for her any more."

I feel sick as I force away the image that fills my mind, and I tense as I think of Estella living in the underworld, going on without me when I have not managed to do so without her. I feel the force of what has been taken from me rush over me in a fresh fury.

Hades drops his hand and leans a little away from me. "Ara, I will do all I can to keep you safe while you are part of the Immortal Games. If you win, then it is up to you what gift you are given. You must decide how best to act. I don't want to influence you in any way. But I will not aid you in this."

"I ... I..." Words fail me as I realize that I'm so tired and confused, so sad and giddy all at once. I look at him and it feels like I'm lost deep in a secret moment that I will never get back. I run my hand up his arm and as my fingertips discover him, I feel a rush of timeless longing flow through me and out of me and I never want to be without him.

I pull him to me and kiss him again, greedily this time, pushing my lips against his, feeling the pressure run through my whole body as I wrap my arms around him and pull my hands through his hair. He holds me close, pressing every inch of me to him. I pull away as the world spins, and I delight in the feeling.

"Ara, I have waited so long for you, so long to feel this way. There were times when I thought I would always be lonely, that I would walk in the darkness with a heavy heart for all eternity and roam the dreaming forever searching for the person that would fill my heart and soul and being with light, and it's you, Ara, it's you. I will love you till there are no more stars in the heavens, till time stops and the halls of Olympus have faded and crumbled, till the rivers of the underworld have run dry and men have ceased to shudder at my name. I will love you even longer than all of this and when your last breath leaves your lips, I will catch it on my own and carry it with me for eternity."

He runs a finger over my lips before he kisses me, softly and completely like the falling of night, but the darkness shines brightly off the two of us. I close my eyes and still I can see him, feel him, taste him. He gently pushes me back on the bed and as he does, I pull him close, his heart beating in the same place as mine. I kiss him so deeply that I think I too have become the darkness and the dreaming, encompassing the moon, and the stars, and the imagination.

I open my eyes and sit up suddenly, a gasp leaving my lips. Hades is gone and I hold my hands to my heart, widowed by the absence of him. I look around and take in my surroundings. I'm in a comfortable bed in a large room; a gentle breeze drifts through the open window, carrying with it the sounds of revelry and drawing in the night.

I move my fingers to my lips where Hades' kisses sit heavy and deep. I smile and almost giggle to myself, as I move the blankets to one side ready to leap from the bed and run to the window, and the night, and Hades.

"Ara!" I turn my head to see Theron, sitting next to the bed, hunched over it, lifting his head from his arms. He sees me and his face breaks into a smile, not the cocky smile he has worn these past few days but a real smile, reminiscent of those he wore before the Games.

"Ara, you're awake!" I can hear the relief in his voice as he makes his way around the bed and stands in front of me. He embraces me and I hold completely still, wincing a little. "Sorry, does it still hurt?"

I look at him quizzically, not quite understanding what was supposed to hurt, my heart maybe.

"What happened?" I ask him, my voice dry.

"The pterippi, one of them injured you. Slashed through your back and torso," Theron motions, and I look down at the soft white shift I'm wearing and run my hands over the bandages that I can feel crisscrossing my body beneath.

"We landed close to a village just outside Gythion; some of the townsfolk saw the flying horses as we passed over and came to see. We carried you to a villa nearby; we tried to get the water that Hades had given you out of the bag, but the bag was empty, so the healer was called. You'd lost a lot of blood. The healer was unsure if you'd make it," he says. "But I knew you would." He snatches up my hand and squeezes it to his lips.

I pull it away from him and stand up, my legs feeling shaky as I cross to the window.

"How long was I asleep for?" I ask, as I look outside to the garden of the villa and see some kind of party going on.

"Two days." He joins me looking out at the garden. I can see Thalia sitting at a table smiling with one of the village girls. Ajax is trying to get Danae to dance, and I look around for the others and realize that it's only Heli left to find.

"What about the quest? The trials?" I ask.

"It's all been a bit quiet ... well, on the questing front," Theron says, with a hollow laugh. "The villagers have been entertaining us tokens. You know how it is: it's a great honour to have the Games pass through your lands and the people here have been keeping us very well. I think we've all been a little relieved to have some time to relax – even Thalia, although she keeps threatening to go off on her own and claim the crown if we stay here for too much longer."

"That sounds like Thalia," I say with a grin, and I can't help thinking that it sounds a lot like Theron too.

I finally spot Heli, deep in conversation with a few villagers just below the window. She looks up at us and smiles. Theron waves to her and she waves back before she rushes off towards Ajax and Danae.

"Ara!" I hear Ajax yell from below, and look down to see him running across the garden, followed by Danae and Heli. Even Thalia is rushing to the villa, her hand in that of the village girl as she drags her along.

"I've been thinking about the nature of the Games and the Gods," Theron says, moving closer to me.

"Really?" I move my head to one side to look at him.

"Really, I do think deeply from time to time." He smiles at me, and I give him a disbelieving look.

"And what revelations on the nature of Gods have you come to?" I'm genuinely interested in what he has to say.

"I've realized that they are always playing a game, their own games, sometimes with each other, sometimes with us, but ultimately every game they play is against us. The dice are loaded, the board is skewed, the winning line is drawn by them, and they don't play fair."

I nod. "Yeah, that sounds about right."

"All of them, Ara. Even Hades," he says, looking at me seriously. "I heard you calling to him while you slept, muttering his name. I've seen the look you have when you talk about him – your kind and friendly God."

I shake my head. "You don't understand..."

"I do understand. He wants you and he's manipulating you, Ara." Theron holds on to my arm. "But you're not his, you're not some token to be claimed." Theron gives that sly smile and I feel a little uncomfortable. "I've decided to play my own game. I've been waiting for you to wake up and now that you have, we need to split from the others, make our own way to the Forgotten Isles, take the ship waiting in the port, maybe find a way so that the others can't leave for the island, and then we claim the crown, together."

"What? Theron, you're not serious?"

"Of course I'm serious. We deserve to win; it's what we've always talked about: winning, making our names, claiming our place among the heroes of the Immortal Games, our place among the stars. Together, Ara, you and me." He runs his hand up my arm, his touch firm. He grasps the top of my shoulder, his fingers pushing into my flesh, holding me in place. "It's always been you and me."

I shirk his hand from my arm, "So, what, we leave everyone behind and make our way to the Forgotten Isles without them; we abandon them?" I can feel myself becoming more and more assured as I confront Theron.

"We're not abandoning them. Let's be honest, apart from Thalia, the rest of them don't have what it takes to win this, and you wouldn't last a day without me."

"Excuse me! I've been holding my own, thank you."

"You'd be with Hades right now if it wasn't for me. I saved you from the flying horse and that sand snake."

I take a step closer to him, feeling the anger rushing through me.

"I brought you back from Hades' gate in the swamps and *I* saved *you* from the sand snake! And if you had been playing the lyre then the pterippi would never have behaved like that, and Solon might still be alive."

"You think I care about Solon? Zeus has put his trust in me, he has equipped me for success; what has Hades given you – a broken compass and a length of rope?"

"It's not about the gifts, Theron. It's about our actions. I'm not about to leave anyone behind, they don't deserve that; I can't do that to them."

"Then you'll lose." Theron walks away from me. "You shouldn't even be here." He turns to face me. "You should have died in the fire; that would have been easier for me to bear than watching you die in these trials, watching you suffer, and swoon over Hades. You think that you're capable of taking this on, all of it, but you're pathetic, Ara. You'll end up just like your sister, your body returned to your parents, and they'll place you in the crypt with her. That's the only way that you're ever going to get to see her again, in death."

I'm shaking as he leaves the room and the others come running in, whooping. Ajax runs towards me and hugs me, lifting me into the air. I'm crying with fury as I look at the door behind him, at Theron's shadow being cast on the wall. I smile at my friends and wipe my tears away as I make them tell me what they've been up to, and I push Theron as far from my thoughts as I can.

27

THE TOKEN OF BETRAYAL

I'm not sure what time I wake the next morning. I'd stayed up talking with Ajax and Danae long after Heli and Thalia had turned in for the night.

The healer wakes me and when she removes the bandages, I can see the deep red slices on my body. It looks as if my torso has been constructed from two different bodies, as the jagged edges of the two halves on the front and back don't quite match up, but the healer assures me that the wounds are doing well, and I should be healed by the time the harvest comes. I have to use all of my self-control not to laugh out loud. By harvest, if I have not won the Games, I will be dead, I think, and then I realize that even if I win the Games I still might be dead. I think of Hades and his kiss on my lips, and how I mean to kill his brother. I give the healer the water skein and ask her to clean the wounds with it. The restorative waters of the Eridanos feel soothing on my skin and the wounds.

I make my way through the house; the cool tiles of

the floor are fresh on my feet and remind me of home. For the first time I feel a sadness and a longing to see my parents. Down the stairs I follow the smell of fresh bread across a mosaic floor and into a large breakfast room set out with fruit and yoghurt, honeycomb and grains. The bread that lured me is sitting in the middle of the table, and I snatch up a small round bun and bite into it greedily; it tastes sweet and warm, the inside soft with runny honey. I swallow it down and as it hits my stomach, I realize how hungry I am. I pick up some cheese, which crumbles in my mouth, rich and salty, and I let out a deep "umm" of satisfaction.

"You made it through another night then!" Ajax calls from the doorway and I turn to smile at him, wiping my mouth with the back of my hand.

"Just about!" I say, as I pick up two plates, passing one to him. I load mine with more rolls and cheese and anything else I can get my greedy little fingers on.

I follow Ajax outside to a stone table on a sunny veranda. He and Danae had filled me in, in extreme detail, about all the festivals, feasts and theatre the tokens had been invited to over the past two days, and he now continues the conversation.

"Are you sure it was only two days and not two weeks?" I joke, as Thalia joins us.

"Have you seen Theron?" she asks, as she loads a plate and sits down at the table.

"I saw him last night," I say. "He was there when I

233

woke up." I realize I should probably go and find him, but I'm still angry with him for suggesting that we ditch the others.

"Theron was worried about you," Ajax says, giving me a nudge and a daft look. "He's been grumpier than ever since we got here."

"He's just serious sometimes." I try to defend him both to myself and the others. "He gets focused on something and it's hard for him to see past it. This quest, the crown, it's one of those things." But I know that this is more than just that and I'm not sure why I'm not being honest with myself or Ajax and Thalia.

"Ajax!" Danae shouts from inside the house, the sound of running footsteps accompanying her curses. "They've gone!" She sprints out on to the terrace.

"Who's gone?" Thalia asks.

I know what she is going to say before she says it. "Theron and Heli, they've gone to get the crown before us."

I feel a rage rise within and any loyalty I felt towards Theron a moment ago is gone in an instant.

"He tried to get me to leave with him last night," I confess. "But I said no. It didn't feel right to me; we're a team, I mean. We've been through a lot, we've lost some good people and I don't want to lose any more of us. I didn't actually think he'd go through with it."

"So, what, he just traded you out for Heli?" Ajax pulls an incredulous face.

"Let's be honest, Theron has been focused on winning the Games since day one, and Heli, well, I was never really sure about her motivations, but I guess we know now," Thalia says, bringing her knife down in the middle of a fig.

"Yeah, well, they can have each other," Danae says. "I'm sure he'll double cross her if he gets a chance; he probably only took her along so that he can feed her to a sea serpent or something!"

Ajax lets out a hollow laugh, and I worry for Heli.

"Heli's younger than the rest of us, but she's smart," I say. "She has Athena to guide her, who knows, she might just double cross him and win it all."

"I thought you and Theron were … friends?" Thalia half asks.

"So did I," I say with a shrug. But the truth is that I'm not sure that Theron and I are friends, not the kind that I want anyway. "I feel like since the Games began, I've been seeing Theron, really seeing him, for the first time, and I'm not so sure that I like what I see."

"I think the Games have made us all do things that are a bit out of character," Thalia says, then she cracks into a smile. "For example, I am actually extremely laid back when not in situations that put my life in constant danger!"

We all laugh at that, even Thalia.

Then I remember something. "Last night, when Theron said that we should leave, he suggested that we do something that would mean the rest of you wouldn't be able to follow to the Forgotten Isles."

"Like what?" Ajax asks.

"I don't know, but if there's one thing I know for sure about Theron it's that once he has something in his head he usually sees it through."

I rush to the bedroom and find my black tunic cleaned and repaired, waiting for me on the bed. I slip it on then grab my bag and begin to pull out each of the objects Hades has given me, laying each of them on the bed: the bag itself, the water skein, the compass, the ring. I touch my lips and remember the kiss. On the back of a chair lie the seven strands of the rope. I gather them up and hold them as one and, as if the rope knows what to do, it becomes whole again, reassembling itself.

I place it and all the other favours into the bag along with some fresh bandages and food. I can hear Thalia calling and as I swing the bag over my body I wince slightly. I'm not sure that I'm ready for what's about to come.

I'm not as fast as the others, as we walk from the villa in the hillside down to the port. The pain in my wounds is a constant dull ache and there's a sheen on my forehead that has nothing to do with the blistering summer heat.

"You look terrible," Thalia tells me. "You should have stayed behind, rested a few more days." She's right but I don't have that luxury; if Theron and Heli find the crown before us then I lose my chance to win, and I need to win.

"I'm fine," I say, and lengthen my stride. I don't want to be the reason that holds us up from getting to the port. I see the look that Ajax shoots at Danae and I know they are both thinking that there is no way I'll make it through another trial, but I have to.

The town is busy as we make our way down the dirt-packed streets that lead to the harbour.

"What was it that Melia said we had to look out for?" Ajax asks.

"The sign of Hermes, his caduceus," Danae says.

Through the gaps between the sun-washed buildings I can see the deep blue sea, the waves sending patches of shimmering silver sunlight dancing across them, and I long to dive in and quench the heat that is running through my body.

I reach for the water skein again, drinking deeply from it, then I pass it to Thalia.

"Hades may be all kinds of weird when it comes to the Games, but I am so glad for this gift." She says, passing it to Ajax.

"Honestly, this and the cornucopia that Demeter gave Acastus were the two best gifts. If I win, I'm going to ask for both of them," Ajax says as he passes the skein to Danae.

"No, you're not," Thalia tells him flatly.

"What *are* you going to ask for?" Danae asked.

Ajax shrugged. "My village used to be prosperous, the farmland was fertile, but for the past few years the harvest has been bad. People have died, some moved away; the whole region is failing. I'd ask for a bountiful harvest and fertile soil forever to help my family and my home and, besides, after all of this I think I'd like to spend the rest of my days growing things."

"So you kind of *are* going to ask for the cornucopia and my water skein," I say with a smile, as I think about how selfless Ajax's gift would be.

"Yeah, I guess so," Ajax replies. "What about you, Thalia?"

"I'd ask for the right to rule my father's kingdom without having to get married."

"What?" Ajax said. "Hang on a minute, your... Oh, you're Princess Thalia of Elaea?" Ajax's eyes are wide as he stares at Thalia, and I think mine might be mirroring his. This explains a lot.

Thalia looks at Ajax, her jaw set, before she nods solemnly.

"I've heard about you. When suitors come to win your hand, you make them perform impossible tasks so that no one is ever worthy of you."

Thalia gives a low grunt. "The last suitor came close, too close. And besides, all the men who have tried and failed would be terrible for the people of Elaea; my people deserve better, they deserve to be looked after, to have their needs met and to be allowed to be who they want to be. We all do."

"That sounds like a worthy thing to ask for, and you would make a brilliant leader to your people," Danae says.

"You?" Thalia asks her.

"Easy, I'd ask for my freedom and the freedom of my family, for the freedom of every slave if I can."

"You're a slave?" Ajax asks, and I am reminded that I know nothing about any of their lives.

"After my mother died, my brother and I were sold by our uncle. I became a slave to a master, and now I am the slave of a God, but at the end of these Games I want to be my own master. No one should have the right to own someone as you would a goat, or a pair of sandals."

A heaviness descends on all of us as we continue through the streets towards the harbour. Danae's words press down on me and I think about what I want to ask the Gods for; one part of me feels ashamed and another feels furious at the Gods.

"Look!" Ajax points to a building and there, painted on the side of it, is the caduceus. A stick surrounded by two twisting serpents with wings at the top, just like the ones on Hermes' sandals. "Do you think...?"

"Definitely!" Thalia says, as she bounds forth and pushes open the door.

THE FEAR

It's dark inside the building, but not any milder; if anything it's hotter, and the sweat collects at the back of my neck and runs down my spine, soaking into my bandages.

"Hello," Thalia calls out. "Is anyone here?"

As if in answer the door behind slams shut. Ajax opens the locket of moonlight, bathing the room in a silvery glow.

In front of us appears Hermes. "Tokens, you have made it this far, but you are not the first to make the port; two tokens are already on their way to the Forgotten Isles. But fear not, the tide always rises and there is a vessel in port set to sail that way on the next high. But before you leave this land you must face a fear. Only those who conquer their fears will be able to leave."

"Another trial?" Danae asks.

Hermes smiles; his teeth glow in the shine from the moonlight and I feel uneasy.

Hermes hits his caduceus into the floor and four doors

appear behind him, each one containing a symbol of the zodiac. I can see the scorpion on the door to the right, its tail curling and ready to strike.

I look over at the others. There's a moment of hesitation before Danae nods her head and moves forward. "See you on the other side," she says over her shoulder as she pushes open the door marked with the sign of Pisces. I can hear the sound of revelry beyond, but that disappears as the door closes with a thud.

Thalia is already pulling open the door with the lion on, a bright light filling the room, and then she vanishes.

I don't glimpse what is behind the door marked with the sign of the crab because Ajax and I open our doors at the same time.

The roar of fire is deafening as I step in and look around. I cough and pull my cape around me to cover my mouth. I'm back in the central chamber of the Temple of the Zodiakos in Oropusa.

I spin slowly on the spot. There is fire all around me, each of the twelve chambers of the zodiac are ablaze. I take a step towards the staircase down to the crypt, and as I do I see someone slumped on the stairs, pulling heavily on the handrail as they try to stand. It takes me a moment to realize that it's "Estella!"

I rush forward and embrace my sister, supporting her, throwing my arms around her and holding her close to me. I can smell the delicate rose of her hair and the lavender of the soap she always used.

"Estella," I sob, as I bury my face in her hair. I never want to let her go.

She looks just as she did the morning that I found her in our bed, the morning that Zeus returned her, except now she is alive. Her yellow robes are identical to Heli's with bronze-coloured Gemini symbols covering them. She is wearing golden armour with lightning bolts on the breast, like Theron's, and she is clutching her side as she holds me with her other arm. I push my hand against the wound that has made her yellow tunic red.

"Ara," she says, as she hugs me back. "I've been waiting for you for so long. I've missed you."

"Oh, Estella, I've missed you more than you will ever know."

She looks at me and smiles. I remember that smile, so free and easy and bright, like the sun as it dances on the golden ears of a plump harvest. "You grew up without me," she says, as she tucks a stray hair behind my ear. And I realize that she's right; I've grown, but she is still the same.

"None of it matters; all that matters is that I've found you. We've found each other," I tell her.

"But Ara, I am not really here. You know that, right?"

I shake my head. "You are real, I can feel you, you are alive. You are here and so am I."

"I am alive here in this place, in this moment, only here," she says. "Before this I was in the fields of Elysium. I've been there … well, I'm not sure how long I've been there, come to think of it."

"Five years," I tell her.

"That long?" She looks at me again. "I watch you sometimes, you know; there is a pool that shows the reflections of those we love, and I often go there with Erastus and we watch our families. I worry about you, Ara. I worry that you aren't happy."

Her words stick in my throat. "I'm happy now," I tell her, and it's true, my whole being feels alight with joy to be near her again. To hear her voice and hold her hand.

She shakes her head. "But this isn't real, this isn't true happiness."

"It could be," I say. "Come on, let's get out of here. Let's go home." I start to lift her to her feet and then up the staircase.

"Ara, I … I can't leave with you. If I pass out of the temple I will die again. I'm alive here and I'm alive there, in a way." She points down into the crypt, except it isn't the crypt below but a meadow of sweet grass, the fields of Elysium, and standing in the field is a young man.

"Hades?" I call, but as he walks towards the foot of the stairs, I realize it's not him and I feel a plunge of disappointment.

"Estella," the young man calls up.

"Erastus," Estella calls, and she looks down at him with an intensity that I feel both privileged and awkward to witness.

A crack fills the air and part of the chamber of Aries collapses.

"Estella, I … I don't want to lose you again," I tell her, and I cling on. "We could stay here, on the steps. Just the two of us, we could stay here forever." I start to sob. Then I look down at the boy and the beautiful fields behind him. "Or … or we could go down there, I could come with you."

She's shaking her head before I've even stopped talking.

"No, Ara, no. You have not lost me; you never have, and you never will. I am here with you always," she says, as she places a hand on my chest. "And you are here." She releases her wound and places her hand to her heart.

She looks at me with a pained expression on her face, puts a hand to my neck and pulls the chains. Her token slips from under my tunic and clangs against my own. She holds them both together in her hands and lets out a low moan.

"I am so sorry that they took you too," she cries.

I have no words that will match the grief I can hear in her voice.

"I … I am a willing token," I tell her, and she looks at me incredulously.

"Why?' The question comes out on a billow of air, as if I have just punched her in the stomach.

"You, Estella. I want to make Zeus pay for killing you, I want to kill him for what he did to you, to mother, to father … to me. The only way I can do that is to be a token, to win the Games and claim Zeus' death as my reward." My voice breaks and my older sister wraps me in her arms, and I feel that I will never stop crying as the comfort of her embrace rolls over me.

"I don't want this for you, Ara," she whispers into my ear. "I don't want you to die for me. And I don't want you to avenge me, either." She tugs at the tokens and pulls hers from me. I gasp as I feel the weight of it leave my neck. "I want you to live the life I never had; I want you to love those that I can't: Mother, Father, Ida."

"But I don't want to leave you," I tell her.

"And I don't want to leave you, either," she says, "but one day we will meet again in the fields of Elysium and when we do I want you to tell me all about your long life and how you made the world a better place despite the Gods."

The pillars of Taurus fall inwards with a mighty crack and Estella looks at me. "We don't have much time, Ara. I need you to help me down the stairs to Erastus, then I need you to leave and live and love. Will you do that for me?"

I take her hand and guide her down the stairs as she holds on to the rail. I realize that when I had first seen her, this was what she was trying to do, she was trying to descend the staircase to Elysium, to Erastus.

As we reach the bottom step, we stop.

"You cannot go any further," she tells me. "If you do, you will die, and if you stay in this temple you will die too." She kisses me on the cheek and holds me close one last time before she releases me and reaches a hand to Erastus. He takes it and she steps on to the grass.

The moment she does, she changes: her clothes become a beautiful long, flowing gown and her skin is smooth and radiant; all the wounds of the Games are gone, and she looks healthy and alive, and older. She too has lived without me, lived a life of love with Erastus in Elysium.

"Go, Ara," Estella tells me. "Go, use the compass that Hades gave you to guide you towards what you want."

I plunge my hand into the bag and pull out the compass. I look at the needle – it is pointing at Estella.

She smiles, glances at Erastus and then her eyes find me again. "I'll be here, waiting for you, in the underworld, at the end, at your end, but that is not now. Promise me, Ara, promise me that you will live."

Her gaze is so intense it reminds me of when I was little when, as the older sibling, she would chastise me for doing something wrong. "Promise me," she says again, "that you will live and love for the both of us."

"I promise," I say through my tears, and as I look down at the compass the needle has shifted.

My feet feel as heavy as my heart as I walk up the stairs. I don't glance back; I don't think that I am strong enough to carry on walking if I see her again. I keep my eyes on the compass and the promise I have just made, as I walk through the central chamber of the temple. I don't look up at the antechamber that I walk through. I don't see the flames that are around me, although I hear them roaring and I see their light and feel their warmth.

"Ara!" I look up and see that the heat I felt and light

I saw have been replaced by the sun and the roaring of the sea. Ajax is running across the sand towards me, and behind him, stepping into the surf, is Thalia. There is a boat anchored just offshore and when I look down at the compass its needle is pointing straight at it.

THE NAVIS

I wade into the sea after Thalia; when it gets to waist height I start to swim. I've always loved swimming in the rivers and lakes near my home, but the sea is different. I've only swum in the sea a few times before and each time I've felt like I'm both connected to something greater than me and that I am nothing more than an insignificant piece of flotsam on the waves; today is no exception.

As I get closer to the boat, I look up at the figurehead that sits on the bow. It's unmistakably Hermes, holding his caduceus aloft, pointing out across the sea.

Thalia reaches the rope ladder that is drifting down the hull of the boat. She climbs it swiftly then disappears from view. I follow her and as I climb, I turn back to the shore to see Ajax still standing there, looking around for Danae.

When he reached me on the shore, he had hugged me tightly; he'd been crying and his whole body trembled. I didn't ask him what his fear was, what he had faced and conquered in the trial. I look away from the beach and keep climbing up the ladder. That's what Estella had wanted, for me to keep climbing, to keep going on … without her, that was the fear I had been avoiding for so long and now I must face it.

I take a deep breath and it catches as I think of Estella, how I had found her in the fire and then how she had looked when she had taken Erastus' hand and stepped into the fields of Elysium. I hope it wasn't all just an illusion, that she really is happy in the underworld. I stop climbing and frantically place my hand to my chest; I pull out my token on its chain, but Estella's is missing. She pulled it from me in the trial. I find a deep comfort in its loss as I haul myself up and over the side of the boat. If the token is gone then the trial was real; Estella took it back into the underworld.

I smile and hold my head up to the sun, feeling its warmth, and I wonder how long it has been since I felt so light.

I open my eyes and look around the deck of the ship; save for me and Thalia, it's completely empty.

"Where are the crew?" I ask.

"I have no idea!" Thalia says from the stern of the ship where she's looking at the rudder.

It's eerie. The oars of the boat sit waiting for rowers; the ropes of the anchor are ready to be hoisted. The sail is full of wind, which moans, eager to set the boat in motion, like an arrow pulled back in a bow ready to be shot. But there is no one else on board.

"You don't think that we're supposed to sail it ourselves, do you?" I ask Thalia.

"I hope not. I wouldn't know where to start!" she says back. "But if we are supposed to sail it, we're going to need help."

Thalia cups her hands to her mouth and calls to Ajax. He turns and looks at us then back to the beach.

"She's gone, hasn't she?" Thalia says, and I can hear the sadness in her voice.

"I think so. I really liked Danae; she was kind and funny and brave."

"Yeah, the way those birds pecked out her eye and she still carried on, fearless."

I feel my fingers curling into fists, and I say the names of all those we have lost: Philco, Kassandra, Xenia, Acastus, Nestor, Solon, Danae.

Ajax falls over the side of the boat and on to the deck and lies on his back in a puddle of water, looking up at the blue sky.

I'm just about to move towards him when the anchor rises and the ship starts to move forward.

"Look at that!" Thalia calls, and I rush forwards to see that the rudder is moving all on its own, guiding the boat out of the bay and into the sea.

"OK, so what, this is a ship governed by the Gods or something?" Ajax asks. He's on his feet and looking weary as he moves towards us.

I look around and something catches my eye. Under

the rudder arm there's a gap in the deck; I get down on my hands and knees to peer into it.

"Ha, it's a machine ship of some kind; down there are gears and cogs, all moving!" I say.

Thalia and Ajax are beside me in a moment, nudging me to one side so that they can get a good look at the complex array of machinery.

"Hephaestus?" Ajax asks.

"It has to be his handiwork," Thalia says.

"I guess we just sit back and wait till we get to the Forgotten Isles." Ajax rolls on to his back and puts his hands behind his head as he looks up into the blue sky again.

"I guess so," I say, feeling uneasy as I sit next to him. The Gods are not likely to make this a pleasant experience, I realize, as the *Navis* makes its way east at a fast clip.

"Look at the harbour!" Thalia says, and I stand up and move to the side of the deck that's looking northward. The entire port of Gythion is on fire.

"Theron," Ajax says from behind us.

"We don't know that for sure," I say, and I can't believe that I'm actually defending him; he told me he'd do something like this and here it is, the charred and fiery husks of every boat in the harbour.

"He must really want to win," Thalia says, and I know that he does, he really, really does.

The ship sails away from Gythion and soon I can't smell the fires any more, the wind has shifted, and the ship has somehow sensed it, as it folds the sails and the man-less oars begin to row.

"It's creepy, right?" Ajax says.

I nod in agreement. It is definitely creepy to see the oars moving on their own, pushing the boat forward against the new wind and the sea swell that it brings. I settle down in the stern of the boat, Ajax close and quiet. It's not the time for him to talk about Danae yet. I know what that's like, not wanting to give voice to the loss, which once spoken about becomes real.

"Any idea how long it will take, you know, to get to the Forgotten Isles?" I ask.

Thalia shrugs as she scoots closer to me, and the three of us huddle together on the deck against the crisp edge of the wind. "I asked around the town during the festival; no one had ever heard of a place called the Forgotten Isles."

"Be a bit of a nonsensical name if everyone remembered it, I guess," Ajax says.

I give a hollow snort of laughter. "Yeah, I guess so."

I pull out some of the food I have stored in the Trojan bag, and marvel at how everything is just as perfect as when I put it inside: the rolls are still warm from the oven and the honeycomb still on the plate. We eat and drink and barely talk as the day, and its trials and losses, hits us.

As the skies darken and the sea becomes wilder, I think of Estella, of the instant that she stepped away from me. In that moment I had wanted to follow her, and not just so that I could be with her, I realize. Hades. In that moment

I had been thinking of him and his kiss upon my lips and his arms around me, and the way he looks at me with those too-blue eyes and the way he says my name and how it makes my whole body tingle. But I'd promised Estella I would win the Immortal Games and live, live for us both, live fully, and now part of me worries that I will never be able to do that, not without him, not without Hades.

I wrap my cloak around me and just as the waves begin to grow uneasy around us, I feel myself slip into a troubled slumber.

THE ONLY ONE

"Poseidon, as much as it pains me to say this, Zeus is right; he had nothing to do with Danae's death," Hades says, as he stands between his brothers.

"How can you even say that?" Poseidon bellows. "He plays games by his own rules, he bends the truth and breaks a lie so he can present each part of it to you and before you know it you've eaten the whole thing. I will not eat his lies any more; I will bend him to my truth."

Hades raises his bident and slams it on the floor; Poseidon wavers as the ground beneath him quakes.

Zeus stumbles, quickly regaining his footing, "I should strike you down with my thunderbolts, throw you from Olympus and dash you to the bottom of the sea."

Hades turns to Zeus, his face full of a quiet disappointment that only makes his brother more enraged.

"Do not look at me that way, Hades. I will cast you back to the underworld too."

Hades gives a mock bow. "If this is what you wish,

I will gladly go. And I take with me my token and my wager."

Zeus shoots a look at Hades and then beyond him at Poseidon. Hades knows what is going through Zeus' mind; it is the opposite of his own thoughts.

If Hades is thrown from Olympus then his place in the Games is void, Ara will be released from the Immortal Games and he will be freed from his wager. But Zeus is so close, close to having it all. Not just control over his brothers, but ultimate control over their realms, over every aspect of their existence.

"Let us not be hasty," Zeus says, and Hades feels the weight of the knot in the weaving shift back upon him. "I did not cheat, Poseidon, how could I have? Obviously your token is not worthy of you, or us, or these Games," Zeus says.

"Are you questioning my judgement?" Poseidon bellows again, and once more Hades steps forth.

He knows the rage of his brothers well; they both follow a similar course. They will storm and thrash and lash out until they are done, and then like the winds and waves after a hurricane, a calm will eventually settle over them and it will be as if nothing had happened, but the scars of their actions will be carried by others.

"Poseidon, Danae was a strong and brave token; the fear she faced was extreme and brutal and, worse than that, she has faced it twice now, once in real life and once in this trial, which to her would be real. She deserves your sympathy right now. You owe her that much for the sacrifices she has made for you.

"And you, Great Zeus, own that honour too. Show us your greatness in all ways, not just in the might of your sword or your mouth."

"Do you dare speak to me that way, brother? Do you dare tell me how to command?" Zeus says.

"Aye, you know I am the only one who ever does. And it is my fault that I do not do it often enough." Hades hangs his head in disappointment for his own actions.

Zeus looks stormily at Hades and then around at all the other Gods, who are silent and watching.

He gestures towards the adjacent hall and Hades follows. "Not you!" Zeus bellows at Poseidon.

As he follows Zeus, Hades looks back at his brother and can tell that another wave is rising.

"How dare you?" Zeus rounds on Hades as soon as they are out of earshot. "How dare you speak to me like that in my own halls?"

Hades rises to his full height and stands tall over Zeus; his face is a mask of fury and his bident looms heavy.

"How dare you, Zeus? How dare you make sport of us, of your kin? You are so removed from all that is Godly that you know nothing any more. Your existence has become centred on your own selfish gratification; you are our father's child." Hades knows he has wounded Zeus, the lighting strike above Olympus only confirms this. "You will never be happy. You can take my kingdom and that of Poseidon, you can seduce every mortal woman who takes your fancy and make war with every man that crosses you, but you will never be happy. Do you know why, dear brother?"

Zeus looks warily at Hades. "Why?"

"Because whatever you do, you will still be you. You are incapable of seeing what is around you, incapable of owning your actions; you are incapable of happiness. You have a Goddess in your bed and yet you turn to others. You have brothers who love you and yet you scorn them. You have mortals who worship you and yet you torment them. You hold all that should be most dear to you in the greatest of contempt and this has been happening for so long, too long, dear brother. The winds are changing, and you will not win this time."

Hades turns to walk away, and Zeus steps forward. "You think that because you have found love with your token that you know what happiness is, that you know how I should live my life."

"No, brother, I know happiness because I worked for it, because I sought it out in the darkness of the underworld. I found my place and I found my purpose and I found myself. You cannot see me for who I am because you cannot even see yourself. I am happy with my deeds, my actions, my path. I haven't always been, and I make amends for that. But I was happy before I found Ara and I was loved; she just increases that. I feel sorry for you, brother, sorry that no matter how much you have, it will never, never be enough for you."

Hades walks away from Zeus, back into the hall, and sits at the board, ready to finish the Games.

31

THE CALM IN THE STORM

Hades is there, standing on a rocky outcrop overlooking a troubled sea; around him rages a terrible storm, the sky a foreboding grey, full of dark clouds that glow from inside as lightning crackles through them.

I duck forward, leaning my body against the wind as I head towards him. His back is to me, and he stands serene, unaffected by the storm that whips around me, pulling my cloak and hair behind me. I hold my bag close to my body with one hand and shield my face from the wind and rain with the other.

"Hades!" I call out to him, but the wind snatches his name from my lips. Every step is an effort, every inch closer to him is a victory, and as I come close enough to reach him, I extend my hand and touch his arm.

I gasp as I step forward swiftly; the wind and the rain have ceased, although I can see it all around me. The look of confusion on Hades' face recedes in a moment as he reaches out and pulls me to him, wrapping his arms around me, pulling me closer still. It is as if I have reached the eye of the storm, and the realm of calm is Hades.

"What's happening?" I whisper up at him, as my head rests on his chest. It's so quiet next to him that anything above a whisper would sound deafening.

"My brothers, my brothers are what is happening," Hades says, and he sounds so weary.

I look out at the angry sea, the waves reaching high in a relentless stream, crashing into one another, cresting in white peaks, and pounding the sea with the frothy spit of fury.

"Danae?" I ask.

Hades nods. "She is part of this; she darkens my gate and now Poseidon is angry. Zeus and he had words and, as with all things that happen in Olympus, the effects are soon felt in the realm of mortals."

"So, this is really happening? It's part of the Games?"

"Yes, and no," Hades says, his jaw fixed and his eyes burning with flecks of stardust. "It is happening, but it is not part of the Games any more than Apollo racing across the sky."

"But they can't kill us with this storm, can they? It was in the rules."

Hades gives a little hollow laugh. "Technically, neither of them will cause any destruction to the tokens," he says, pointing.

I squint to see what he is indicating and my heart sinks as I see it, a giant sea serpent swimming through the waves, churning the water in its wake, driving up then crashing back on to the seas, jaws open and hunting.

"That is your trial, not the storm, although it is not helping matters."

As I continue looking, I see something that makes my blood turn to ice. "Is that our boat?"

"No," Hades says flatly.

"Theron and Heli?"

"Yes."

"Can you save them? Can you make sure that they are safe?"

"Ara, I can't even make sure that you are safe," he says as he looks down at me, holding me tight. "If I can't save you, I definitely can't save them."

My eyes grow wide as I watch the small ship tossing around on the mighty waves. From the clifftop vantage point, I can see it all, the small boat, the crashing waves, the sea serpent writhing within the water.

I think of the Gods on Olympus and how they are privileged to see the whole picture from their lofty dwelling, and I shudder at how they can see it all and let it play out. A bolt of lightning strikes, illuminating the clouds, and from within them it looks as if a hand is stretching out, fingers looming towards the ship.

"Zeus is trying to even the odds for his token," Hades says. "He has rolled an advantage; he is allowed to take an action."

I realize at once the power that the Gods have, the

strength and might and size of them, and how small and insignificant I am, we all are. How could I have ever thought that I could take them on, that I could win against mighty Zeus himself. He would crush me as surely as the waves threaten to crush Theron's boat.

"What about you, what did you roll?" I ask.

"Defence," he answers.

I give a shrug. "That's not so bad." And he looks down at me, that small smile tugging on my heart. "I'm used to looking out for myself and besides, I've come this far, and I don't plan on joining you in your realm anytime soon."

"No?" He almost raises an eyebrow.

"Well, not unless I'm invited and I'm still alive. I have a promise to fulfil," I tell him, and he strokes my cheek before kissing me. In the middle of all that destruction, beneath his fighting family and before the churning sea, he kisses me, and I feel complete bliss flow through every part of me.

I look up at Hades as he sighs, and then his eyes focus on the storm, reflecting back the colours of the sea and the sky, and I realize he is just as powerful as the sky and the sea and the Gods within them; the large looming hand is present in my mind.

"What do you look like?" I ask him. "I mean truly look like."

He looks at me blankly and I can tell that I've caught him off guard, his eyes pinching at the sides as he tries to process what it is that I'm asking. Then his face relaxes and he offers that familiar small smile.

"I take this shape because it is how you see me," he says.

"But I want to see the real you," I tell him.

"I'm not sure that you can," he answers. "The true me is not too dissimilar to the true you. You are a spirit experiencing a mortal body, living an existence in this realm, and you will return to that spirit when you enter the underworld where you will hold a shape that you find familiar, that you identify with.

"I am a spirit but a much older one than you can comprehend, and I am having a Godly experience as you are having a mortal one. I, like you, am much larger than this vessel that you see me in, my shape is more of a tone. Here." He takes my hand and places it on his chest. "Close your eyes." I give him a playful, cautious look.

"Close them," he commands, and I smile as I do as he says.

"Now I want you to think of me, not just my face, or my body; I want you to listen to the sound of my voice and think of the colours that it contains."

I see a deep crimson colour, with a swirl of richness to it and a splash of golden light. He has moved his lips closer to my ear as he says, "Now think of the way that I smell." The air is suddenly full of the dark and deep heavy scents of the earth. "Add that to the colour," he instructs. "And think of how I feel." He runs one hand along my arm up to my shoulder, my neck, my face where he cups my jaw and strokes my cheek. Then he kisses me deeply. The whole of my body tingles with a deep longing that fills each and every nerve ending in my body, flooding it with a fire deeper than the flames of Prometheus.

Then his lips are close to my ear again and he says, "And what echo of me is left when I am not with you?" His touch is gone and the storm slams into me, the wind and the rain rushing around me while inside I keep hold of the sensations of Hades: the calm of him, the way the darkness bends towards the light of him, and the dreaming folds to embrace him, the unyielding power he has and the way that he uses it, the respect that he has for it, for the souls he cares for, for me. I hold on to all that he is, and I let it grow within me. As I stand in the middle of the storm, steadfast and adamant, and I let him dance through my being, I delight in the sensation of it. I feel the very essence of not only him but of the way that he makes me feel about myself: stronger, bolder, braver. He makes me a better person and I feel that I make him a better God in return. And laced through all of this, like a thread that binds the two of us together, is a deep love, not just longing and want, but reverence and knowing. I *know* him and through him I know myself, my true self. He had once told me that I was the sun, and if that is true then he is the light that I shine.

I open my eyes and expect to see him, but he's not there.

"Hades!" I call out, spinning around as the storm pulls my hair, and there he is, standing a little behind me and closer to the cliff edge.

"Hades!" I reach out for him, the storm dying around me as soon as I touch him. I pull him around to face me. The look on his face almost floors me, anguished tears that I reach up to wipe from his cheeks.

"Is that really how you see me, how you feel me, and experience me?" he asks, looking at me in a way that makes me feel so full.

"Yes." I can barely hear my voice even though everything around me is so still and silent and calm.

He shakes his head. "I have never... Not even my fellow Gods see me like that."

"Did I do it wrong?" I ask, knowing I hadn't; I had experienced him as he truly is and he still thrummed through my being.

He smiles. "Ara, I think that you see me as I would hope to be."

"No, I see you as you are." I reach up and place my hand around the back of his head, lowering his lips to mine. As the world crashes around us I feel my spirit grow and burst as I entwine my fingers in his thick dark hair and slip my other hand around his waist. He holds me so tightly to him that I'm sure the two of us are one.

When I pull my lips away from his I feel breathless and unsteady. He rests his forehead on mine and strokes my face as I loosen the grip on his hair and smooth my hand over his locks.

"I was going to give you a gift, a walking stick."

"A walking stick!" I say incredulously.

He smiles, then traces a hand over my face. "But I fear I have given you something that I didn't even know I was offering," he says, his face a delightful puzzle of surprise and joy.

"Oh, and what's that?" I ask.

He looks at me more seriously now, moving his head away from mine. "My heart, Ara, if I have one, I'm not entirely sure. But my love, affection and adoration, all of it is yours."

I feel my head and heart spin at the intensity of the feeling.

Outside the calm the two of us are sharing, another tremendous lightning strike fills the sky. I feel scared and secure all at once. Surely no one is supposed to feel this way; to hold the heart of a God is a terrifyingly powerful thing.

Hades looks beyond me to the sea. I follow his gaze and watch in horror as Theron's ship breaks apart on the rocks that surround the Forgotten Isles like jagged teeth.

"Theron!" I call out and move away from Hades, back into the storm, my hair whipping around as I call to Theron again, my voice nothing compared to the roar of the wind.

Hades is beside me; he doesn't touch me; the storm still has me but, on the wind, I hear his voice. "He has not entered my realm."

I scan the sea; small dark parts of the broken ship litter the tossing waves, but I can't see Theron or... "Heli?" I ask, as I turn to Hades.

I don't need to hear his answer, I can tell by the look on his face. "She is at my gate." I look back towards the floating wreckage. "Ara, if you and your friends are to avoid joining her, you must wake now," he says.

I turn back to him and reach out a hand. He takes it, moving closer to me, and bows his head, rubbing his cheek along mine, filling my body with fire. As I close my eyes, he whispers in my ear.

"Wake up, Ara."

32

THE SEA SERPENT

My eyes shoot open just as the first large wave bears down on the boat, filling the deck with saltwater and soaking us all.

"What's going on?" Ajax cries.

"A storm and a sea serpent!" Thalia calls back.

"Awesome, my God literally tells me nothing!" Ajax says.

"Hera gave me this." She holds out an almond. "She told me to hold it in my hand and not let it go, it would make me float."

"Brilliant," Ajax says. "Artemis gave me a feather; she said it would help me to remember – but I can't remember what I was supposed to remember. Maybe she told me a secret way to get to the Forgotten Isles and avoid the storm?"

I push myself up on to my knees and lean towards Ajax to touch the golden circlet around his neck. "Or maybe she already gave you something to help with the sea," I tell him, remembering myself that the circlet would keep his head above water at all times.

"Of course, that Goddess is a genius! But she could have given me a heads up."

"Ha-ha!" I say, then smile because in the middle of all of this it is actually funny.

Another wave hits the boat, and we all pitch to one side.

"It's about to get way worse than this," I tell them. "Theron and Heli's ship was destroyed. Heli didn't make it," I shout above the squall.

"What did Hades give you?" Ajax calls.

I hesitate. I can't very well say his heart. "Nothing that will be of much help in the middle of a storm!" I say, but then I realize that the courage he has in me, the faith and love, might be the best thing he could have ever given me.

At that moment something hits the hull of the boat, knocking the vessel at an odd angle.

"I'm guessing that's the sea serpent!" Ajax says, his eyes wide.

The oars on the *Navis* continue rowing in perfect unison, trying to bring some order to the chaos of the storm, carrying us straight up the crest of a mighty wave. Inside the wall of water in front of us I can see the dark swirling shape of the sea serpent heading straight for us.

"Get down!" I shout, as it breaks from the wave and heads towards the ship, its jaws open as it snaps off the figurehead from the prow and pulls the wooden Hermes into the depths.

As the boat reaches the top of the peak it teeters there for a moment. Suspended between waves. I reach inside my bag and pull out the rope, ready to tie us all to the side to stop us from falling overboard. But as I take a step the boat pitches forward, plummeting down the wave. I slide along the deck and manage to grab hold of the mast; the sail is still attached, torn and flapping about in the wind.

"Ajax!" I scream as he slides past me, down the deck and straight through the hole that the figurehead has left behind.

As the *Navis* reaches the bottom of the wave and the oars begin to row up the next, I take the shift in momentum as an opportunity to right myself. I put my back against the mast then pass the rope around it, tying myself to the ship before making the rope shrink as tightly as I can stand while still being able to breathe.

"Thalia!" I scream out. But all I can hear are the waves and the thunder and the sound of my heart pounding in my ears.

The next wave is even steeper.

"Thalia!" I continue to shout.

"Ara, I'm OK," Thalia shouts from behind. I turn to see her, but I'm so tightly bound I can barely move.

The wave suddenly begins to crest towards us and instead of the boat reaching the top, the top reaches us. I am sure that, just like I saw a hand in the clouds, I can see a face in the waves; it belongs to Poseidon, his deep green eyes full of vengeance and watery wrath.

He roars, opening his mouth wide and screaming as the wave moves forward, swallowing the boat, crashing water all around us. For a moment that lasts a lifetime, the ship becomes submerged in the depths of the sea. The pressure of the water pushes down on me before the buoyant hull rises the boat up out of the watery depths to the surface.

I gasp as I cough up seawater and look around, eyes bleary.

"Thalia," I shout, but only the waves shout back at me as another one hits the ship, plunging it under the waves like a leaf in the rapids of a stream. I feel the ship twist this time and a vibration thunders through the mast. As I look up, the water stinging my eyes, I see the top of the mast split off and drift slowly in the sea; still connected to the ship by the sail, which fans out like hair in a pool. I feel the push of the hull again and this time I'm prepared for the ship to break the water, but what I'm not anticipating is the sail coming down on the deck, wrapping around me, the broken top of the mast falling over the side of the boat, pulling the sail tight over me.

The heavy sail, thick with the sea, pins me against the mast, and I start to panic; I can't see, and every breath is full of water from the soaked sail. I cough and splutter as I try to push the sodden sail from my face so I can breathe. The ship is making its way up another wave; I brace myself for the fall.

"Hades," I call out into the darkness that surrounds me, but it's Estella's voice that I hear.

"Promise me!" she says.

And I did promise her.

I manage to move one hand in front of my face, trying to keep the sail from my mouth. The other hand I move to touch the rope. I think about the rope growing longer, giving me room to move, the knots loosening and coming undone as I hold it in my hand, and the boat rushes down the wave and plunges under the water.

The sail lifts from me and floats in the water above me like a giant jellyfish. I pull myself out of the rope and into the open water. I see the jagged rocks that litter the seas around the Forgotten Isles loom out of the depths. The ship crashes into them and I twist away, kicking with all of the strength in my legs up to the surface and away from the wreckage of the boat. I still have the rope in my hand, and it follows me through the water, its soft light glowing as it shrinks.

As my head breaks the surface, I take a huge gasp of air. The waves throw me about like the rest of the wreckage from the boat. I have no idea which way I should be swimming. All I can do is try to keep my head above water and, in that moment, I think of Ajax and his circlet and choke back a hysterical laugh.

I try to swim but I am at the mercy of the waves, which push me back under with no warning.

The ship is below me, drifting underwater, and I wonder whether the oars are still rowing as I see it collide with the rocks again and again, the hull splitting apart more each time. The sail and mast have become untethered from the ship now and I turn just in time to see them looming towards me. I realize that if I'm caught in the sail, I'll never escape it, so I swim up to the surface and hope that I can make it before the sail sweeps out and captures me.

As I move upwards, I look back to make sure that I've missed the sail and see that just below it, drifting serenely, is the sea serpent, heading straight for me.

My lungs burn, my body aches. Adrenaline courses through me at the sight of the creature. Its long, scaled body is powerful, and its open jaws are full of teeth. I break the surface and take a lungful of air then try to swim as fast as I can in the direction of the current. I know I can never outswim the sea monster and, in a moment of recklessness, I dive back under the waves and swim towards the sail. I see that the serpent has changed its direction but is still heading for me.

The sail billows open in the water and I swim along it, looking for a rip in the fabric big enough for me to swim through. When I find one, I gather my courage and I turn to face the sea serpent, waiting till it is close enough for me to see the iridescent green–grey scales that cover its smooth body, then I slip through the rip and swim upwards as fast as I can. Below me the sail bulges and distorts as the sea serpent tries to free itself but instead manages to twist the sail and mast into a knot of fabric and rope, trapping itself inside.

As I near the surface I can feel stars forming at the edge of my vision. I need to breathe so badly. The urge to open my mouth and fill my lungs becomes all-consuming, and darkness begins to descend. I kick with my legs and reach out with my hands, my fingertips breaking the surface, hitting something hard. I latch on to it as I pull in breath after breath. As I grab hold more securely, I realize that I'm clutching the caduceus of Hermes, the figurehead from the ship, and pull myself on to it. As I lie there I only have enough energy for my next breath. My thoughts drift like the sea as I shiver, and breathe, and cry, clutching the figurehead and letting it take me wherever it wishes.

33

THE FORGOTTEN ISLES

I can't remember when the rhythm of the sea changed, when the large waves were replaced with a gentle lapping, when the lapping then stopped and I washed up on the shore. I do remember lying on the beach in the darkness with the summer stars shining above me, as the sand stuck to every inch of my wet and shivering body. And I remember Hades, his strong arms lifting me, holding me close, and carrying me through the night into the tall coarse grasses that line the sandy coastline.

Warmth now seeps into my body as something soft and warm is wrapped around me, cocooning me as I lie on the sandy earth, surrounded by the sharp sea grass, the sound of the waves filling my ears. My head is on Hades' lap, and he strokes my hair until I finally stop shivering.

I'm not sure how close I came to dying, but I think Hades knows. As if he can read my thoughts, he says, "For a moment there I felt that you might be joining me in my realm after all."

"I would have thought that you'd like that," I say, as I turn to look up at him. "I'd never have to leave you."

He sighs. "But you would, Ara, you would leave me slowly and completely. As your soul journeyed through the underworld you would in time forget me, just as you would forget your life and all that you have done, and when you were ready you would enjoy another experience of life and I would be nothing to you but a God to fear. Whereas I, I will live forever, forever loving you and missing you, and as someday I am to live an eternity without you then I want you to live a long and full life so that I have much to remember and love when you no longer know me or even yourself."

"Is that what happens when we die? We mortals, we forget?" I think of Estella and how she knew me and I her, but then I remember how, when she had stepped into Elysium, she had got older; she lived there, a different type of living, but it was something.

He carries on stroking my hair as he looks down at me with a sad smile. "Eventually, over the eons, yes, and for you it will feel like forever, but forever is so much longer for me than it is for you."

After a while he reaches into the Trojan bag and pulls out the water, then some food, then the ring. He gives all three to me, slipping the ring on to my finger.

"I never did tell you what this does. If you twist the sun and the moon around so they change positions, you will become invisible. Twist them back to be seen again."

I give out a light chuckle as I look at the ring on my hand. "I wish I'd known sooner; I could have had fun with that. Ajax will love it. Wait, Thalia, Ajax, did they ... are they...?"

"Thalia is not in my charge."

"But Ajax? Artemis gave him the circlet." I'm confused and then I remember the sea monster. "I ... I don't think I can do this any more," I say, and I hate how weak my voice sounds, how cracked and small.

"You're so close, Ara, so very close."

"Everyone keeps dying and ... and I..." I don't want to tell him that I can't watch Theron die. He may have abandoned me, but he has been my friend for a long time, and I feel as if I've lost enough friends to the Immortal Games. I can feel hot tears running down my face. I feel empty and defeated; before I had a fire, I had revenge, and now what do I have?

Promise me. The memory of Estella's voice echoes to me.

I have made a promise, a promise to live, and I'm not sure that I know how to do that.

The sky is lightening in the east, bringing with it the warmth of summer, and as its light grows so do all the expectations of the day.

"Humour me, Hades. Tell me what it will be like, when this is over, when I return home."

Hades looks up, as if he can again see something that is just beyond my vision.

"You will return home and your father will be relieved;

he will embrace you and tell you how much he loves you. Your mother will see you; she will glimpse your light and lean towards it, and she will start to know herself again as you live, every day a little bolder and brighter. You will let more people in; you will find joy and happiness, friendship, and love."

He looks down at me now and I reach a hand up to his face.

"Will you be there?" I ask him.

"You have my heart; I will always be there." He places his hand over my chest and then his lips on mine.

I wrap my arms around his neck and pull his kisses deeper to me.

We sit there for a little longer, watching Apollo chase the night away, and then I hear my name being called, followed by Ajax's.

"Thalia!" I sit up and look along the shoreline.

"Go to her," Hades says. "Take the cloak; it is but a small gift, but the red side will keep you as warm as the fires of the Furies and the grey side as cool as a winter's night."

I stand up, pulling the cloak around me, and he grasps my hand. "I will see you after the next trial," he says.

I nod. "I promise." As he drops his hand I run in the direction of Thalia's calls.

I see her on the beach but have to slow my pace, holding my side; the cuts from the pterippi are sore and my head spins a little from the exertion. I remind myself that I did almost drown and when I get to Thalia, she looks like she may have actually succumbed to the waters only to have been revived again.

I take off the cloak and throw it around her, red side towards her body. I rub my hands over her and hug her close, trying to warm her up. She's soaking wet, her skin looks pale and her lips a little blue. I guide her from the beach, out of the lingering winds of the storm and into the shelter of the long grasses, just as Hades did with me.

Once there I settle her down and start to look for some driftwood above the tideline. I don't find much but there's enough for a small fire to warm Thalia and dry her. I sit close and curl my friend in my arms. When she stops shaking, I offer her some fresh water; she drinks deeply then throws it all up on to the sandy ground. Then she starts crying and I hold her again, fighting back my own tears.

"Ajax?" she eventually asks, and I shake my head.

"Just us two." And then I add, "And Theron."

"Any idea where we need to go?"

"As a matter of fact, yes," I say, as I plunge my hand into the bag and pull out the compass. It's pointing east, towards the sun that is fully above the horizon now, the grey wispy clouds passing across it every now and again.

I pull some food out of my bag too, and Thalia and I eat in silence. When we've finished, she is more like herself. Her colour has returned and with it her solid determination.

"Come on, Ara, let's see what fun new way Hermes has planned to kill us with next."

I smile; she is not wrong. We follow the compass inland, the sandy beach quickly giving way to rocky terrain. With tall outcrops and sheer cliffs of mostly limestone, and little vegetation, the ground is littered with small white rocks that slide under my feet. Every so often we come across signs of a rockslide and have to double back to find a different path.

Around midday the sky clears, the grey clouds evaporating to a beautiful kingfisher blue. Then around mid-afternoon, just as Thalia is leading the way back along the path we had been travelling, after finding yet another of the rockslides, I hear a rumble like thunder, and freeze.

"Did you hear that?" I ask Thalia.

"Hear what?"

I hold up my hand and we stand still and quiet. Then I hear it again, a deep rumble but not from the sky, from the earth. I look up just as a rockfall starts. Thalia turns and runs towards me, and we double back again. The sound is deafening as the rocks fall and tumble, kicking up a cloud of white dust that rolls our way as we run. I pull my cloak over my mouth as the dust fills my lungs and I start coughing. Thalia grabs hold of me and the two of us fall to the ground, huddled together as the rumbling slowly fades and the dust settles.

I pull Thalia up. The air is full of a dusty haze and through it I can see that we are now blocked in on both sides.

I take a few steps along the ravine path and then stop as I can see something else looming in the haze, something big that is moving towards us.

"Thalia!" I point and she turns to look behind. I plunge my hand into my bag and call out my rope as the dust settles a little more and I can see what it is.

"By the Gods!" Thalia says. We both look up at the giant cyclops as it rises above the cloud of dust. "First some weird swamp creatures, then birds with blades for beaks, followed by giant three-headed snakes, flying horses, sea monsters and now, *now*, one-eyed giants? I've had enough!"

"Thalia, I have an idea. I can use this to bind its feet and when it falls you can kill it," I tell her, as I gesture to her sword and spear.

"No, it's too dangerous; it'll squish you if you get too close," she says, and I reach down and twist the ring that Hades gave me. Thalia's eyes widen.

"It can't squish what it can't see. Make sure you get back," I tell her, and I don't wait for her to object as I rush down the path to the rockslide that the cyclops is just stepping over. I see his foot coming down through the dissipating cloud and dodge aside. The ground shakes as he steps forward and I feel myself pitch towards the ground. I roll out of the way of his other foot as it comes down then I push myself up and get to work.

Somewhere in the dust ahead is Thalia and I can't let the cyclops reach her before I'm ready.

I tie a rock to the end of the rope and drop it to the ground before I run around the foot that's on the floor then snatch up the end with the rock and tie it off to form an anklet of shimmering starlight. As I'm securing the rope the cyclops moves off. I hold tight as I'm lifted into the air, high above the ground; at the top of the cloud of dust I can see Thalia. She's almost reached the first rockslide we found on the path and is running out of room to flee.

As the cyclops lowers its foot, the rope swings forward, sending me flying out. I land with a thud that knocks the wind from me, but I scramble to my feet. I run forward, the rope lengthening with me. When his other foot lands, I'm ready. I keep lengthening the rope till it's round his ankle; he starts to take his next step and I keep extending the rope as I tie it off; only when I know it's secure do I stop. I hold on to the rope and think about it getting shorter and shorter. The effect is almost instant; his feet are suddenly together, and the giant is falling towards the ground. I fall over too, as he lands face down. The giant lets out a single deafening roar and for a moment he thrashes about wildly before coming to rest. His whole body blocks the ravine path, so I seize the moment and jump up on to the back of his legs and run up his body.

"Thalia," I yell. "Thalia!"

I stand on the shoulder blade of the giant, looking around for her. I stand still, searching, and that's when I realize that the giant isn't breathing. I get on my hands and knees and press my ear to his back. I can't hear any breathing, no heartbeat, nothing; she did it.

"Thalia, you deserve your own epithet for that – Thalia, Princess of Elaea, Token of Hera, Slayer of Giants!"

281

I slide from the cyclops' shoulder and on to the rocky ground. He is face down in a puddle of blood and under his forehead, where his eye used to be, I see her.

Thalia's arm is outstretched, her blood-covered sword still clutched in her fist, her gold tunic slowly turning red.

I shake with rage and scream out so loudly that I think the dead might be able to hear me. Thalia's body begins to glisten, and disappears. I don't cry this time. I have no more tears left, I just have anger, and grief and a promise.

This time when I say their names I don't keep them in, I shout them out for the world to hear: "Philco, Kassandra, Xenia, Acastus, Nestor, Solon, Danae, Heli, Ajax, Thalia!" Their names are not just the outpouring of my grief, not just a tribute, they are also a promise.

I pull the cape that Hades gave me, the one that Thalia had been wearing, out from under the giant's face; it is covered in blood. I stuff it into the bag then retrieve my rope. When the giant landed, one arm crushed the rocky barrier that had trapped us. I climb up his arm and over what remains of the obstacle, jumping from his open hand to the ground.

The ravine splits just up ahead. I pull the compass from my bag and follow it east.

34

THE TEMPLE OF THE ZODIAKOS

I walk for several hours through the rocky paths that grow smoother and greener as the compass leads me on. I'm feeling heavy, not just my body but my heart and spirit too. There's a deep loneliness running through me that I haven't felt since those early days after Estella was taken.

I place my hand to my heart and as I do I realize that I never twisted the ring back; I'm still invisible, and that's how I've felt for so long now, wandering unseen through the days. I twist the ring. I want to be seen, I want to be noticed and I want to take notice of everything around me.

I start to look, truly look, at the green of the leaves on the bush, its white flowers fragrant in the warm summer sun. I listen to the sound of the soft wind as it stirs through the canopy of trees that are growing thicker and closer together with every step. The light on the path dances in the breeze and I feel the air become cooler under the protection of the trees.

The shady path opens into a meadow and in the middle

is a twelve-sided stone Temple of the Zodiakos. It is bigger and far more elaborate than the temple in Oropusa. I walk around the sides of the temple till I find my symbol, the scorpion emblazoned on the door in golden stars. Then I walk up the stone steps and enter.

It's pitch dark inside the temple, and I am instantly reminded of the night of the Blood Moon when Hades picked me for his token, as I find myself in an identical room. I look around and see the bronze statue of Scorpio looming above me and the stars in the ceiling, and I see no reason to think this is not the same place.

I expect to see Hades stepping from the shadows as he did that evening. I remember how I had felt about him, his dark robes flowing and his eyes almost glowing in the blackness, and I realize that from the first moment I saw him I had felt it. I had fallen for him with no warning, with no realization until it was too late.

I hear a shifting behind me and turn hopefully; I'm disappointed to see Hermes floating theatrically in his winged shoes.

"Token of Hades," he addresses me, "you have made it to the final trial. Beyond this door is the Labyrinth of the Zodiakos. It is full of many dangers and at the centre lies the Crown of the North and victory. However, the dangers of the labyrinth are not the only things in your way; there is a token who has made it here before you and he is already mastering the maze."

Theron, he's alive, he made it past the giant. I'm more

relieved than I thought I would be, but then the fear of what lies ahead floods in.

"The rules as set out at the beginning of this quest are still very much in play." Hermes reels them off quickly in a bored tone: "All favours from the Gods belong to the token to whom they are given. A token must pledge their full allegiance to the God that chose them; no alliances or bargains are to be made between tokens and any other Gods but their own. And no mortal token may wittingly draw the blood of another; instant disqualification will be bestowed upon the token and their God, and great punishment will be given, blah blah blah!"

He turns to me and smiles. "Now we want this to be an interesting showdown between the two tokens from Oropusa, friends for so long, maybe even a little something more! What can I say, we Gods are invested! Look to your strengths when you're in the maze, and to the gifts of your God, speaking of which…"

He extends a hand and offers me his caduceus, but when I look at it, I realize that it isn't his caduceus at all, it's Hades' double-pronged bident. I hesitate before I reach out to take it.

Surely Hades is not giving me a weapon; after all his protests, all of his useful gifts, all of the dangers that I have faced and it's now that he gives me a weapon?

But as soon as I hold it, I understand. I can look around the dark chamber and see in clear detail, as if the sun were shining on everything. And I realize that the light that

285

is shining is coming from me. I gasp as I remember that Hades, his hand on my cheek as he looked deep into my eyes, told me, *Ara, you are the sun.*

"You must hurry now, token, if you are to have any chance of claiming the prize for your God," Hermes says. He waves his arm and the door at the back of the chamber opens.

I walk towards it, fear rising in me. This is it, the final trial. I've come so close to claiming victory, to claiming the gift of the Gods that I have coveted for so long.

As the door closes behind me, I take out the compass. I have no idea which way is north but that doesn't matter, I don't need to know, all I need to do is think of the thing that I want. The needle is pointing behind me at the door. I stand still for a moment and close my eyes, clearing my mind, and then filling it with the idea of the crown. I see myself lifting it victoriously, placing it on my head. I look down and the compass needle is pointing to the right. I journey down the path of the labyrinth and take the first right; the needle then twists and I look for the next left. The walls of the labyrinth are narrow, claustrophobic. I keep hold of the compass in one hand and the bident in the other. I'm sure that without both I will soon become disorientated in the dark passages, and I hope that is exactly what Theron is feeling now.

The night sky is swirling above me, the stars moving much faster than they really do, and I wonder if time is moving differently inside the labyrinth or if this is an illusion of the Gods, another thing sent to disorientate.

The stars look as if they are radiating down in myriad

colours, lighting the sky in ways that I have never seen before; I wonder if it is the effect of the bident. As I make a left I slink immediately back. Ahead of me is a creature I've only ever heard about in stories.

I twist the ring to make myself invisible and feel a small semblance of security pass over me, as I berate myself for not using it before. I glance back down the path. The harpy's face is that of the most beautiful woman I have ever seen, but then it opens its mouth and squawks so loudly that I have to resist the urge to drop the compass and the bident and cover my ears. It stretches out its wings and lifts from the ground, its talons curled and vicious.

I move into the passageway and look up at the bident. The two points have a wicked edge that will easily cut through the harpy. But as I take another step forward, I stop and wonder if there isn't another way.

The compass is pointing dead ahead, and I realize that there's a left turn between me and the harpy. I slowly and quietly shift towards it, pulling some of the food from my bag as I do. When I get to the opening, I throw two of the sweet honey rolls down the passageway; they make a dull thud that captures the harpy's attention. As she darts forward I push myself up against the wall, the rush of air from her wings hitting me as she swoops around the corner. I waste no time and hasten down the passageway to the sounds of her devouring the rolls.

I move faster now, keeping the crown in my mind and following the compass at every turn. The passages feel as if they are becoming narrower and time feels as if it is slipping from me. Somewhere in the maze is Theron; he may be closer to the crown than I am.

As I make the next turn, a wave of heat hits me and I scramble back. The floor of the passage is lava. I turn around but see that the right turn I had just come from is no longer there. I stare at the solid wall in amazement and wonder if the labyrinth has been shifting around me the whole time. I look up at the stars, the strange radiations coming from them, and wonder if the shifting of the paths is part of the game that the Gods are playing.

I could really do with Hades rolling something good, as I realize that not only is it getting hotter but also the lava is closing in on me. But when I peer ahead I can see that it ends further down the passage. There is no way I can jump the lava in one go, but I think I can make it in two. From my bag I pull out the cloak; the red side will warm me, and the grey side will keep me cool. *I just need it to keep me cool for a moment*, I think to myself, as I throw it out over the lava, hot side down, cool side up. The cloak is smoking around the edges as I leap on to it then off again, making it to the other side where the passageway forks in two.

I look at the compass and take the path to the left. Ahead I see a strange glow that's moving fast and, as I turn the next corner, I see that the glow is coming from a familiar figure. I feel my heart lift. "Theron!"

He turns to look in my direction, but I remember that

I'm still invisible. I move to twist the ring, but something stops me; it's the way he's standing, his arm up, a lightning bolt in his hand as if he is ready to strike me, his face full of anger. And there's something else about him. Just as there is a light glowing out of me, there is one glowing out of Theron. His light is small and dull as if it is shrouded in a cloud of red dust. I wonder if he is just on edge from the things he's seen in the labyrinth, but then he stands up tall and calls to me.

"Ara, are you here? Hermes said you were coming, that you were the last of the tokens, that all the others were dead. I told you they were pathetic, do you remember?" There's a taunting in his voice that is ugly, and I keep still and quiet.

"Ara!" he calls my name, making each of the letters long; the sound vibrates off the walls and trembles within me. He's stalking up the passageway slowly, the lightning bolt raised and flickering across his face.

"You know you can't beat me. You couldn't in the training fields, and you can't here," he says.

I clutch the bident more tightly. He's right, and I feel a little despair fall over me that turns to anger as he rounds the bend and makes a throwing motion with his hand. A bolt of lightning hits the wall, exploding it. I hear the blast and see the rubble fly from further down the passage where I'm inching away from him. He uses his shield to protect himself and that's when I realize that he's using the light of the shield to see by, like a searchlight. I wonder if he'll be able to see me when the light extends to where I'm standing; if the godly light will expose me or if it will burn me like it did Nestor. I decide not to take the chance and move faster, back up the way I've come and take the right-hand path instead.

My whole body is trembling, images of Theron and the thunderbolt running on repeat. A weapon capable of killing a God would obliterate me. But surely he wouldn't use it; not only is it against the rules to draw the blood of another player, but it's Theron, he's my friend, and at one point he wanted to be more than that.

I hurry down the passageway, looking back over my shoulder as I run, and it's too late for me to realize that I'm walking into danger until I'm in it. I turn to see a large lion blocking my way, pawing at the ground. He lifts his nose into the air and sniffs deeply. I guess it doesn't matter if I'm invisible because it's obvious that he can sense me. He stares in my direction, his eyes locked on to the space that I occupy, and then he opens his jaws and roars. I don't think, I just run towards the nemean lion. As I get close, I dig the ends of Hades' bident into the ground and leap into the air, gliding over the lion as it carries on running forward. I hit the ground and run, faster and harder than I've ever run in my life and not just because I know the lion has turned and is chasing me, but because I can see the centre of the labyrinth and the crown.

I drop the compass as I extend my hand to grasp the

crown and just as my fingers graze it, I feel a jolt rush through my body, throwing me to the floor, as the crown skids to a halt just behind me. I'm completely stiff as lightning sparks course through my body. I can't move a muscle, and I can't pull in a full breath; my body is completely out of my control and fear is running rife. All I can do is hold on to the moment and watch as Theron shoots a lightning bolt at the nemean lion, stands over its dead body, and then he turns and walks over to me, trapping me in the light from the shield as I lie on the floor. I'm amazed that the light isn't burning me like it did Nestor, although I think it might be better if it was because the look on Theron's face is terrifying.

He crouches down and tries to pull the bident from my hand, but my fingers are tightly gripped around it and refuse to let go. Theron pulls each one of them off and I hear them snap; I feel the pain, silent tears running down my face, but I still can't move; the jolt from the lightning bolt has paralysed me. Then he pulls the ring from my finger and lowers his shield.

"There you are, Ara." He smiles at me, all teeth; he reminds me of the Children of Sorrow. "You never could beat me."

He grabs me by the hair and pulls me up. My body is useless. I want to hit him, to strike out, as he moves me like a doll. He strokes my face then kisses my unmoving lips.

"Don't cry, Ara," he says, wiping my tears away. "You didn't cry on the night of the Blood Moon." He kisses me again. I want to lash out, to pick up the bident and run it through him. I want Hades to appear and save me. I want Thalia to come and gut Theron, or Danae to throw her net over him, or Nestor to set him alight with the Promethean fire. But it's just me and Theron alone in the dark; no one is coming to save me.

I draw in a ragged breath; as I do, I say his name. He moves his ear to my lips, and I draw in another breath with his name on it. I can feel the tips of my fingers moving. I flex them a little and feel something unyielding and metal next to my left hand. The crown. All I have to do is grasp it, claim it, just as Theron is trying to claim me.

I lengthen my broken fingers, the pain coursing through them, as Theron holds my face cupped in his hands.

"I told you, it's you and me, Ara. It's all part of the Gods' plan for me. Zeus has told me what I've always known, what my mother said was true. I am the son of the king of Termera, and once I return victorious to Oropusa he will send for me and give me his kingdom. And you, Ara, you will come with me as my wife."

I let out a little yelp of anguish in part from what he said but mostly because my twisted fingers have slipped on the crown, pushing it a little further from me.

"Don't worry," he coos to me. "I have always known what I would ask the Gods for when I won. I know that you never truly loved me, that you never thought of me in the same way that I do you. In the way that you do *him*." Theron's face is full of anger. "But once I ask for you as my

292

reward, he will not be able to have you; you'll be mine, not Hades'."

I let out a little yelp but this time of triumph, as my fingers latch on to the crown. I feel my grip becoming firmer and surer as a warmth moves through my fingers and up my arm, slowly flooding through my body, restoring it. I keep my eyes locked on Theron's and lift my arm, placing the crown on my head. His eyes widen as I push him from me and stand up. He cowers on the floor for a second then in a swift movement he stands up; thrusting his hands towards me. I blink and look down, then grasp the end of Hades' bident – the sharp points are buried deep inside me.

"If I can't have you, no one will," he says, tears falling from his eyes, as blood spills from my body and trickles from my mouth.

As I fall backwards, I feel Hades grab me, sweeping me into his arms. He looks at Theron, his eyes shooting stars of fury. "I am going to enjoy hosting you in Tartarus for the rest of eternity," he tells Theron, and I can hear a sinister edge to his voice that makes me shudder.

Zeus appears next to Theron and places a hand on his shoulder, then gives Hades a sneering smile.

I feel like I've missed something as I lift a hand and place it on Hades' chest.

"Hermes!" Hades calls.

Hermes arrives, floating in mid-air, and when I look back at Theron he looks just as angry as Hades does, maybe even more so.

"Hermes, fix this!" Hades calls. I can hear the urgency in Hades' voice as I feel myself drifting away.

35

THE PASSAGEWAYS OF THE SOULS

Darkness is all around me, suffocating and deep. I am no longer in the arms of Hades, but someone much larger and older.

My carrier looks down on me and I know who he is: Thanatos, collector of souls, warden of the dead. I look down at my torso; two dark patches stain my tunic from where Theron used the bident to stab me.

"Am I dead?" I ask, knowing it's true, but not believing it yet.

"Yes," Thanatos says, his voice as deep as the darkness that we walk through.

I look around, expecting to see him, but he's not there. "Hades!" I call into the darkness, and I remember him telling me that it was not his privilege to escort the dead. I didn't really know what he meant then. He also said that when I died, I would be forever removed from him, just as I am now. I place my hand to my heart, and I can no longer feel the surety and warmth that was there.

"Hades!" I whisper his name as Thanatos carries me on; he is gentle with me, almost motherly as he cradles me in his arms like a baby.

"He cannot hear you," he tells me softly. "The passageways of the dead are for the souls of the departed and me to travel alone; no living thing can come here and that includes a God."

"You're not a God?" I ask.

He looks at me with empty eyes. "I am the last breath you took, the last beat of your heart, the last thought you had. I am made of an eternity of endings. If I am a God, I am the God that never was, the God that ended before he began."

I feel the tears run down my face and wonder how that can be. I have no body and yet I can feel; I feel Thanatos' arms around me, I feel the pain in my broken hand, in the wounds Theron gave me, they are dull but there. And I feel the tight grip of grief around my heart, grief for the life I have slipped from and the future I know I wanted. But most of all I feel the aching pain of the loss of a love I will never have again.

All at once there is a soft glow of light in front of us and I see the gates to the underworld; they are impossibly large, reaching up into the continuous darkness that surrounds us.

As we near them, I can hear running water. I close my eyes and am reminded of the river that runs at the back of the villa at home in Oropusa, and I think of my parents and Ida and feel a pang of sadness. They will find my body just as I did Estella's.

Estella. I think of the promise I made her and how disappointed she is going to be to see me in Elysium.

I hear a dog barking and, as Thanatos gets closer, I can see people standing around outside the gate.

"Ajax? Danae?" I call.

"Ara!" I hear Danae call my name and then Acastus.

"Acastus!" I shout.

I can see them all now. All ten of them. Thanatos places me down before the gate and Thalia rushes towards me and embraces me, Nestor following her, and then we are all a knot of hugging and voices, as they ask what happened. Below their voices is the babble of the river and above it the barking of the dog.

"So, Theron won?" Heli asks, an awkward and disappointed expression on her face.

I shake my head. "No, no, I won," I say, and I reach up to find that I'm still wearing the crown.

"Then why are you here?" Ajax asks.

I look down at the wounds in my tunic. "Theron killed me."

"That's against the rules." Solon's voice is stony.

"I'm not sure that the Immortal Games really has rules," I respond, and there is a deep tiredness in my body that I am struggling to shake.

"Yes, yes, it does have rules," a panting breath says, and I look up to see Hades standing on the opposite side of the gates, his dog, Cerberus, beside him. I rush to him and push my arms through the bars to hold him.

"I'm sorry," I say. "I didn't mean to die. I didn't mean to leave you."

The lock in the gate clicks and Thanatos starts to push it open.

I reach for the gap, to slip through and go to Hades, but Cerberus barks at me and Hades leaps on the gate, pushing it closed.

"No," Hades shakes his head. "I refuse to let her in my realm."

I feel his words hit me like a whip.

"Take her back," Hades commands Thanatos, and for a moment I can see why most fear the God of the underworld.

"I can't do that, my lord," Thanatos says. "Her thread has been … her fate is…"

"Still twinned to mine," Hades says. "And I refuse to see her pass into the land of the dead. The Games are not finished, no threads have been snipped, no prize has been claimed. Take her back."

I look at Hades, at the conviction on his face and the almost imperceptible tremble of his lip.

Thanatos looks at the lord of the underworld for what feels like an eternity before he turns the key and locks the gates once more.

Hades releases his hand from the gate, then presses his forehead against it. Cerberus nudges him with one head and licks his hand with another. Hades strokes the top of the third head as he looks up at me, his eyes large.

"What does this mean?" I ask him.

"Go with Thanatos," he tells me, his voice hard.

"Not until you tell me what is happening."

"Zeus, Zeus is happening, he is trying to control the Games, to manipulate it and win. If you come through the gate, if any of the fallen tokens come through the gate, then the Games are over, your thread will be snipped and you will die, Ara. I can't let that happen, I..."

Hades is lost for words, and I feel the fire of revenge inside me again. Even now when I've won, Zeus is trying to get his own way.

"Go with Thanatos, back to your body in Olympus, I will meet you there."

"What about us?" Danae asks.

I look around at my friends. Hades does too. He remains silent but I can see him thinking things through, as if he is looking to those possibilities that I can never see, the ones that call and distract him.

"I'll not leave without them."

"Ara, please go with Thanatos, return to your body, claim your prize as victor of the Games." He reaches through the bars and strokes my cheek, and I lean against his hand.

"I can't just leave them," I tell him again.

I see him nod to Thanatos, who scoops me up in his arms and carries me off.

"No!" I yell, as I reach out towards my friends. "I'll not leave without them." I struggle and twist and try to break free as Thanatos carries me away from the gates, from Hades, from all of the tokens, from everyone I care about.

36

THE GAME ROOM

I open my eyes. Everything around me is bright and white. I look up slowly into a ceiling of baby-blue sky and white fluffy clouds. I give myself a moment to test my body. It all seems to move so I sit myself up and look down at my stomach where the bident pierced it. My tunic is perfect; no bloodstains, no signs of the trials mark the fabric or me. I run a hand over the places where I have been injured and lift my broken fingers; all are restored.

I'm sitting on a marble slab and as I swing my legs over the edge, I see that the slab is on a plinth; around the bottom of the plinth are all the gifts that Hades has given me throughout the trial.

I'm in a huge temple-like room with a domed ceiling that opens up to the sky beyond. There appear to be no walls, but the area is defined by large columns which hold the gaping ceiling aloft and I can tell that there are chambers beyond, although I can't define where they begin or end.

"Olympus," I whisper to myself, as I slide from the plinth and cross to the table in the middle of the room and the thirteen chairs around it.

The table holds an intricate map of the world.

Something catches my eye in one of the alcoves of the room; it is similar to where I was lying, but I have to put a hand over my mouth to stop from calling out when I see what is on the plinth.

"Thalia." I move towards her and look more closely, realizing she is not on the plinth but suspended above it.

She doesn't look as she did when I saw her moments ago at the gate, and I'm not prepared to see the brutality of her body, crumpled and broken, the blood fresh and glistening as if she has just been crushed.

On the base of the plinth where Thalia's gifts are placed there is an inscription – TOKEN OF HERA.

There are more alcoves, more tokens.

I move towards Heli; she floats just above her plinth, her neck at a strange angle. Ajax's eyes are open wide, his mouth gaping in surprise and his body ripped in two, a jagged tear running across the centre; both parts float one above the other. Danae is curled up like a ball, her knees drawn up to her chest, her hands wrapped over her head, pulling it in towards her. I start sobbing when I see her and think of how scared she must have been. Solon is next, his face caved in on one side from the pterippus' blow.

Nestor's eyes are closed just as I left them. I reach out and touch his hand then run my fingers over the rivulets of his burn scars; his flesh feels warm. Acastus is next and the tears come thick and fast. His eyes are closed too, and he looks so peaceful; he could have been sleeping were it not for the puncture wounds on his torso, poison and blood glistening in both.

Xenia is just as I remember, a red halo of blood surrounding her head, her leg curled under her at an unnatural angle, which now that she is floating upright makes her look as if she is standing on one leg. Even in death we are a spectacle for the Gods, something to bring them amusement.

Kassandra is soaking wet. Dead branches and decomposing leaf-litter cling to her hair and clothes, her mouth and eyes are wide open, and I choke back a cry at the memory of her before all of this. Last is Philco. I never met him. He's so young, younger than all the rest of us; his round face is serene, his dark curls shining against the white of Olympus. One hand is hanging beside him, the other at his neck, reaching for the dagger that has pierced it.

I feel a hand on my shoulder and turn to see Hades looking at me.

"What is this?" I ask him, extending my arm towards my fallen friends, my voice harsh.

"Ara." He moves towards me, and I take a step back.

"Is this what you do? They die, and you bring them here so you can, what – gaze upon their destruction? Is it not enough that you take their lives, you have to ridicule them in death too?"

"It's not like that, foolish mortal," a sing-song voice says from behind. I turn and see Hermes floating near the table. "We Gods honour our tokens, even if they have not lived up to their potential. We keep them here until the end of the Games, their bodies frozen at the edge of their deaths, their spirits suspended at the gates until the Fates snip them free."

"Their spirits suspended!" I think of my friends outside the gates of the underworld, waiting in the darkness in the space between life and death. Then I think of Estella and how her body must have been on display like this, how her soul was kept prisoner till the Gods had finished, their fun and games officially ended.

"And what now, now that the Games have ended?" I demand. I hear the edge in my voice and I see the flare in Hermes' eyes.

He smiles and opens his arms wide. "Hades waits an eternity to win the Games and when he finally does, his token is the most spirited victor we have seen in eons."

I look around and realize that all the Gods of Olympus are here, each one standing by their dead token, except Zeus who stands in front of an empty marble plinth.

"Token of Hades, these Games are drawing to a close, but we are not yet finished. There is a matter of punishment and reward to be dealt with. But as soon as that is done, we will return the mortal parts of the tokens to the earth and hand over their spirits to Hades."

I turn and look up at Hades, who towers above me.

Here in the halls of the Gods, he feels unreachable, but his hand slips into mine.

Hermes turns towards Zeus.

"Zeus, your token broke the rules of the Games; he injured the token of Hades with intent to kill."

"Now, now," Zeus says, "we all know what it is to feel the passion of battle, the heat of the moment when the thunder and lightning come. My token was swept up in the Games, in the emotion of it. After all, he is in love with Hades' token, he professed his heart to her, and she scorned him."

Aphrodite lets out a sigh and Athena a scoff.

"That does not give him the right to hurt me, to kill me!" I shout, and both Hermes and Zeus look at me as if I am nothing more than an annoying fly.

"Besides," Zeus continues, as if I'm not there at all, "I'm sure you will find that technically the Games were over when she died. Hades had won, his token had the crown. If she dies after that then surely that is fair. She dies, but he wins the Games and the wager. Whereas if Theron is found to have broken the rules and she is restored as victor, then I think you will find that my token and I are disqualified from the Games."

Zeus smiles at Hades and I know that something important is happening, but I can't quite put my finger on what it is.

Hades squeezes my hand then steps forward. "I demand justice for Ara. For the damage done to her."

"I hear your claim," Hermes says. "It is the will of the Games that justice is served. Zeus, present your token."

Zeus claps his hands together and Theron appears in the middle of the room, standing on the table below the hovering Hermes.

Theron looks around wide-eyed, taking in the Gods, the dead tokens, me. When he sees me, he cowers.

The rage builds inside me. I want to pick up Hades' bident and thrust it straight through him, just as he drove it through me.

Hades strategically steps to the side, blocking my path, then he looks over his shoulder at me and something in his eyes makes me still. There is more happening here than I am aware of.

Zeus steps towards the table, his eyes flashing.

"Ara, please, stop them, I didn't mean it," Theron calls to me and I feel conflicted. "I don't want to die." He is looking at Hades. And I realize that Theron is not sorry for what he did to me, rather he's scared of what his fate might be.

"Worry not, mortal, we will not kill you; what use is a punishment if we cannot see the suffering?" Ares, God of war says, his voice booming like a drum, a cruel smile on his lips.

Hermes raises his caduceus and clears his throat. "Theron, token of Zeus, by your own free will you have broken the rules of the Games and as punishment you will live out the rest of your natural life not as a hero but as a monster."

There is an "oooh" from the collected Gods. Aphrodite shrieks and hides her face as Ares claps in eager excitement.

"Please, I beg of you, be merciful," Theron pleads, as Hermes hovers over him.

Theron drops to his knees as his body contorts. I take a step forward, but Hades stretches out an arm, holding me behind him. I watch as Theron's handsome face is transformed. Large boar-like tusks erupt from his jaw, his eyes become small and red and his brow heavy and protruding. His feet grow hooves, his shoulders round as thick coarse hair grows all over his body, his fingers turn to claws. I'm stunned as I look upon him weeping as he lifts his hands and feels his face.

"Please," he moans.

"I will not have it said that the Gods of Olympus are not merciful," Hermes says. "So, I will offer you this cure. When you right the wrongs that you have done, and those you fought with fight for you, then you will be restored. But till then you will be shunned by your fellows, hunted by those greater than you, and despised by all who are fair."

Hermes lifts his caduceus high and a blast of light floods the room. Then Theron is gone.

"Where did he go?" I ask.

"He has been sent home," Hermes says with a mean smile. My mind is flooded with images of Theron's mother – and the villagers – seeing him. I wonder if they'll try to attack him and then I remember he tried to do worse to me.

"Now, token of Hades, it is time for you to name your reward." Hermes beckons to me, and Hades stands aside. I make my way towards the table.

I look around at the Gods and I can't believe that they are so removed, so unkind and unfeeling, except Hades. The difference is marked. He feels everything I feel, whereas for the other Gods, emotion is extreme; it has to be big for them to feel it; they have no awareness of the subtlety in emotion or anything else for that matter.

I stand before Hermes, surrounded by the Gods and by my fallen friends, and I look back at Hades. When I was with Thanatos, when I was walking through the darkness and I couldn't feel Hades, when I thought that I would never see him again, my heart felt as if it would wither. For a moment I think about asking to be with Hades forever as his equal, as a God. But that is against the rules and as much as the Gods bend the rules for themselves, I don't think they will bend them for me.

"What is your reward?" Hermes asks, his smile wild. "Name it and we, the Gods, will give it to you."

I glance over at Zeus. I could ask for a thunderbolt, just one, one is all I need. I know I can throw and at this distance I will hit my mark and hit it well.

Promise me. Estella's voice fills my head, it tears me away from Zeus and I look over at Hades. He is staring at me. His jaw is clenched and his whole body is tense. *Promise me.*

I take a deep breath then stare at Hermes. "I want you to restore my friends to life. To give them back their good health, and return them to their homes, their families, to long and happy lives. Philco, Kassandra, Xenia, Acastus, Nestor, Solon, Danae, Ajax, Heli, Thalia ... and Theron too."

There's a silence and it pulls on for longer than makes me feel comfortable. "I said I want you to..."

Hermes waves his caduceus impatiently in the air. "Yes, yes, we heard what you said, it's just ... well, wouldn't you rather ask for riches, or a kingdom, or a flying horse?"

I let out a small "ha" at that. "No, thank you. I want you to restore them all to good health, and then return them to their homes, to long and happy lives." I try to cover all the bases to make sure that what I ask for can't be interpreted in any other way than what I intend.

The Gods begin to murmur among themselves, and I risk a glance over at Hades. I have learnt to read the small expressions that he wears and right now he is looking at me proudly.

"What is the point of the Games if the risks can be undone by a mortal's words?" Zeus declares.

"It is in the rules that we grant them what they want, *whatever* they want," Artemis says, and her voice is full of authority.

"Except to become a God," Ares says.

"Well, yes, but that is in the rules," Athena says.

"And maybe this should be too," Zeus replies.

"But what of Theron?" Hera asks. "He defied us, he broke the rules, his punishment must be allowed to stand."

Hermes looks at me seriously. "Yes, token. There will be

no negotiations on the fate of Theron; he has been punished, but he is alive and has been returned to his little life."

I nod in agreement. "But the others, I wish for them…"

"Yes, yes, we know what you wish for them," Zeus says, a bitterness in his voice.

"It is possible," Hades says. "Their threads are yet to be cut, their souls are still connected to their broken bodies, which are easily fixed. Their spirits are still outside my gates; they have not set foot in my realm. I have not claimed them as my citizens yet."

There is a long pause, and all of the Gods look from Hades to Hermes and then to Zeus, who sighs as he shakes his head. "It *will* be in the rules by the next Blood Moon!" he says, glaring at Hermes.

"Very well! As master of these Immortal Games, I bestow upon you your gift." Hermes waves an open arm around the room and as he does, each of the tokens on the plinths is restored to life, their mortal injuries erased, their health restored. They look as they did at the very beginning of the Games.

I look around and smile as I see them all floating in the air in amazement, taking in the Gods around them, the halls of Olympus. Before any of them can say anything, Hermes strikes his caduceus on the table and they are all gone.

I feel my joy turn to hope, hope that they all live their lives, truly live them for themselves, doing the things that make them happy, in spite of the Gods.

"And now all that is left is for me to send you home victorious, and declare Hades winner of the Games."

"What about the feast?" Dionysus calls.

"Ah, yes, and to open the feasting," Hermes adds. "We'll send you back after that." He glances at me.

Hades smiles and a ripple of warmth spreads through me as the Gods around us begin to clap in celebration.

"Wait." A soft voice fills the air.

I turn to see three women walking through one of the vaulted arches and into the room. One is young, one middle aged and one old; each of them holds weaving tools in their hands, and at once I know that they are the Fates: Lachesis, Atropos, Clotho.

"There was a wager, and it must be settled," a dry voice says, and Clotho moves forward. She studies Zeus, Hades and Poseidon in turn, pointing a bony finger at each of them. "You three made a godly bargain, a sworn deal that must be upheld." Her voice is stern. I watch as each of these powerful Gods shrinks a little before the Fate, looking almost as childlike as we mortals do before them.

Zeus looks from Clotho to his brothers, and I see a smirk on his lips as he steps forward to address the Fates.

"Sisters of the threads, weavers of the world, I am sorry that you have wasted your time in venturing so far from your domain, but there is nothing to resolve. The wager is void. I am afraid that when my token expressed his free will and chose to harm the token of Hades, my place in the game was forfeited. I have been disqualified, you see, so the wager between the three of us cannot be upheld."

Something about the way that Zeus sniggers makes my blood curl and I wish I had asked for a thunderbolt and used it to wipe that smile clean off his face.

Atropos steps forward; she is holding a small pair of golden scissors and as she points them towards Zeus, he flinches. "Ah, I see. But you, mighty Zeus, do not. I and my sisters are in the fortunate position of being able to see all the threads of the world."

Lachesis joins her sister, in her hand a spinner. "You can only see as far as your own thread, and while that is long, it is not very wide."

"You may have left the Games but not the wager," Clotho adds. "The conditions of the wager were woven into the world when the three of you made it."

"The knot of your pact was pulled tight," Atropos says.

"If one of you three were to win these Games then the other two would give him their thrones," Lachesis says. "And one of you has won."

Poseidon and Zeus both turn from the Fates to face Hades. He is standing tall and very still, his face unreadable.

"Absurd! I was disqualified because of the actions of my token; how could I have won the Immortal Games?" Zeus says.

"Not you and Theron! Ara and Hades had won before Theron acted. You, Zeus, had a choice; we saw the way your thread moved, we witnessed the stitches you made with Theron, how you pulled his thread along and used it to your own advantage," Lachesis adds.

"Did you cheat?" Poseidon asks, his voice low, his eyes flaring with the promise of choppy waters.

"How dare you accuse me of cheating after you tried to aid your token in her final trial."

"These lies again!" Poseidon rages.

Hades steps in. "Brothers, this rivalry and feuding is what led to this wager. You are so deprived of purpose and have strayed so far from your charges that you are in constant pursuit of self-gratification. You care not for each other, and you care not for the mortals in your charge; look how you treat your champions: this tells us all we need to know about the start and end of your characters."

"How dare you!" Zeus' eyes blazed. "Under whose authority do you seek to school me – me, Zeus, mightiest of all the Gods, your Lord?"

"Except, you are not," Clotho says.

Zeus turns on her, his face contorted with anger.

"You entered into a wager and the rules were clear: the victor would win it all. Hades is the ruler of the underworld, the seas and the skies. Now Hades is the God of all Gods."

I look up at Hades in disbelief. All the time that we were playing the Games together I thought I was the only one who was risking anything, but he was risking it all and trusting in me every step of the way.

Zeus storms, lightning bolts filling the dark skies that swell and surround Olympus.

Poseidon lets out a low laugh then claps Hades on the back. "Well played, brother. I cannot say I am happy with the situation, but rather you than... Well, I expect there will be some changes around here."

"Some," Hades said. "But to start with, some things will remain the same. I will keep to my realm and have charge over it, and I hope that you will keep to yours, Poseidon, as no one knows the seas better than you, and you too, brother Zeus, that you will both keep watch of your domains and do your duties as were set out in the beginning, when we bested father together and set out the treaties.

"But I would like to add to the treaty that, from this day on, the three of us rule together, that we three will work as one to fulfil the promises of our offices, taking council from the other Gods of Olympus as we do."

"Together?" Poseidon says, rubbing his beard in thought. Then he cracks a smile. "I like the idea of this alliance. After all, the last time the three of us combined forces we changed the world; imagine what we could do together again."

Hades extends a hand to Poseidon, who shakes it. "If we do change it, then let it be for the better and with no bloodshed this time," Hades says. And I smile; only he would think that the world could be changed with some rope and handy accessories.

"And what of you, Zeus?" Hades asks, his face solemn. "Are Poseidon and I to rule alone?"

"You two, you couldn't rule over a line."

"So, you'll join us?" Poseidon asks, and I realize that the whole court of Gods is clinging to what Zeus is about to say.

"Someone will have to show you both how it is done." Zeus hesitates for a moment before extending his hands. Both Poseidon and Hades grasp them, and I feel a shifting in the air.

"The tapestry has straightened," Clotho calls.

"The knot undone," Lachesis adds.

"The pattern restored with vibrancy and intricate precision," Atropos says with a smile.

"Let it be known that this is a new age of the Gods, an age of unity, prosperity, harmony and richness, the likes of which have never been witnessed before," Clotho declares.

"Come, brothers, let us celebrate our new union," Poseidon says, as he pulls Zeus over to the banquet tables and the other Gods follow them.

Hades approaches me and I feel nervous. The Games are done. There is no longer any need for me to be here.

"Ara." He sighs my name and moves his hand to cup my face. He kisses me deeply.

"So, you're in charge now!" I say, and he smiles.

"It is more of a coalition of Gods, but yes. And the first thing I am going to do is make sure that my brothers spend some time in the underworld – I feel both of them need a little perspective."

"I think the world is in safe hands," I tell him, as I entwine my fingers in his. "I guess it's time for me to go." I look up at him, a lump rising in my throat.

"Oh, I thought … I thought that you might stay," he says. "We could probably make you a God. We did it for Dionysus; when he was mortal he invented wine and we honoured him with eternal life. You have managed to unify the Gods, which is a comparable feat, I think."

I smile and shake my head at him. "Comparable."

"Stay, Ara. Stay with me forever," Hades says, and I feel a pull so great that it threatens to overtake me.

"I will, but not just yet," I say to him, locking his too-blue eyes with mine. "I fought so hard to stay alive during the Games, and I made a promise that I would live, so I want to do just that. I want to live a life full of experience and being, so that when I join you, I will have much to tell you. Will you wait for me?" I ask.

"For the whole of eternity if I have to," he says. "But please, Ara, don't keep me waiting that long." And he scoops me up in his arms and kisses me.

"May I visit you, in the dreaming?" Hades asks.

"Every night," I say and kiss him back.

PRONUNCIATION GUIDE

GODS

Aphrodite (a-fruh-dai-tee) Goddess of love and beauty

Apollo (uh-pol-oh) God of the sun, music and poetry

Ares (air-eez) God of war

Artemis (ahr-tuh-mis) Goddess of the hunt

Athena (uh-thee-nuh) Goddess of wisdom and strategy

Demeter (dih-mee-ter) Goddess of the grain and harvest

Dionysus (dai-uh-nai-suhs) God of wine and revelry

Hades (hey-deez) God of the underworld

Hephaestus (hi-fes-t*uh*s) God of fire

Hera (heer-*uh*) Goddess of women, children and the
home

Hermes (hur-meez) The messenger God

Poseidon (puh-sai-dun) God of the sea

Zeus (zoos) God of the sky, God of all Gods

OTHER GODS

Thanatos (than-*uh*-tos)

TOKENS

Acastus (a-kas-tuhs) Sign of Virgo, token of Demeter
Ajax (ay-jacks) Sign of Cancer, token of Artemis
Ara (ar-*uh*) Sign of Scorpio, token of Hades
Danae (duh-nay) Sign of Pisces, token of Poseidon
Heli (he-lee) Sign of Gemini, token of Athena
Kassandra (k*uh*-san-dr*uh*) Sign of Taurus, token of
    Aphrodite
Nestor (nes-ter) Sign of Sagittarius, token of Hephaestus
Philco (fil-co) Sign of Libra, token of Apollo
Solon (sow-luhn) Sign of Aries, token of Dionysus
Thalia (th*uh*-lee-*uh*) Sign of Leo, token of Hera.
Theron (th-air-on) Sign of Capricorn, token of Zeus
Xenia (zee-nee-uh) Sign of Aquarius, token of Ares.

THE FATES

Atropos (a-tr*uh*-pos)
Clotho (kloh-thoh)
Lachesis (lach-uh-sis)

OTHER

Aeacus (ee-*uh*-k*uh*s)
Cerberus (sur-ber-*uh*s)

Eridanos (ih-*rid*-n-os)
Fury (fyoor-ee)
Minos (my-n*uh*s)
Rhadamanthys (rad-uh-man-th*uh*s)

MORTALS

Erastus (ih-ras-t*uh*s)
Estella (es-tel-la)
Ida (eye-d*uh*)
Melia (meh-lee-uh)

CREATURES

cyclops (sai-klops)
psammophis-hydra (sam-o-fiss hai-dr*uh*)
pterippi (terr-o-pee)
stymphalian [Birds] (stim-fey-lee-*uh*n)

WEAPONS AND TALISMANS

bident (bi-dent)
caduceus (kuh-doo-see-uhs)

AUTHOR NOTE

Heroes are not born they are made and the way to make a hero, in my humble opinion, does not come from the things that happen to us, the trials and the quests that we find ourselves in, but from the way that we tackle those experiences.

There is a great power that we all have full command over each and every day and that is the power of choice; we choose how we react to those trials, those quests that we find ourselves a part of. We have the power to choose how we will be in that and every moment. We choose what we want to grow inside our hearts and souls and minds. We choose how we want to be, and we can choose to be better, to do better. We can love and we can live a life of joy and personal integrity, or we can choose not to.

I believe that we become the total sum of our choices and our actions and that acting with grace is always worth the extra effort. I believe that all it takes for the world to change is for more of us to use our power to lean towards the things that unite us, the things that we know are good and positive.

We are most powerful when we deliberately choose who we are and how we will act. The trials in front of us are hard, but we can defeat even the largest of monsters, especially if we heroes band together and show up every day as the most authentic, powerful, and positive versions of ourselves and then take action to embody our values and integrity in all that we do.

So choose to become a hero, every moment of every day.

ANNALIESE AVERY

ACKNOWLEDGEMENTS

When I was first set the task of writing this book by my quest master and glorious editor Yasmin Morrissey, I definitely felt more than a little trepidation as I set off. Luckily, I had the closest thing to a Goddess on my side, my amazing agent Helen Boyle! She, along with Yasmin, supplied me with the belief and encouragement that I needed, and I set off into the unknown to seek out and claim the story you have just read.

I didn't do it on my own; I had a merry band of writers to support me along the way with writing sprints and words of encouragement. We have a common quest that binds us, and journeying along with you all is a pleasure, Ian Hunter, Gemma Allen, Kate Perry, Alice Jorden, Teara Newell, Simone Greenwood, Leoni Lock, The Write Magic Sprint Crew, The Good Ship 2022 Debut Group and my fellow Undiscovered Voices – thank you.

My huge thanks also goes to my glorious writing friends Cathie Kelly, Nicola Whyte, Kirsty Fitzpatrick, Vikki Marshall, Abs Tanner, Chrissie Sains and Kate Walker, for reading early versions of *The Immortal Games* and all becoming the founding members of the Hot Hades Appreciation Society!

Vanessa Harbour, as always, your friendship and giggles have smoothed my trials.

My Pizza Pals, Yvonne Banham and Anna Brooke – you are both brilliant and I value our friendship and the pizza that we share as much as any gift from the gods.

Dominique Valente, you and Chrissie Sains have been so supportive and such a joy to spend time with, I would fly wild pterippi with you any day!

And to my family The Awesome Avery's, Jason, Liberty, Krystal and Oakley, thank you for steering me straight and helping me battle the waves of my voyage to write this story; the seas got a little rough there in the middle bit, but we soon found calmer waters and a safe harbour.

As always, the team at Scholastic have moved with the grace and wisdom of the greatest of gods, special thanks to Jamie Gregory, Sarah Dutton, Penelope Daukes and Harriet Dunlea. And also to my lovely friend Nicki Marshall for her brilliant copyediting skills, she wields a red pen with an accuracy matched only by Zeus with a thunderbolt!

There is one person I need to give an extra big thank you to and that is cover illustrator Tom Roberts. I have been a huge fan of Tom's work for years now and when Scholastic told me that he was available to do the cover for *The Immortal Games* I didn't think I could get more delighted … I was wrong! That delight was surpassed when I saw the cover rough and then eclipsed when I saw the final cover. Tom, you are so deeply talented, and if it was within my powers, god like or other, I would immortalise your art in the stars forever.

And lastly, to every bookseller, reader, and librarian, the three powerful Fates of the book world, that has fallen in love with Ara (and Hades) and journeyed through this Immortal Game and supported all its tokens, I give the Crown of the North, for you are the true winners of these Games.

BOOK CREDITS

Editor
Yasmin Morrissey

Managing Editor
Sarah Dutton

Assistant Editor
Tierney Holm

Copyeditor
Nicki Marshall

Fiction Publisher
Lauren Fortune

Designer
Jamie Gregory

Cover Illustrator
Tom Roberts

Map Illustrator
Julia Bickham

Agent
Helen Boyle

Publicists
Harriet Dunlea
Hannah Love

Marketer
Ellen Thomson

Production Manager
Alice Pagin

Sales Team
Antonia Pelari
Tina Miller
Lucy Page
Laila Dickson
Danielle Knight
Rachel Cotton

Rights Team
Emily Landy
Ruth Middleton
Tanya Harris-Brown
Sarah Bardell
Hazera Khatun